W9-CNR-204

She
Wore Red
Trainers

Withdrawn

She Wore Red Trainers

Na'ima B. Robert

KUBE PUBLISHING
CHILDREN'S BOOKS

She Wore Red Trainers

First published in 2014 by
KUBE PUBLISHING LTD
Tel +44 (01530) 249230, Fax +44 (01530) 249656
E-mail: info@kubepublishing.com
Website: www.kubepublishing.com

Text copyright © 2014 Na'ima B. Robert
5th impression, 2021

All rights reserved. No part of this publication may be reproduced,
stored in a retrieval system, or transmitted in any form or by any
means, electronic, mechanical, photocopying, recording or otherwise,
without the prior permission of the copyright owner

Author Na'ima B. Robert
Book design Nasir Cadir
Cover design Fatima Jamadar
Editor Yosef Smyth

A Cataloguing-in-Publication Data record for
this book is available from the British Library

ISBN 978-1-84774-065-6
eISBN 978-1-84774-066-3

Printed by Elma basim, Turkey

To all those who are striving to
'keep it halal'

1

She was still looking at me, I could feel it.

You know how it feels when someone is staring at the back of your neck; it's as if they're sending off radio waves or something. Of course, she was expecting me to turn around and look at her again. I caught the look she gave me, just before I sat down by the window on the bus. I knew what it meant.

I took out my phone and started to play a game, hunching my shoulders to show that I was *not interested*.

A year earlier, when I had started praying regularly and paying attention to halal and haram at last, Dad had reminded me of the Islamic guidelines on girls, now that I was finally ready to hear them: no second look, limited interaction, definitely no dating and, of course, no physical contact of any kind before marriage.

There's no point pretending it wasn't hard.

Some days, I thought I would literally go crazy, I was so tense and wound up. And all the girls in their summer dresses didn't help things, trust me. Plus I was still thinking about my ex-girlfriend, Amy.

'Fast, son,' was Dad's advice. 'Work out, play basketball or something. It will give you an outlet.'

'To be honest, Dad, it's not that easy...'

'Oh, I know it's hard, son, we've all been there. But you can do it – you just need to practice a little self-control. And don't allow yourself to get into any sticky situations, keep your distance.'

So, getting girls' numbers was definitely out. Back in the day, I wouldn't have hesitated. Even when I was in a relationship, I was a mega flirt, I had to admit it, and I'd have had that girl's number so fast, she wouldn't even have had time to notice the tattoo on my right forearm. She would probably still have been checking out my hair, the stud in my ear, my light eyes.

Girls always loved my light eyes.

But that was last year, practically a lifetime ago. Before I realised how short this life is, how something you think belongs to you can be snatched away at a moment's notice.

Inna lillahi wa inna ilayhi raji'un. To Allah we belong and to Him we shall return.

I couldn't wait to get off that bus.

2

* * *

When I got home, to our house which still ached with Mum's absence, I found Dad in the light filled kitchen, his laptop open on the marble tabletop, a cup of cold tea beside it. He was on the phone. He was always on the phone these days. I felt irritation at his extreme attachment to his smartphone and computer. They were his distractions, I felt, his way of avoiding a reality that no longer included his wife of 20 years.

'No, Kareem, I really don't think so. I mean, I appreciate

the gesture but I couldn't, I just couldn't...'

My ears pricked up. It sounded like Dad was talking to his old friend, Kareem Stevens, someone we hadn't seen in forever. What was he offering him? And why was Dad turning it down?

Dad turned then and saw me standing there, watching him, and he nodded at me, gesturing for me to wait for his call to finish. Then he turned away from me and went out on to the balcony, the phone jammed against his ear. I went to the fridge and opened it to find the shelves bare aside from a half-finished bottle of milk and a carton of orange juice. Time to do the shopping again. The fridge had never looked this bare when Mum was around. I felt a twist of nostalgia as I thought of the boxes of cream cakes, the covered trays of cubed mango and watermelon, the bowls of spicy tuna salad and leftovers that tasted better than the day they had first been served. Mum hated an empty fridge.

3

I took the lonely carton of juice out and poured myself half a glass.

Through the open French doors, I could hear snatches of Dad's conversation as he paced up and down the overgrown path through Mum's herb garden.

'But South London, Kareem? I don't know whether I'm up to parenting my boys in the inner city... '

What was he on about?

There was a pause, then I heard Dad sigh. 'OK, Kareem, OK. I'll give it a try. It's not like we have any other options at the moment, anyway.' It hurt me to hear the defeat in my father's voice. But then his voice lifted again, strong: '*Jazakallah khayran*, thank you I really appreciate it.' I could practically hear him pulling himself up by his bootstraps, straightening his shoulders. Dad never was one for self-pity.

When he came back into the kitchen, I looked into his face and braced myself for unpleasant news.

'Well, son,' Dad said in a fake, cheerful voice. 'How's it going?'

I raised an eyebrow and looked at him, warily. Whatever it was, it was making him extremely nervous.

'Sit down, Ali.' He gestured towards the stool by the counter. 'I've got to talk to you about something.'

I waited to hear the momentous news.

'We'll be spending the summer in London, *inshallah*...'

'London? Brilliant!' My face lit up as I imagined spending the summer in London, as we had done before, shopping on Oxford Street and visiting Tower Bridge, riding on the London Eye. But my face fell when Dad shook his head. And that was when he told me: his business was in trouble, serious trouble, and we needed to do something drastic to keep the house. So that was why we were moving to London for the summer, to rent out our place to another family visiting from abroad.

'I need you to understand, it won't be a holiday, son. I'll be working all the hours God sends so I will need you boys to be responsible and to look after yourselves, pretty much.' Then he smiled hopefully. 'The good news is that we've got somewhere to stay for a few months... just until we get back on our feet and business picks up again and we can come home...' I saw the look in his eyes: he wanted me to believe him, to trust him to make everything all right, like he had always done. To be a superhero once more.

You see, when we were little, Dad used to tell us that he was a superhero with secret super powers. Of course, we were always begging him to show us his powers, and he always said that he could never show them to us, but that we would know them when the time came. I'll never forget the day I realised that the powers he had been talking about weren't about being able to fly at warp speed or turn into a ball of fire; his powers were much more subtle than that. But the effect was the same: just like Superman, he made us feel safe, like there was nothing that could touch us, that he was always there to shield us from the baddies, from the harsher side of life.

Until Mum died, that is. Because then our superhero lost his powers and fell to earth, broken. And there was no one around to shield us anymore.

When I think about it, maybe that was what led us to find Allah again: the realisation that there is only One superpower on this earth, only One who can protect us. *La hawla wa la quwwatta illa-billah*. There is no power or might except with Allah.

5

But that afternoon, in the kitchen of my beautiful family home in Hertfordshire, I let my dad be my hero again. I wanted him to believe in himself again, to see a stronger version of himself reflected in my eyes. 'OK, Dad, that's great. *Alhamdulillah*. Where will we be staying?'

'Your Uncle Kareem's leaving his place for a year to live and work in the Gulf. He said we can stay there. It sounds nice: three bedrooms, garden, close to the mosque... There's only one problem...'

'What's that, Dad?'

'The house is on a housing estate.'

My jaw dropped. 'You mean it's a council flat?' Whatever I had been expecting, it wasn't that! An image of our beautiful house here in Hertfordshire flashed through my mind and it was as if a knife had twisted in my heart. A council flat?

Dad must have seen the look of horror on my face. 'No, Ali, it's not a council flat. It's a house and Uncle Kareem owns it. And it's not a real estate; it's in a compound with a gate so you don't have to worry, it is really secure.' I must have visibly relaxed because he smiled then. 'And the best thing about it,' he continued, 'is that all our neighbours will be Muslims. That'll make a change, won't it?'

I smiled weakly, trying to process what he was telling me. A new journey was about to begin.

2

I woke up to the sound of Mum crying. It wasn't loud or anything, but my ears had grown used to detecting the sound of her sobbing through the thin wall that divided our rooms. So that was how I knew that my brother Malik's dad, my mother's fourth husband, had left the night before, after their row.

I felt my insides contract, just a little. Must have been anxiety. Or the thought that I might actually get a peaceful night's sleep again, a night where my body wasn't on high alert. Abu Malik leaving may have pushed Mum to tears, but it brought me relief.

Some stepfathers are more toxic than others. Let me leave it at that.

Here we go again, I thought as I pushed my little sister's sleeping body off my arm and towards the wall. I swung my legs over the side of the bed, the mattress creaking beneath me. 'I wonder how long it will last this time.' It wasn't the first time one of their arguments had ended in a walkout.

I knocked on Mum's door, knowing she wouldn't want me in there, wouldn't want me to see her crying. 'Mum,' I called softly. 'Would you like a cup of tea?'

I didn't wait to hear her muffled response. I didn't need

to. I knew she needed a cup of tea. Soon, she would need me to give her her pills, too. Just to take the edge off the pain.

As I made my way down the stairs, stepping over piles of clothes, both clean and dirty, toys and books, I found myself growing irritated by the damp spots on the wall of the bathroom and the dust that had gathered in the corners. What with me spending so much time studying for my A levels, I could see that things had slipped around the house. I would need to whip everyone back into shape.

I put the kettle on and padded towards the back of the house, towards Zayd's room. I knocked and waited briefly before sticking my head in. As usual, he was all tied up in his duvet, just the top of his head and his hairy feet sticking out, like an overgrown hot dog. I stepped in, narrowly avoiding the crusty glass and plate by the side of the bed.

'Zee,' I called out, giving him a nudge with my foot. He mumbled and groaned in reply. 'Abu Malik's gone, yeah. Just thought you should know.'

Zayd didn't come out of his duvet sandwich. 'Yeah, I know. I saw him last night, innit.'

'Did you say anything to him?'

'What's to say, Ams? It's the second *talaq*, innit, their second divorce. One more chance.'

I kissed my teeth and walked out of the door, disgusted. 'Men,' I thought to myself as I banged Mum's favourite teacup on the chipped enamel counter. 'They're all the same.'

So, that morning, it was up to me to get my little brothers and sister – Abdullah, Malik and Taymeeyah – ready for madrasah at the mosque.

'Taymeeyah, give me that hair grease... we're going to have to take your hair out soon, those plaits are looking kinda tired.'

As Taymeeyah ran upstairs to find the hair grease in the bomb site of our room, I rolled Malik's sleeves up. His eczema was getting bad again. I grabbed the pot of aqueous cream from the counter and began to rub it into the rough, reddened skin on the inside of his elbows. 'You haven't been using that soap with the bubbles, have you, Malik?'

He just nodded, his finger in his mouth.

I sighed and shook my head. 'You know you can't, babe. Not until your skin gets better. And no more milk, OK? You have to drink the soya, you know that...'

Malik made a face. 'But I hate it, Ammie,' he whined. 'It's yucky!'

Taymeeyah had reappeared. 'It's true, Ams,' she said. 'It *is* yucky.'

I poked her in the belly. 'And how would you know, young lady?'

She grinned at me, a guilty look in her eye.

'You drank the last bottle, didn't you? Admit it, Tay.'

She nodded sheepishly and I gave her a look.

'That's not right, is it, Tay? Malik's milk is expensive, y'know. And he can't drink the regular stuff. Promise me you won't touch the soya milk again.'

Taymeeyah nodded. 'I promise.'

'Muslim's word is bond, remember?'

'Yeah, I remember, Ammie.'

I felt a tugging on my nightshirt and turned to see Abdullah looking up at me.

'Where's Uncle?' he asked, using his podgy fingers to sign out the words.

I faltered. What should I tell him? What *could* I tell him?

9

That his brother's dad had just walked out on his kid in the middle of the night? That I had no idea where he was or when and if he would be back, either to see us, to drop some money for Mum, or to stay? No, I couldn't say that, so I gave him a quick hug and flashed him a smile.

'I'm not sure, babe,' I signed back, 'but if we don't hurry, you'll be late for madrasah. Come on, you guys, hurry up!' And I made a big show of getting the value pack of cornflakes down from the shelf and filling up their little bowls.

As I watched them eat, I felt the knot in my stomach tighten. They would all be depending on me again – me and Zayd.

OK, so now of course the question was, where was the human hot dog in all of this? Well, Zayd, my older brother, and I had a strict division of labour in the house: he did the weekday school run and I took the weekend mornings.

'What with work during the week, it's the only chance I get to sleep in, Ams,' was his reasoning. 'Now that you've finished school, you'll get to join all the other sisters, living the easy life at home, while we brothers sweat it out at work every day. *Subhanallah*, you sisters have got it easy, man!'

I had given him my most superior look. 'Anyway, who said I'll be sitting at home? Uni is only a couple of months away, remember? And then there's the fat job afterwards, inshallah. You do know that I'll be working after I graduate, don't you? No signing on or benefits for me. And no waiting for some useless man to take care of me.'

Zayd groaned. 'What's with all this women's lib stuff? Is that what they taught you in that school of yours? A woman's place...'

I put up my hand and started shouting over him. 'OK,

OK, Zee, give it a rest! Let's just agree to disagree, yeah? Because, if you think I'm going to be one of those deadbeat sisters on the dole, popping kids out every year, you've got another thing coming.'

I could have slapped that look of pity off his face. 'You have much to learn, young grasshopper,' he said, smiling. 'For now, though, you can do the kids on Saturday mornings while I sleep in, all right?'

'Yeah, yeah,' I growled. 'I guess that's fair enough.'

Zayd knew just how to wind me up. Most girls who had been brought up in a strict, conservative Muslim family like mine, praying, wearing hijab since the age of seven, with a stay-at-home mum who never finished school herself, would have had no problem with my brother's jibes. What he was teasing me about was the reality for most of the girls I grew up with: finish as much school as you can (GCSEs, if possible) and then hurry up and get married. Getting married was the biggest milestone, the one piece of news a girl's parents would make sure they shared with the whole community. Once you're married, you're safe: you're off the streets, you're not a *fitnah*, a trial, you've got someone to take care of you. This was my background, these were the ideas I grew up hearing. But I was never like the other girls. You could say I was cut from a different cloth.

* * *

I looked in on Mum just before I left with the kids. I wanted to remind her that I was planning to go to the park to do some sketching after I had dropped the kids. I knew that she probably wouldn't remember and would start worrying if I didn't come straight back after the *masjid*.

The curtains were drawn and the room felt hot and stuffy. Mum was curled up in bed still, her hair spread over the pillow, a frown line between her eyebrows. I stroked her hair, tucking it behind her ear, and kissed her cheek. Her skin felt hot and damp.

'I'm sorry, Mum,' I whispered. 'I'm sorry.'

As we left the house and walked down the close to catch the bus on the main road, I looked up at Mum's window. The left side of the curtain was sagging badly, right where the broken glass had been sealed with masking tape, months before. Abu Malik was meant to have had the glass replaced but, obviously, he'd never got round to it.

O Allah, I prayed silently, *take me away from all of this.*

12

3

The drive into London took forever, mainly due to an accident on the motorway. We drove down with Dad on Thursday afternoon to make sure that the house was ready for the movers who were due over the weekend.

I must admit, even though Dad took great pains to explain the difference between a housing estate and a housing association, I was expecting the worst: grim estates decked out with rusting swings and dog mess on the scratchy lawns.

But our route took us through the bustle of Brixton, up tree-lined roads, past a beautiful park with a country house perched on a hill, to the gates of our new home. Looking around as we drove up the driveway, I could feel my heart rate start to slow down and the dread I had been unconsciously holding onto, easing away. The houses were neat, well looked after. Good cars stood in the private driveways and the close was flanked on one side by sky-high oak trees.

'You sure this is it, Dad?' I asked, suddenly anxious to check that this was the right place, that I hadn't got my hopes up for nothing. 'It doesn't look that bad...'

Dad smiled, 'Uncle Kareem wouldn't invite us to stay in a dump, Ali.'

Umar kissed his teeth and scrunched down further in his

seat, his eyes fixed on the phone he held in front of him.

'I can't wait to see what it looks like inside!' Jamal was jumping up and down with excitement.

Dad chuckled and tossed him the keys. 'Do the honours, son.'

And Jamal duly unlocked the door of our new home and let us in.

* * *

We went to pray the Friday prayers at the local mosque the next day and, as far as I was concerned, we stuck out like sore thumbs, even amongst other Muslims. We were obviously strangers, new to the community: we dressed differently, spoke differently, didn't know anyone. But one of the brothers made his way over to us like it was the most natural thing in the world.

'*As-salamu 'alaykum.* My name's Usamah.' As tall as Dad, maybe even taller, dressed in a brown linen *thobe* with a crisp white turban tied around his head, he greeted us with such a smile, such easy confidence, that Dad was caught off guard. '*Mashallah*, fine set of boys you've got here, sir,' he smiled, shaking us all by the hand, and giving Jamal a mock punch on the shoulder. 'Y'all new to the *masjid*?'

'Yes, we are,' Dad answered him. 'It's our first time here as a family.' Then he frowned. 'Well, the boys' mother – my late wife - and I visited a friend here a few times when we were newly married. But we moved out of London and didn't come back here again...'

I stared at Dad. It wasn't like him to speak so candidly –

14

and to a stranger at that.

Usamah bowed his head slightly and said a brief prayer, then looked up at all of us. 'May Allah make it easy for all of you,' he said quietly. 'Losing someone that close is never easy.'

I shifted on my feet then, feeling bare and exposed in the crowded prayer hall. How are you supposed to respond to a statement like that?

But Dad didn't seem to be having any problems. He answered the brother's questions about our family, where we were living, what we thought of the *khutbah* – totally unlike his usual reserved self.

Although I wasn't at all comfortable with the upfront disclosure that was going on, I found myself warming to Usamah. He seemed laid-back but had a serious, focused look in his eyes; his manner was confident but humble, in that spiritual sort of way that you read about but seldom encounter. I decided to suspend judgement.

Somehow, we found ourselves talking about sports and, once he heard that I had been on the school rugby and basketball teams, he laughed. 'No wonder you're so pumped up, bro!' And he invited me to play basketball with him and some other Muslim brothers the next morning.

'I'll introduce you to the brothers,' he said, full of confidence. 'It will make settling in easier.'

And then he was gone, off to greet the imam of the mosque and get himself some fried chicken from the food trailer parked outside the mosque.

'Mashallah,' said Dad, with a smile, 'he seems like a nice brother...'

Umar scowled. 'What's with the wacky dress sense?' he growled, then kissed his teeth and went to sit on the low wall

15

outside the mosque, his hood over his head, his hands stuck deep in his pockets.

He stayed there, detached, not responding to anyone's *salam* or attempts at conversation, until it was time to go.

'He'll come round,' Dad had said.

'Inshallah, Dad,' had been my response.

* * *

By the time I reached the basketball courts on the other side of the park, the brothers were already there, messing about with the ball, shooting hoops, showing off to no one in particular. When I came the first time with Usamah, things were a little awkward but everyone relaxed once they saw that I could play. Now, it felt like I'd been playing with them forever.

I tossed my bag onto the nearest bleacher and called out, 'Hey!' My feet were itching to feel the heat of the court, my hands eager for the ball's rough surface.

The three of them – Usamah, Zayd and Mahmoud – all turned and returned the *salam*, 'As-salamu 'alaykum, bro.'

Usamah's face broke into a smile.

'About time, akh!' he laughed. 'We thought you had bailed out on us!' And he did a little jump and flipped the ball into the net with a flick of his wrist. 'Ready to get your behind *whupped*?'

I grinned back at him. 'I'm going for 50 hoops today,' I laughed, buoyed by the bravado that came from hanging with 'the brothers'. That was how they rolled. So that was how I was going to roll, too.

16

'Nah, man,' jeered Mahmoud, 'never!'

'Watch me!'

'I'm watching, akh,' called Usamah, 'and I don't see nothin' but talk. Don't aim too high, you might fall hard!'

'That's right, my man!' called Mahmoud, getting ready to throw the ball to Zayd. But, just then, something caught his eye and he turned towards the bleachers.

Two girls sauntered across the bleachers and paused, posing, preening, looking out on to the court.

Mahmoud let out a low whistle from between his teeth and nudged me, a crooked smile on his face.

'Hey,' he said softly, 'have a look at *that*. Now *that* is hotness...'

In spite of myself, I glanced over at the girls and caught a glimpse of skin, glossy hair and flashing eyes. *Fitnah*. Straight up.

'Now, wouldn't you like a taste of that?' Mahmoud was still staring, a slow fire burning in his eyes.

'No, not me,' I mumbled, studying the ball in my hands. 'I'm not into all that.'

Mahmoud looked at me, curious. 'Hey, a man's got needs, right?'

I swallowed hard. 'Yeah, that's right...' I avoided Mahmoud's gaze and looked up at the net. 'But that's why I fast... and play ball.' I needed to ease the tension, to stop all this talk about girls and needs, all the stuff that made life complicated and left you frustrated. I took a run up to the net and slam dunked the ball, sweet as anything.

'That's one!'

The game was on.

***

Well, after that my mind emptied, the intensity of the game sweeping all other thoughts aside. I didn't stop for a moment: running, reaching, twisting, springing, leaping, thrusting, driving the ball into the net again and again and again.

The others were like shadows on either side of me, a blur, merging with one another. But I was aware of everything else: the hard slap of my trainers on the ground, the grainy texture of the ball, slick with nervous sweat, the strain in my calf muscles, the tension in my forearms, the sweat soaking my scalp, trickling down my back.

I lost myself in the game and left the others floundering, panting, struggling to keep up, to slow my flow.

But none of them could match my focus.

Not today.

Then came the moment of truth: I held the ball in my hands, my fingers splayed, my palms burning. The others hovered around, breathless, their shoulders heaving. I got ready to shoot my fiftieth round. Victory was within reach.

Then – 'Zayd!'

A clear voice rang out across the court, a girl's voice, cutting the air like a knife, a cool wave over the hot tarmac, and I felt the tiny hairs on the back of my neck stand up. Stupidly, I turned to look. And the world stood still.

It *was* a girl, but not like any I had ever seen. Her black hijab and *abaya* were stark against the sun-drenched colours of the bleachers. A fresh breeze came and whipped her long hijab up and it swirled around her like a cloud, like a dream, like a spell.

She brought her hand up to move the fabric away from her face and, in that moment, I froze as if a bucket of ice had been poured over me. My breath caught in my throat.

I noticed everything: the tiny hands, the pale fingernails, the cleft in her chin, its defiant tilt, the nose ring, the piercing eyes, the long eyelashes. I noticed it all in the space of about 3.5 seconds, the time it takes to have one look, and in that moment I smiled without meaning to, an involuntary smile, the kind you get when your heart leaps for no reason, when it skips a beat. Then I looked down. And I saw her trainers. Red Converse trainers, just like mine.

Woah

My breath came back to me and the world began to move again.

I didn't realise I had dropped the ball until I caught sight of Mahmoud, on the other end of the court, jumping high to land the ball into the net. The ball banged against the backboard and spun around twice before dropping through the hoop and bouncing off the court. Mahmoud and Usamah cheered, exultant.

'You almost had it, man,' Mahmoud panted, his wild eyes dancing.

'What did I tell you?' laughed Usamah. 'Too much talk! Now, watch and learn from the experts, boy!' And he ran down the court and did his favourite move, sailing through the air, arms and legs outstretched, swinging from the net as the ball fell through it.

I laughed as I watched him, panting. My mind was on other things.

But when I looked back to the bleachers again, the girl was gone.

4

I wasn't supposed to be at the basketball courts. Zayd was playing with his guy friends and that generally meant that the court was off-limits.

'I don't want you coming around the brothers, sis,' he'd always say. I would roll my eyes every time. Not like there was anything there I hadn't seen before.

'Nah, it's just that I know how guys' minds work, OK? Trust me, it's better you stay away.'

Then he'd keep going on in that earnest way of his about the Islamic rules on modesty – *ghayrah* and hijab, niqab, lowering the gaze etc. I'd usually tuned him out by that point. I got it. He didn't want his friends eyeing up his sister. I could respect that.

But that day was different. After I dropped the kids at the mosque, Mum started ringing my phone, asking where Zayd was. Apparently, he had promised to take the kids to the park after madrasah while she went to her appointment at the doctor's, and she was still waiting to hear back from him. I shook my head. Zayd may have been the world's most dutiful son, but he had a terrible memory.

Anyway, that Saturday morning, I knew that he had his regular basketball practice so I decided to go over and tell him to call Mum before going off to do some sketching.

I recognised all the other players: I had seen most of them outside the *masjid* at one time or another.

I saw Usamah, the exchange student from the Bronx, studying fashion and design at Central Saint Martins, a cross between a 'loud 'n' proud' New Yorker and a twenty-first century Ibn Batutta. And he scored a very respectable eight in our totally naughty but hilarious Muslim hottie chart: the 'Mottie Scale'.

Then there was Mr Smooth, Mahmoud. I only knew him because we'd been at primary school together but I never gave him much more than a nod and quick *salam* in recognition of the fact that he had once pushed someone over for bullying me in the playground. Other than that, I stayed away. Some guys are just too dangerous. You can't let them get too close because they don't know how to be 'just friends'. Mahmoud and guys like him were officially excluded from the Mottie rankings. We girls know better than to play with fire.

But then I noticed that there was someone else on the court, someone I hadn't seen before. He was playing some serious ball, making everyone gasp and pant to catch up with him. He seemed to be aiming for some sort of record, slamming the ball into the net again and again. There was something about the way he moved – strong, graceful, rippling, like a cat – that made something flutter in my stomach.

What a gorgeous specimen, I thought. From a purely artistic point of view, of course.

For a split second, I imagined myself framing the contours of his arms the colour of caramel, the biceps flowing into the sinewy forearm, the powerful hands with the perfect nails. Charcoal, for sure. That was the best way to capture the glow

AMIRAH ♀

of his skin and play of shadow and light that highlighted the muscles.

But those thoughts only flashed through my mind for a second.

Astaghfirullah.

What was I doing there again? Then I remembered: I was here for Zayd. But he hadn't seen me yet, he was so intent on trying to block the guy with the ball. I would have to interrupt.

'Zayd!' I called out, my voice perfectly controlled to sound mature and businesslike: my 'brothers voice'.

All four of them turned towards me and, for a brief moment, the stranger's eyes met mine. They were the lightest eyes I had ever seen on a mixed-race boy, light and clear. Trusting. As soon as our eyes met, he smiled, almost before he could catch himself, and dropped the ball. It was as if his smile had eclipsed the sun; I wasn't aware of anything else, just shadows that made him shine even brighter. My heart flipped a couple of times and my mouth went dry.

Oh, wow.

Then, out of the corner of my eye, I saw Mahmoud running up to grab the ball. But it was as if the stranger couldn't hear him – either that or he didn't care.

A moment later, he had lowered his gaze, the ball was out of his control and Zayd was running towards me, his face red, his hair plastered to his forehead.

'What are you doing here, Amirah?' he frowned, guiding me away from the court. I heard the ball slam into the net on the other side of the court. Seemed Mahmoud had interrupted Mr Light Eyes' flow.

'Well, *as-salamu 'alaykum* to you too, brother,' I smiled, only mildly irritated by his over-the-top protectiveness.

♀ AMIRAH

He mumbled a greeting as he approached.

'Your mother has been trying to reach you,' I said as he fumbled around for his phone in his bag. 'Something about a doctor's appointment?'

Zayd groaned. 'Subhanallah, I completely forgot!' he cried, slapping his forehead.

'Well,' I said, 'you'd better get your backside over to number 6 Seville Close quick time before the Wrath of Mum descends on you.'

Zayd turned to his friends, 'Yo, *ikhwan*, I'm out. Got to take care of some family stuff.' He looked over at the sharp shooter and smiled. 'Great play, Ali, mashallah...'

So, his name was Ali.

Another piece of information to add to the fact that he was quite possibly the most gorgeous guy I had ever laid eyes on.

But I had to stop that train of thought before it got out of hand because, for a start, the only reason a strictly practising Muslim girl like me would have anything remotely emotional to do with a boy is if she were ready to get married.

And I was *never* getting married, ever.

End of.

23

5

'You did good, man, mashallah,' Usamah smiled over at me as we cooled off after the game. Mahmoud was already gone, off to meet one of the girls who had stopped by earlier, no doubt. Usamah rubbed his towel over his bald head and sat down to drink some water from his bottle.

'You didn't play too badly yourself,' I said, leaning back onto the bleachers and looking over at him. 'But you know I could have got 50, don't you...'

'Uh-huh,' Usamah took another swig from the bottle. 'If you hadn't gone and gotten distracted, you might have.'

I coughed and let out a little laugh, embarrassed. But Usamah just shrugged his shoulders and looked out over the court, smiling. I glanced behind me and thought to myself, *This is the spot, right here. This is where she was standing...*

We got up to go and Usamah turned to me. 'You hungry? There's a great West Indian place around the corner. And I could show you around your new hood.'

And he did. He showed me the station tucked away under the bridge, which bus to take into Brixton, which one to take down to Croydon. He took me to try the best halal Jamaican patties in South London, and told me which stalls in the market sold the best incense and perfume oils.

And as we walked and ate and rode the bus, we talked.

'So why did y'all move from out in the country to the big, bad city?'

I took a deep breath. I hated this bit: explaining why we had left Hertfordshire. Usamah noticed my hesitation and put a hand out towards me.

'I don't want you to think I'm nosey or nothin', it's just that I've got a habit of asking questions about everything. So any time you feel you want me to shut up and stop asking you about your life story, you go right ahead and say it, OK?'

'OK,' I laughed, thinking how unusual this Usamah guy was. 'It's not a problem. You remind me of one of my school friends, Pablo. He was like that, always asking questions, wanting to get to the bottom of things.'

'Good at getting those 'Oprah moments', huh?'

'Yeah, you could say that...' An image of Pablo flashed across my mind: it was the last day of school, the day after we had finished our exams. We were both dressed in our school uniform, and I was telling him that I wouldn't be coming to the end-of-year dance. The look on his face – incredulity, incomprehension, disappointment – only made my words seem harsher than I intended. I didn't trust myself not to buckle, not to allow him to sweet talk me into fulfilling our pact, as he always did. So I got it out and over with, as quickly as I could, and walked away.

That was the last time I had seen him.

I had decided that I couldn't trust myself around him. His lifestyle was too tempting, and my fledgling Islamic identity was too weak to withstand the attraction. Or so I had thought at the time.

Now, with his face vivid in my mind, I wondered whether

25

I had been too harsh on him – and too doubtful of my own strength of character.

Usamah's voice snapped me back to the present. 'So, is that why you don't sound like most of the brothers I've met from London?'

I laughed, embarrassed. 'You mean my accent?'

He nodded, smiling.

'Well, I went to a public school – what you Americans call private school – so my accent is a little different. You're from New York, right?'

'That's right, the Bronx, baby.'

'So what are you doing in London?'

'Well, I always wanted to travel, to see Europe and all that jazz. And I thought studying abroad would be a way to do that – don't ask me how I ended up living in South London studying fashion, though, that was just fate, the *qadr* of Allah!'

'Seriously, bro – *fashion*?'

He laughed again. 'Yeah, I'm that straight guy with the queer eye, I guess. I just always loved clothes: drawing them, making them, y'know. My sisters loved me 'coz their Barbies were the best dressed in town!'

An image of a child-sized version of Usamah fitting clothes on a Barbie popped into my head and I spluttered.

'OK, maybe I'm missing something here. I mean, I don't mean to judge or anything, but how does the fashion industry fit in with your beliefs?'

Usamah sighed and scratched his head. 'I'm trying to make it work, akh. But I can't deny the gifts God gave me. I can't pretend I don't love what I do. So I've got to halalify, y'know? I design clothes for young Muslims – or anyone into funky, individual style with a modest edge. And I sell them from my website. As for the other stuff, the shows, the models and all that, I'm trying to find a way around it all.'

I felt really relaxed around Usamah. He didn't have his guard up like so many other young men, and he wasn't afraid to be himself, to be an individual. Me, I tended to want to blend in, picking up slang and ways of being that were alien to me, simply to fit in with the group: first, the English boys at school and, now, it seemed, the Muslim boys in South London. Usamah, on the other hand, was quite confident in his identity: his roots, his accent, his quirky dress sense and interest in fashion and spirituality. He wore it all with pride. I admired that.

'So, what about you, akh? What do you love to do? What can you not live without?'

My mind flicked through various possible answers: rugby, PlayStation, studying, basketball, but none of them felt right. I felt so far away from them all now. Six months ago, my response would have been immediate, 100 per cent sure. But now...

'I don't know, bro. I guess I'm trying to figure myself out, too. I've only been on the *deen* for the past eight months so a lot of it is still new to me. And I've had to leave a lot of stuff behind...' Pablo. The band. Amy.

Amy.

'Ahh, the baggage of *jahiliyyah*, huh? All that haram stuff we used to do? That's a hard one. But don't worry, bro, you'll get there. You'll find your niche, that place where you belong, inshallah.'

So, as we walked up the high street toward the bus stop, I plucked up the courage to mention what had been dancing around in the back of my mind since our basketball game.

'You know that girl who came to the court during the game, the one with the nose ring and black hijab?'

Usamah gave me a look. 'You mean Zayd's sister? Man, I try my best *not* to know who she is! Zayd don't take to that kinda thing, y'know. He gets kinda defensive – angry – any time anybody mentions his sister... why, you know her?'

'Of course not, I don't know anybody! I'm the new kid on the block, remember?'

'Well, if I were you, I would just look the other way. That's Zayd's sister. She is off-limits, man, totally off-limits.'

So, I had my answer. Now I could finally stop thinking about her.

The girl in the red trainers.

6

After leaving the basketball court, I went back to my favourite spot to sketch: a bench under some oak trees at the top of the hill, overlooking Brockwell Park and the surrounding neighbourhood.

This park was definitely my favourite place in the whole of London, especially early in the mornings when the mist rolled down from the hill and gave the green slopes an unearthly, magical feel. That was my favourite time to walk, when I shared the park with no one but the dog walkers and running enthusiasts. This was before the park filled up with yummy mummies and their toddlers in their state-of-the-art buggies, before the groups of teenagers coming out to use the basketball courts, the school kids determined to conquer the climbing frame, before the families carrying bags of stale bread came to feed the ducks and the Canada geese, before the barbecues, the Frisbee games and kite flyers.

This was my time to be alone with my thoughts, to process, to reflect. To be honest, I often felt like praying when I was up there, surrounded by the sounds of nature and the miracles of creation. It would be easy, really. Just work out the direction to pray, the *qiblah*, stand up and offer two *raka'at*, simples.

But even though I longed to feel the earth beneath my fingers and smell the scent of the grass as I touched my forehead to the ground in *sujud*, I had never plucked up the courage to do it. What if someone saw me? What if people stared? Would they take me for some extremist nutter and call the park ranger?

No, safer to sit and contemplate. I could always read from my pocket-sized Qur'an without attracting too much attention.

Sigh.

The life of a post-9/11, 7/7 Muslim in London.

It was almost *Zuhr* time, around midday, so I knew that my sketching time was limited. I would have to go and get started on the housework before long. I opened my bag and took out the heavy sketch pad. I had started a drawing the week before, a landscape that stretched from one end of the park to the other.

I looked at it again, my head tilted to one side. It was quite good, very good in places. I moved my fingers lightly over the page, unsure where to start. I did a bit of shading, hardened a couple of edges, smudged some outlines. But I just wasn't feeling it anymore. Was it the fact that the empty green I had been sketching the other morning was now dotted with people? Or was it that I had other things on my mind?

My phone vibrated in my pocket. I took it out and saw it was a text from my best mate, Rania. *Need to get outfits and heels for UMP show this Sun! U in?*

Rania's mum, Auntie Azra, was an event organiser and was arranging the annual Urban Muslim Princess (UMP) fashion show and dinner party. She had invited us girls to come along to celebrate the end of our A levels – and to launch

Rania's first designer clothing collection. I was way beyond excited because I had seen the collection grow from the mood board stage to actual outfits that we were going to wear on the catwalk! How awesome was that?

All money raised was going to help a Muslim charity that worked with orphaned victims of war. The irony of laying on a lavish three course meal in order to feed starving orphans was not lost on me but I had learned to live with it. Some people help by going without, others help by going out into the field to volunteer, and still others help by paying to have a halal version of a prom. Don't judge.

I texted her back: *No doubt!*

I turned the page of my sketch book. I felt like doing something different...

I chose a slim stick of charcoal and started to skip it over the paper, concentrating on the picture I could see quite clearly in my head. Lines blended into others, shading deepened the shadows, the flat side of the stick gave me the coverage I needed. I drew, deliberately ignoring the implications of the image I was creating, deliberately focusing on the technical side, not the emotional memory that was fuelling it.

And then it was done. I closed my eyes and turned away, clearing my mind. I always did that before looking at my work after I had finished. It helped me to look at it with fresh eyes and spot the mistakes.

I turned back to the sketchbook that lay open on the grass in front of me. My breath caught. It was good. It was really good, possibly the best I had done in a long time.

It was a drawing of a hand, a strong, beautiful hand, the fingers tipped by perfect fingernails. A hand holding a basketball with a mole below the little finger.

And it was obvious who the hand belonged to.

Mr Light Eyes.

* * *

If there's one thing I've learned about life, it's this: when you are not supposed to do something, you will find it near impossible to resist and when you have to do something, you'll find any number of excuses to avoid doing it.

Take that morning. As soon as I saw that boy – Ali – and saw the way his face lit up, I knew that there was something potentially wonderful there. Wonderful or dangerous. And, given my circumstances – being a practising Muslim and expected not to even be able to recognise a member of the opposite gender (ahem) – it could only be dangerous. Tragic, even. You see, in my community, it doesn't really work the way it does in the movies: boy meets girl, boy fancies girl, boy asks girl out, they go out, discover they are amazingly compatible soul mates and begin a torrid affair with lots of romantic dates and passionate encounters and a nice dose of happily ever after at the end of the movie.

In my community, a 'boy meets girl' romance normally results in heartbreak, betrayal and a damaged reputation – for the girl, of course! In every scenario I had ever seen, it was the girl who paid the price for entertaining the guy's advances. Because that's what guys do, right? They try it. They keep knocking and knocking and knocking until someone lets them in. That's their job. The job of a girl with her head screwed on is to not be the fool who opens the door to the *fitnah* dressed up like Prince Charming.

♀ AMIRAH

So, back to the paradox of the human condition: I knew all this. I was painfully aware of the price to be paid for embarking on a pointless obsession that could so easily lead to the haram, the forbidden. So I mastered myself. Every time he popped into my head, it is like I was closing the curtains, shutting him out. I probably wouldn't ever see him again, anyway.

I would not talk about him.

I would *definitely* not ask Zayd about him.

I would not even think about him.

At all.

No one needed to see my drawing. It could be my little secret.

AMIRAH ♀

7

We had decided to start unpacking after a week or so.

A few hours in, we were still at it and Dad said he needed a cup of tea.

'I'll make it,' I sighed.

As I waited for the kettle to boil, I thought of Umar still lost in sleep in his room. He had point blank refused to wake up and help unpack. 'I think he may be coming down with something,' I had muttered vaguely when Dad asked where he was. I thought it would be easier than Dad going in after him. Besides, it wasn't like we couldn't manage without him.

It had been harder than I expected to talk Umar round to the idea of leaving the home we all loved, all his friends, to stay at an unknown location in strange, far away London for the summer.

'Why? Why do we have to leave?' he had yelled at me when I first told him what Dad was planning. I knew why he was so upset: his whole life was in Hertfordshire where he was part of a tight-knit group of friends at school; he'd started making music – and there was a girl in the picture somewhere. I understood his frustration, but what could I do?

'We can't afford not to, Umar,' I had said, as gently as I could. 'Dad's business is in trouble and he needs the rent from this house. Please try to be reasonable. We'll be back after the summer, inshallah, don't worry.'

'But I don't want to go to London – or anywhere else!' He had jumped up out of his seat, his eyes blazing. I had never seen him so angry. 'Why does everything have to change? Why can't we just stay here? We could stay with Nana Jordan for the summer...'

But I knew there was no way Dad would go for that. I shook my head.

'I'm sorry, Umar, but this is the way it's got to be. And it's only until the end of the summer, inshallah...'

'Don't we get to have a say about *anything* in this house anymore? It's become more like a dictatorship than a proper family!'

He had turned and stormed out, shrugging on his jacket. His sleeve had caught the edge of the lamp on the side table. It toppled, then fell onto the hardwood floor. I bent down to pick it up as the front door slammed: a crack had appeared in the base. The lamp had been one of Mum's favourites, a memento from her and Dad's visit to Venice. I was sure I could fix it somehow.

I needn't have bothered: Dad made me leave that in storage, along with all Mum's other things.

The steam from the kettle scalded my wrist. My eyes were stinging with unshed tears.

That was when I heard the revving of a motorbike engine. I leaned over and peered into the parking lot to see a rider getting off the back of a huge, glossy motorbike, with yellow and blue flames painted on the side. He took off the massive helmet he was wearing, looked up, and waved. It was Usamah.

The rider in front got off and took off his helmet, revealing

35

short, black hair and a neat, curly beard.

'This is my main man, Yusuf,' Usamah said after I had let them into the house, still shocked that they were actually there.

'*As-salamu 'alaykum*, bro,' Yusuf smiled and shook my hand.

'*Wa'alaykum as-salam*, brothers!' Jamal piped up, determined to be part of the conversation.

'I'm not a kid anymore, Ali,' he had said to me just that morning. 'I'm nine – almost ten! You have to stop treating me like a baby. If I'm old enough to have to pray, I think I'm old enough to get a little respect around here!' And he'd puffed out his puny chest at me.

'Respect, huh?' I'd teased him. 'How about you start with those dishes sitting in the sink, waiting for a little respect?'

'Oh, no,' he'd laughed, dancing off into the bathroom. 'I said respect, not responsibility!'

But now, here he was again, wanting to play with the big boys. 'Ready for some responsibility now, eh, Jamal?'

He stuck his tongue out at me just as Dad came in, rolling up his sleeves. Usamah and Yusuf greeted him. '*As-salamu 'alaykum*, what do you want us to do, sir?' Usamah smiled. 'We're at your service.'

'You boys don't need to do that,' said Dad. 'We can manage. What do you think I've got these strong lads for?'

Usamah chuckled then turned to me, 'Yo, where's Umar?'

I made a face. 'He's still asleep. I thought it would be best to just let him sleep while we get on with it.'

'Yeah, I remember when I was that age – I would have slept all day if my mom let me!' We all laughed.

Just then, Umar stomped into the living room, rubbing

his eyes and yawning. He took one look at the mess and all of us standing with boxes in our hands and growled, 'What's going on here?'

'Umar!' Dad's voice was sharp, edged with embarrassment. 'Is that any way to greet people? Where are your manners?'

But Umar's response was simply to kiss his teeth and stalk back out of the room, muttering under his breath.

'Umar!' Dad quickly followed him and, a few moments later, we all heard his raised voice, going back and forth with Umar's monotone. Everybody pretended not to hear anything and, a moment later, Usamah was asking for a dustpan and brush and Yusuf was kneeling down in front of Jamal.

'And how old are you, bro?

Jamal drew himself up to his full height. 'Almost ten.'

Yusuf's eyes were wide. 'Really? Subhanallah, I thought you were at least 12! Since you're such a big guy, you won't mind helping me shift these boxes, will you?'

Jamal shook his head and followed Yusuf to the far side of the lounge where the full boxes were stacked.

With everyone – except Umar – working together, it didn't take long for everything to be unpacked and put away. I put the kettle on again and Yusuf took a tin foil package out of his bag.

'Chocolate cake,' he said by way of explanation. 'My sister made it. She thought we might like something sweet after all that hard work.'

'Mashallah,' said Usamah, hurrying to the sink to wash his hands. 'May Allah bless your sister. She's always got a brother's back.' Then he turned to me. 'Yusuf's sister, Sister Yasmin, can bake the hind leg off a giraffe!'

Jamal giggled as he took a bite of the rich, gooey chocolate cake. 'You always say such funny things, Usamah!'

'Well, Allah made me funny, little brother. What can I say?'

'Yusuf,' I said, turning to him, 'what's this all about?' I was pointing to his leather jacket, and the embroidered insignia across the back. It said 'Deen Riders'.

'Oh, that?' Yusuf grinned. 'That's our Muslim biker club.'

The look on my face must have said it all.

'I know, it sounds crazy, right?' Usamah shook his head. 'But these brothers are for real – good, solid brothers. And their bikes are amazing, man, straight up!'

Yusuf smiled modestly. 'A group of us met at a motorbike show – the brothers with the beards are kind of easy to spot, y'know. And we decided to make a club of our own, with our own insignia and everything.'

38   I was puzzled. 'But riding bikes isn't haram, is it? Why bring the *deen* into it?'

Yusuf looked at me. 'We would go on these weekend rides' he mused, 'and I would think, yeah, this is the life. It can't get much better than this. But then I realised that, although I loved riding, it wasn't necessarily helping me *deen*-wise, y'know? I didn't feel like there was much benefit in it, in terms of my Islam. So we started thinking about how we could make our love for bikes into something that benefitted us and others. And Deen Riders was born.'

'Wow, that is so cool.' Jamal's face was bright. 'Brothers on bikes!'

'Hey!' Yusuf hit him lightly on the back. 'That's a great name, bro! Why didn't I think of that?'

'Little brother got there first, bro. Stay in your lane!'

Yusuf looked over at me. 'So, Ali, have you ever ridden a

motorbike?'

I shook my head.

'Would you like to ride out with us one day? There are some great roads outside South London, clear and fast. And we've got a rally coming up in a few weeks, too. Funds going to charity.'

I smiled and shook my head. 'Nah, bro, I think I'll have to pass. I'm not much of a risk taker. Not anymore.' I ruffled Jamal's hair. 'Got to keep my feet on the ground.'

Yusuf raised an eyebrow, shrugged, and looked over at Usamah. 'Suit y'self, bro. Usamah, you're coming, innit?'

'Wouldn't miss it, akh.'

'*I wonder if Zayd's sister likes guys on bikes...*' The thought just popped into my head, out of nowhere and an image flashed before me: the girl in the red trainers and me, speeding through the countryside on a motorbike. She was laughing, holding on tight. Thrilled.

So much for keeping my feet on the ground...

39

8

The tension in the house was too much for me. What with Mum on anti-depressants and the kids bouncing off the walls, I was just about holding it together. I had really wanted to continue working on my secret drawing of Mr Light Eyes' hands but the kids didn't give me any space at all. Between breaking up their squabbles, making their lunch and keeping the house from becoming a tip, I had to deal with Malik who had been clingy all afternoon, crying whenever Taymeeyah teased him. Even Abdullah was on edge. He kept tugging at my sleeve and signing, 'What's wrong with Mum?' I found it really hard to reassure him when Mum had basically retreated to her room and refused to talk to anyone, let alone sign with Abdullah to let him know that she just needed a bit of space.

That was when I decided to set them all up at the table with some paints and paper. That kept Taymeeyah and Malik busy for about thirty minutes but it was better than nothing. By that time, Zayd was back from his Saturday job and I was like, 'Bro, you need to take over. I need to get out of here.' But then I noticed that Abdullah was still at the table, hunched over his paper, totally engrossed. I stepped up behind him to take a look and gasped with surprise. Abdullah had painted a figure in a box surrounded by angry black and red swirls. All

40

around the box were words like 'tired', 'scared', 'Mum' and 'tears'.

'Abdullah,' I called out, touching his shoulder. Immediately, he shielded the paper with his arm but I gently moved it away. 'What does the picture mean, babe?' I asked.

He shrugged. 'Means what it says,' he signed.

And that was when I got the idea to introduce Abdullah to my world, the world of art as an escape. You don't need to be able to hear to be able to appreciate beauty, or know how to use a box of paints.

I would start in the morning.

But first, I had to save what little sanity I had left: I had to get out of there and Rania's house was just where I wanted to be when things got too hectic at home.

We had developed a Saturday ritual over the previous six months: Taymeeyah and I would go over to Rania's house to escape the boys for the night. In the run-up to the exams, Rania and I had studied while the younger girls played, but now that school was over, we spent the evening talking, eating, doing henna and cackling over silly YouTube videos. Occasionally, we would listen to an Islamic talk. But with the Urban Muslim Princess event just a few weeks away, Rania had me working on her fashion show: the backdrop was my main responsibility, but I was also meant to be both Creative Director and one of the models on the catwalk.

'And to think,' I grumbled, 'you're getting all these services for free, all because you're my best friend.'

Rania snorted. 'Girl, please, you know you love it! And one day, when my brand is famous and I'm flying you to Dubai for my latest show, you'll be able to say, "I was there when it all began."'

I pulled a face. 'Yeah, yeah, keep saying that while you treat me like a slave.'

Then we both laughed and went back to picking the accessories we wanted for each outfit in the show.

'I wish my dad was here to see this.' Rania's voice was low and I could tell that this was something that had been playing on her mind for a while. She always missed her dad when things were going well, like when she had played Lady Macbeth in the school play, or the time her design was chosen for the new school sports kit.

'He would have been so happy,' she always said. 'He always told me I could do anything.'

A lump in my throat appeared at that moment, just before the tears pricked my eyes. I didn't know what that felt like: having a father who not only stuck around and played the role of 'Dad', but encouraged me to achieve my potential, and who was my biggest fan. Rania was so blessed. Really, she was.

Then Rania looked up at me. 'What about your stepdad? Is he still troubling you?'

I had confided in her about Abu Malik months ago. Now I told her how he had left the house and that my mum was in her waiting period – the *iddah* – before the divorce would be finalised.

She heaved a huge sigh and hugged me. 'Do you think that's it then?'

I shrugged and did my very best 'I-don't-care' fake out. 'Hey, what can I say? Let the merry-go-round begin. It's only Round Two, remember? A lot can happen in three months so he could be back again.'

'Don't, Ams,' Rania said, and my heart twisted at the sadness in her voice. 'I hate it when you talk like that, all hard, as if you don't care.'

I heaved a sigh. 'Rani, I had to stop caring a long time ago. This isn't the first time, remember? I've been through all this before, so many times I've lost count. Of course, I hate the upheaval, especially for the kids, but, to be honest, I sometimes wish there were no stepfathers on the scene at all. Just us. Then, at least, we could have some stability. My mum doesn't handle the *iddah* well at all.'

Rania closed her eyes and shook her head. 'It's just too awful, Ams. I can't even imagine it.'

'Of course not, Rani,' I said, suppressing the bitterness in my voice. 'Your parents were happily married for 18 years, mashallah. You had your dad around. You don't know what it's like to have stepdads and divorces and waiting periods going on all around you since you were little. You're not a victim of your mother's chaotic love life, basically.' I felt bad then. It wasn't Mum's fault, not really. She just didn't pick husbands very well. Either that, or she was a magnet for losers, troublemakers and men who just didn't know how to value her.

This wasn't the first time Mum's relationship had failed. She'd had my older brother Zayd when she was 17, and me three years later. Neither of our fathers had stuck around long enough to name us so we had spent our early years with my nan while Mum tried to finish school, get a hairdressing qualification, anything to get some money coming in and some independence.

But then she met Uncle Faisal. He was running a *da'wah* stall on Brixton High Street, telling passers-by about Islam. Mum had stopped to listen and had been moved by the message. She always told us that it was the purity of Islam

– the worship of one God, the clean lifestyle – that had first attracted her to the religion.

So she accepted Islam and Uncle Faisal asked her to marry him, told her he would provide for her and her kids, honour her as his wife. That was more than anyone else had ever offered her. That was how we ended up together in a flat in Stockwell, a family at last. Those were happy years, mashallah. Zayd and I loved Uncle Faisal like a real dad and he treated us just like his own kids, Taymeeyah and Abdullah.

But that marriage had had its fair share of ups and downs, false starts and separations. Then, one day, Mum told us Uncle Faisal was gone and wouldn't be coming back. That was the beginning of the end of my illusions about life and love. I had been Uncle Faisal's princess. Then he was gone.

Mum had married two more times after that – no kids, polygamy each time – before she met Abu Malik. I think she'd hoped that Malik's dad would be the one, the one who would stay, the one she would grow old with as his only wife, who would do the right thing and raise his boy. But even I could see that he wasn't the type to stick around and take care of his responsibilities.

When he left that first time, taking his box of Sahih Muslim and smelly football boots with him, Mum couldn't handle it. She had just seen what she thought was the failure of her fourth Islamic marriage and it was all too much for her.

That was the start of the dark days of her depression.

That was the day I decided that I would never put myself in that position, not for a million pounds.

♀ AMIRAH

9

It is a Sunday morning. I can tell by the uncanny density of my duvet, the warmth and light that floods the room, telling me that it is after eight o'clock. I can tell by the sound of Dad's voice as he sings his version of opera in the shower – his own words, English mixed with snatches of French, Spanish and Patois. I can tell by the sound of Jamal's voice, high and chirpy, as he takes Umar's breakfast order.

And I can tell by the smell of pancakes coming from the kitchen. Mum is making her speciality: cinnamon pancakes with stewed apples and ice cream. And, if Jamal has his way, there will be chocolate sauce and toasted pecans, too.

I can hear her voice so clearly, 'Boys, come and get it! First come, first served!' And her favourite: 'You snooze, you lose.'

Now it is time to throw off the covers, grab my dressing gown and head for the kitchen, beating Dad and Umar to the top spot. Mum will smile at me and shake her head.

'When the meat is on the bone, you will see the people,' she will say with a wry smile, like she always does. Then she will ruffle my hair and kiss my head and put the steaming plate of pancakes in front of me. Jamal and I will be the first to eat, almost finished our first helping by the time Umar rolls out of bed and Dad has finished singing his mash-up in the shower.

I will say to Mum, 'What about you, Mum? Sit down, I'll get yours.'

'*Jazakallah khayran*, sweetie.' And she will smile gratefully and sit down at the other end of the table, on Dad's right hand side, unfastening her apron and putting her feet up in Dad's lap. As I pass by her, she will hold out her arms and give me a hug.

Instead I find myself waking from a dream, crying in the dark and cold. The lights in the corridor off, the whole house silent. Mum wasn't in the kitchen making pancakes because she wasn't here anymore, she'd gone. Been buried far away and the only one who makes pancakes now is me.

And it's time to pray *fajr*.

46

* * *

'Umar, wake up, man,' I reached over to shake my brother, whose head was buried under the bed clothes. I always wondered how he could breathe like that.

Umar moaned and turned on his side, moving out of my reach. 'Leave me alone, man,' he groaned, pulling the covers tighter around his head.

'It's time to pray, man,' I insisted, pulling the covers a little harder. 'The old man said to wake you up.'

No response.

I decided to change tack. 'Just get up and make *wudu* – you'll feel better, y'know...' But the covers stayed firmly over Umar's head.

I sighed and tried again, 'Remember, prayer is better than sleep,' I called out, just like the *adhan* of *Fajr*.

'Yeah, right,' was the response.

I gave up then. What was I supposed to do if Umar refused to wake up? I had my own *salah* to worry about.

At the other end of the hall, I knocked lightly on the door and pushed it open. 'Jamal,' I called out softly. 'It's time to pray...'

Immediately, a tousled head poked out from under the duvet. Jamal sat up and rubbed the sleep from his eyes.

'Have you prayed yet, Ali?' he asked.

'No.'

'Good.' Jamal swung his legs over the side of the bed and stretched. 'Don't you pray without me, OK, Ali?'

'Sure, Jay, we'll wait for you, inshallah.' I turned to go.

'Oh, Ali?'

'Yeah?'

'D'you think you could make pancakes today? I had a lovely dream about them last night.'

I laughed. 'No problem, Jay, I'll make you pancakes today.'

'With chocolate sauce and ice cream?'

I chuckled as I nodded my head. 'Yup, with chocolate sauce and ice cream – if there's any left!' I shook my head again as I watched my nine-year-old brother scamper to the bathroom. That boy sure loved his food!

And Islam. When Dad and I started making changes to our lifestyle – prioritising our faith, the prayer in congregation, *Jum'ah*, and all that – Jamal was totally on board. It was as if this was what he had been waiting for. Not so Umar.

As I walked down the hallway, I saw Dad standing in the

47

doorway to Umar's room, a frown on his face and a hard edge to his voice.

'Umar!' he barked, his fist tight on the doorknob. 'Get *up*!'

'All *right*!'

I could hear Umar rising violently, no doubt throwing off his covers. In a moment, he had pushed past Dad, a scowl on his face, and the bathroom door was slammed behind him.

After the *salah* I sat making *dhikr*. Dad had said that Umar would soon calm down and fall into step with all of us but, from where I was standing, he seemed to be getting more and more rebellious, more resistant to us.

'Oh, Allah,' I prayed, 'please guide him to the straight path. Don't let him forget who he is, what Mum taught him.'

I was worried about Umar. After Mum's death, he had withdrawn into himself. I was hurting so much myself, I didn't have the emotional energy to try to break down his walls. So he barricaded himself behind hostility, resentment, and silence.

He resented everything: losing Mum, renting out the house, moving from Hertfordshire. And he resented our efforts to revive Islam in our lives. He wanted to 'live free', in his words, 'find his own way'. And every time Dad told him to pray, or accompany us to the mosque, or take off his headphones, he bristled.

'It's my life!' he would scream and then he was gone, out of the room, out of the house. There were times when I thought he would storm through that front door and just not come back again.

So, every time he did come home, no matter what state he was in, I breathed a sigh of relief.

Because Umar was Mum's favourite, I had always known that. No matter how much she tried to hide it, I could tell that she had a soft spot for him. And she made me promise to always look out for him.

'He needs you, Ali,' she would say in the aftermath of another row. 'And he does look up to you, even though he doesn't show it. He's a good boy. Don't you give up on him, OK?'

So I had to hang in there. For Mum's sake.

Unpacking our things was the start of a new era for us. Besides, Dad had assured us it would only be until the start of the new school year. After that, we would be able to move back home to Hertfordshire. I was sure we could manage until then.

10

Sunday was our shopping day. The girls and I agreed to meet up to go shopping for clothes to wear to the Urban Muslim Princess event. But we couldn't agree on where to go: would it be further south to Croydon, east to the sparkling new shopping centre in Stratford or west to Westfield? In the end, logistics and finances won the argument and we headed to Tooting, home to our beloved TK Maxx. I'd been saving up for months and was more than happy to spend my cash in cheap 'n' cheerful Tooting, rather than upscale Westfield.

Now, when it comes to shopping, different people have different styles. Take Rania, for example. She is Miss Hijabi Fashionista so, for her, shopping is a real investment. She is always on the lookout for clothes that are stylish yet modest – long skirts, tunic tops, scarves and jackets, always jackets. I swear, last time I took a look in her wardrobe, I thought I had stumbled into the designer womenswear section of Selfridges: she clearly has a jacket fetish in addition to an addiction to shoes and bags. So, in short, shopping with Rania was always serious business: everything needed to be tried on, matching outfits put together, accessories sourced. A total look, no less.

Samia was a different story: for a start, she was never into fashion, even before she became Muslim and started wearing hijab. Samia, formely Sam, became Muslim in high school when she was that random white girl who used to hang around with the Asian girls, learning Urdu and wearing a dupatta with her school uniform. She attended one class at the *masjid* and that was it, she was hooked. She took her *shahadah* just before her GCSEs. But Muslim or not, she was always more of a tomboy, more interested in tracksuits, trainers and footie than heels and accessories. Now she nearly always wore a scarf and an *abaya*.

'I *love* my *abaya*!' she always said. 'Better than PJs, I tell you! No more fussing, no more stress.'

So you can imagine that shopping wasn't her favourite thing to do. But she came along that Sunday because the last thing she wanted was a telling off from Rania's mum. If there's one thing Auntie Azra can't stand, it is when people 'don't make an *effort*!' So she would have to get her glad rags on, just like the rest of us.

'Ooohh, these are soooo cute!' Rania had found herself a pair of sequinned pants and looked like she was about to have a heart attack – joy and elation all over her face. She clutched at the sparkling trousers on the rack and held them to her chest.

She grabbed at least four pairs of trousers and ran off to join the queue for the changing room.

I shook my head and smiled, then looked over at Samia. As usual, she was squinting at the screen of her iPhone, a green jumpsuit dangling from the hanger in her hand. Only Allah knows how she managed to actually live life between Tumblr blog posts, Facebook statuses and Twitter feeds, but Samia's relationship with her iPhone was a bit of a mystery to all of us. The girl had an app for absolutely everything, even calculating her carbon footprint or the *true* cost of a banana from Guatemala! Because those things were *really* important to Samia, Miss Eco-Warrior herself.

'Hey, Samia,' I called over to her. 'You found something?'

'Yeah,' she smiled up at me, sliding her finger across the screen to close down the phone. 'I love this colour...'

'Yeah, it will look great with your red hair,' I agreed. 'And your eyes.'

Samia blushed and looked away, chewing her bottom lip. 'Mashallah...' she mumbled before heading off for the changing rooms. I watched her as she walked away, head down, shoulders hunched beneath her puffa jacket. That was so typical of Samia: the girl just could not take a compliment.

I looked around for Yasmin and saw her standing in front of a rack of dresses, her arms empty. I grabbed a couple of the dresses I'd been looking at and went over to her.

She turned to look at me, a worried look on her face. 'I can't find anything, Ams,' she said. 'None of this stuff would look good on me. I can't even see anything I like.'

I fingered a brown maxi dress with turquoise flowers. 'This one's nice...'

Yasmin wrinkled up her nose. 'Nah, that would make my arms look like slabs of salami.'

'What about this one with sleeves?'

'Oh, no, look how low it is. I'd be falling out of that one.'

I sighed. Shopping with Yasmin really was tough. She just did not know what she wanted – and she was hypercritical of her looks and her weight. Over the years, she had accepted the part of the quiet one, the silent observer, like the grey background that allowed the butterflies to shine even brighter.

But eventually, we made it out of TK Maxx in one

piece; arms full of bags, ready to dress to kill, flushed with excitement, hungry as anything.

Only one place would do: Katie's Cafe.

* * *

'I swear, I thought this year would never end!' Rania said as we all squeezed into the booth at Katie's Cafe. This was our guilty little secret: a greasy spoon with enough calories in the burgers to give you *and* your mum a heart attack. But it was cheap and it was halal so, sometimes, just sometimes, nothing else would do: it just *had* to be cheeseburgers and fries with double thick milkshakes at Katie's.

'I know,' I said, jostling Samia with my elbow. 'It's so cool of your mum to combine her fundraiser with our end-of-school celebration.'

'Well, I, for one, can't wait,' Rania said, waving at the waitress. 'The last time we had a good party was Eid and, after those crazy exams, I think we deserve a good time, don't you?'

Everyone agreed and, when the waitress came, we felt no guilt as we ordered enough carbs, calories and fizz to feed the entire *ummah*.

What can I say? Girls just wanna have fun.

11

I woke up thinking about her. Again.

As I made *wudu*, I looked at myself in the mirror, trying to see whether anything had changed. My lower jaw was covered with a light fuzz of hair and it made me look older, more serious. Did she like serious guys? Did she like beards? Judging by her brother, I thought it was safe to assume that she probably didn't mind them, even if she wasn't necessarily a fan. I puffed myself up and looked at my body critically. I had put on a bit of weight, what with all the takeaways we had been eating. It was time to get back into shape. At least basketball would help.

After *Fajr*, I slipped off my thobe and hit the floor to do some push ups. I was soon out of breath and, quite frankly, disgusted with myself. I had really let myself go. It was time to take back some control of my life, time to get in shape and get my mind focussed on the future. But even as those thoughts ran through my mind, I could feel the adrenalin running out of me.

I missed my mum.

I just did.

And, if I was honest with myself, I was crushing on a girl who was as unattainable as the stars, and almost as distant.

She probably didn't even know I existed.

The summer stretched ahead of me, like a life sentence, and, at the end of it, there was uni. I sighed. The prospect of studying Law had started losing its appeal last year after Mum died and I got over the initial sadness. Ever since then, the dream of being a hot shot lawyer had seemed less and less attractive. But what were my alternatives? And what would Dad say if I dared tell him that I didn't want to study Law? He would hit the roof, for sure.

I slumped back against my bed and let sadness wash over me again.

I missed Mum. I missed having her there to talk to anytime and about anything. She would have known what to do, she would have known what to tell Dad.

Just as the tears welled up, my phone vibrated: a message. I checked the screen. It was a message from Usamah. 'Wanna go skateboarding this morning? Bring your bros.'

And even though I couldn't skateboard to save my life, even though I associated skateboarding with long-haired white dudes from the States, it was just the distraction I needed.

* * *

The skate park in Brixton was small and scruffy. Low-rise estates surrounded it on all sides and the litter and graffiti on the pavement just added to the gritty, urban ambience. I was determined to keep an open mind but I could see that Umar was seriously unimpressed. Jamal stuck close by me and just stared.

But, as usual, Usamah was in his element. He knew

some of the other guys there and, in no time at all, he had introduced us and managed to persuade his friends to lend us their skateboards and give us an introductory lesson. I felt quite silly, wobbling along on wheels but I could see that Jamal was getting the hang of it.

'This is fun!' he called out as he sailed past me for the third time. 'You need to copy me, Ali!'

I was just about to shout out and tell him what a great job he was doing when I heard some raised voices behind me.

'What you sayin', blud?'

I turned around to see Umar literally surrounded by a group of young guys with bandanas and expensive trainers. They all had scowls on their faces. Umar did too, but I could tell that he was completely out of his depth. 'Oi, what's going on?'

56 The boys turned to face me as I hurried over to where they were all gathered.

'What's it got to do with you, man?'

'He's my brother, that's what.'

One of them laughed, covering his gold tipped teeth with his fist. 'Hear dat lickle posh bwoi!'

Another snarled, 'Tell your brother to watch himself, yeah? He don't belong here down these sides. Down here we hurt mans, y'get me? Especially if they've got attitude like this one.' He jerked his head over at Umar who stood there, his hands in his pockets, his eyes blazing. I needed to get him out of there.

'C'mon, Umar,' I muttered, leading him away. 'Let's go…' I ignored the insults they flung after us. Umar was shaking next to me, determined not to catch my eye.

When I told Usamah what had happened, he shook his

head. 'I don't know what's happening to these kids, man. They crazy down here... reminds me of the Bronx, for real. Come on, guys, let's beat it. We can go get something to eat up on the hight street.'

We left the skate park under a cloud, the fun of trying, failing and finally mastering the skateboards now forgotten.

As we left, I looked back and saw that the group of boys were still there, sprawled across the low wall on the side of the skate park. Every one of them was staring hard at Umar as he walked away. I felt a shiver run through me. I didn't think we would be coming back any time soon.

* * *

On the way home on the bus, I told Usamah about my dread of the long summer ahead with nothing constructive to do until A Level results came out.

'Yo, they need some extra hands down at the Islamic centre,' he said. 'I figure you might want to help out, what with you having so much time on your hands and all. You too, Umar. You're welcome to come on board if you like.'

I was speechless. Not only had I not expected Usamah to be the 'community type', but I had never envisaged myself in that setting: youth work. In the suburbs of Hertfordshire and the halls of St Peter's, community work was something you did after a long plane journey, in Africa or South America, just like the school we had worked for in Mexico. But now that we were living in South London, not quite ghetto but close enough, the need for youth programmes was clear: without them, kids were on the streets, getting up to no good.

Umar glanced over at Usamah. 'Don't look at me,' he said shortly. 'I've got better things to do than hang out with a bunch of losers.' And he turned to stare out of the window again. Usamah looked over at me and shrugged his shoulders.

'I've never really thought about it, to tell you the truth,' I admitted, embarrassed by Umar's lack of manners. 'I'm not sure that I'm cut out for that kind of thing...'

'All you need is time, and you got plenty of that! And anyway, I bet you got mad skills from all those years in that fancy school of yours, what did they teach you, riding, fencing, ballroom dancing...'

I laughed. 'OK, OK, I'll help in any way I can. Just don't expect me to be a group leader or anything. I've never done anything like this before. And the boys... they may not take to me, you know?'

58   'Too posh, huh?' Usamah was clearly amused by my discomfort. 'Nah, you'll be fine, akh. Just relax. You can help Brother Omar out with his group and maybe go on the trips with them. You think you can handle that?'

I nodded, swallowing hard. Yes, I was pretty sure I could handle that.

12

'Hey, Samia, what's the latest with your *wali*, Imam Sajid? Has he tried to marry you off to any more serial polygamists lately?'

Samia's face went red.

'Don't even joke about that, Rania, it's really not funny. Just because I'm a revert, my *wali* thinks it is of the utmost importance that I get married ASAP, never mind that the brother doesn't have two *miswaks* to rub together, has three other wives or has just come out of prison!'

'And everyone knows how popular white revert sisters are, eh?' I remarked drily.

'As if I would ever settle for one of those losers!' Samia snapped. 'People think that, just because I'm a revert, I'm going to put up with their rubbish. Well, guess what: I wasn't desperate before Islam and I sure ain't desperate now...'

'Waiting for Brother *Sunnah*-to-the-max to sweep you off your feet, eh?' I smirked. 'Dream on.'

Samia looked over at me pityingly. 'The last thing I want is to be swept off my feet, my dear. I want my feet firmly on the ground where I can see them. As far as I'm concerned, it's all that Western crap about romance and Prince Charming that sets marriages up for failure. That's why I prefer the Islamic approach: don't try to woo me, speak to me plainly, honestly, tell me what you're bringing to the table. I'll judge you on your merits, with a clear head, and make a rational decision, one that is based on fact, not butterflies.'

'Ughh,' Rania shuddered. 'I *hate* the way you make that sound: just like a business contract!'

'But isn't that what it is?' Samia asked. 'A contract between two people to give each other their rights, to fulfil responsibilities: so simple. Beautiful.'

'I don't think it sounds beautiful at all,' Rania pouted. 'If a guy came to me with that kind of talk, I would chuck him out so fast his head would spin. I *want* to be wooed. I *want* the romance. I demand to be swept off my feet! After waiting this long, it's the least he can do!'

We all laughed and made smoochie faces at Rania. She chucked a couple of menus at us. I laughed with the others, of course, but couldn't help asking myself: which approach did I prefer? The no-nonsense, Islamic approach or the romantic, fairytale one? My heart fluttered as I saw *him* again in my mind's eye. But I quickly shut it down. Of course I didn't prefer either of them. I wasn't getting married, remember?

'Rania,' I said, smiling, 'you are wasted on those brothers, sweetheart. You're too good for them, girl, you know that.'

'Oh, come on, Amirah,' Samia sighed, 'haven't you grown out of that guy hating phase yet?'

'I never said I hate guys, Samia!' I said, making googly eyes at her. 'I just don't trust them, OK? And besides, Muslim brothers make lousy husbands.'

'How can you say that?' The expression on Samia's face was one of genuine surprise. 'The Prophet Muhammad – *sallallahu alayhi wa sallam* – was a fantastic husband.'

'Yeah, I know that, Samia. But let's be honest, you're not likely to find anyone like that anytime soon, especially not walking the streets of Lambeth!'

Everyone laughed and, when the waitress came to take our order, we waved her away, saying, 'the usual, girl, the usual!'

Yasmin looked at me. 'Don't you believe in love, Ams?'

I gave her my most incredulous expression. 'Yaz, what's love got to do with it? You can love the guy as much as you want, it doesn't stop him being a scumbag and taking liberties with you.' I was getting warmed up to my favourite subject: useless Muslim men. 'Listen, ladies, let me spell it out for you: Muslim men these days want all the perks and none of the hard work. They want the little obedient wife who will give it up whenever they're in the mood, who will have ten gazillion children and homeschool them all *and* help pay the rent. Why? Because they're spoilt and too lazy to get off their backsides and step up to the plate, like real men.'

'Really?' piped up Yasmin. 'Your brother doesn't seem that type. I think he'd make someone a great husband, mashallah.'

I chuckled to myself. Yasmin wasn't fooling anyone. We all knew that she had had a crush on Zayd practically forever. 'Listen, girl,' I said to her, putting my hand on her shoulder, 'forget about Zayd, all right? He's still in cloud cuckoo land, waiting for Miss Ideal Muslimah to appear.' I took a slurp of my extra-thick strawberry milkshake. 'Besides, he won't consider any sister who's not already wearing niqab.' I saw Yasmin's face fall and, for a moment, I felt bad for being so blunt. I sipped the milkshake it was cold and sweet, just the way I liked it and I thought to myself, *It's better I be honest*

AMIRAH ♀

with her so she doesn't get her hopes up.

Rania took a huge bite out of her burger and rolled her eyes. 'I don't care what anyone says,' she said, her mouth full of beef. 'This is by far the best burger in the south of England. No contest.'

I had to agree. Just the right amount of meatiness – not so much that you felt you were chewing on someone's leg – and just enough crumbliness, with a spicy, salty edge. Teamed up with crisp lettuce, a juicy slice of tomato, pickles and salad cream (no onions), you were talking serious burger beefcake, right there.

'Another cow dies needlessly,' Samia said sourly.

'Oh, no, Sami,' I winked at her, 'that's where you're wrong. This cow *needed* to die so it could end up on my plate right here.' I tapped the plate with the tip of my finger. 'An honourable end indeed for any bovine.'

Samia wrinkled up her nose and sniffed. Ever since she had decided to go vegetarian, she'd become a pain to go to Katie's with. She spent the whole time trying to make us feel guilty for being happy-go-lucky carnivores.

'Samia,' Rania pointed a French fry at her veggie burger, 'how do you square your new vegetarian ideals with the fact that the Prophet Muhammad ate meat? Isn't that a bit of a contradiction on your part?' She leaned in and narrowed her eyes. 'Isn't it, in fact, *haram* to choose vegetarianism as a lifestyle choice?'

'Ooohhh!' That was low and Rania knew it. But then I saw the wicked glint in her eye and realised: of course, she was just trying to wind Samia up.

You see, out of all of us, Samia was definitely the most cautious when it came to religious matters. She even did proper research into things, finding out whether they were halal, haram, disliked or recommended. And the *Sunnah*, the way of the Prophet Muhammad –peace be upon him – was a big deal for her.

Now, I'm not saying that it wasn't a big deal for us born Muslims but she was definitely the most conscientious about things like that. When you're born a Muslim, you do tend to take certain things for granted, accepting the rules pretty much without question and getting on with life. But as a convert – or revert as she liked to be called – everything for Samia was deliberate, a conscious decision to choose the correct Islamic position, to halalify her life in every area. I thought she'd be really offended by Rania's low blow but she just shook her head. 'No, babe,' she said, nibbling on a piece of lettuce, 'I've done research into this...'

'Of course...' I added.

She shot me a look. 'And my decision to be a vegetarian is not haram because I'm not saying that it is forbidden to eat meat; I'm just choosing not to because I disagree with the way animals are treated and the whole way in which modern farming works. Did you know that they have bred bulls that have butts so big that they can't reproduce properly?'

That was it. We all burst out laughing. I laughed so hard that I almost fell off my seat. LMBO, literally. Rania choked on her Coke and sent it spraying across the table. Yasmin squealed, dabbing frantically at her hijab while I tried to control myself, wiping the tears from my eyes.

'I'm serious!' Samia's face was going red. 'If you don't believe me, look at this!' And she whipped out her phone and typed a search into YouTube. When she showed us the genetically modified bulls with their enormous rumps, we started howling all over again.

'Oh, I give up on you guys!' Samia huffed, even though a little smile was tugging at her lips. But soon she was giggling too. 'Yeah, yeah, I guess it is pretty funny...'

'Not for the cows, it ain't!' More howling laughter that earned us dirty looks from our waitress. She probably couldn't wait for us to leave but, hey, we'd been coming here for longer than she had been wearing that striped pink apron so she'd have to just sit down and zip it.

Then Yasmin spoke up in that quiet, deliberate way of hers.

'My aunts were talking about scheduling some marriage meetings with brothers before uni, in the next couple of months.' She said it so carelessly, like it was no big deal. But it *was* a big deal. It was a *huge* deal. The table erupted again, this time with everyone asking about the hows and whys, names, details and Mottie stats.

Rania cried out, 'Hold on a minute! Didn't your parents say that you have to finish your degree first?'

Yasmin sighed. 'Yes, but my mum's older sister, *Khala* Shazia, has a daughter who has a Masters and is still single. She's scared to death that I might end up like her so she's convinced Mum and Dad to start looking now, just in case, even if it means a long engagement...'

'But I thought you had decided to tell them that you want to go to culinary school, not uni...' Samia's voice trailed off. We all knew how much courage it would take for Yasmin to tell her superambitious parents that she wanted to bake cakes for a living.

Yasmin looked down at the table and fiddled with her straw. 'Yeah, well, let's just say it hasn't come up yet. They've all been distracted by this great big marriage debate. But I'll tell them soon, inshallah...'

I watched Yasmin's emotions flit over her face as the others asked her more questions about her aunts' husband hunting plans.

I felt sorry for her then and made a big show of sighing impatiently. 'What's all this talk about marriage anyway? It's so sad: once Muslim girls reach a certain age, it's like that's all we can talk about, like now that we've finished school, that's the next logical step.'

'Well, isn't it?' Samia again with her wide-eyed revert look.

'No, Samia, it isn't,' I said firmly. 'I, for one, have things I want to do, places I want to see, dreams to fulfil...'

'You can do that once you're married, can't you?'

'I'd rather do it on my own, thank you very much,' I sniffed. 'Husbands just get in the way. And then you've got the spawn to contend with...'

'Oh, Amirah, stop!' Rania pushed me away and I almost fell off my chair, again. 'You talk so much rubbish. We all know that you love those rugrats more than anything. I hardly ever see them around without you! Just admit that you're an old softie, really, and all you need is the love of a good man to get you barefoot, pregnant and in the kitchen...'

'Shut it, Rania,' I said, duffing her on the head with my bag, my face burning. 'You don't know what you're talking about.'

Samia got in on the act. 'Well, if I was a gambling woman – which I'm not, of course – I would put my money on Amirah to be the first to get married and have a kid.'

I stared at her, my mouth hanging open. 'And what on

earth would give you *that* idea? If I told you once, I told you a thousand times: I am not getting married. End of!'

Rania threw Samia and Yasmin a knowing glance and smirked, 'Methinks the lady doth protest too much...'

I grinned then, feeling foolish. I *was* making too big a deal out of it. It wasn't as if I knew the future; only Allah knew that. But I felt pretty confident that Samia's prediction would come to nothing. Anyway, who in their right mind would want to marry me with all my issues?

'Well, while you three weird sisters carry on with your Mystic Meg act, I'm going to order dessert. Let me know when you get back down to planet Earth.'

And that was the end of all that talk. There are certain times when one's full attention is required: ordering dessert is one of them.

66

13

'So, son, have you heard anything more from the university?'

Dad sat back from our new dining table after a delicious dinner of roast chicken and macaroni cheese. One of our new neighbours, Khadijah Jones from number 5, had sent it. She had packed a week's worth of dinners in sturdy plastic containers, wrapped in cling film, and dropped them off first thing in the morning.

'*Jazakallah khayran*, sister,' I had said, overwhelmed. I hadn't expected hospitality like that, not in the city.

'You're new to the community, aren't you?' she had chirped. 'And you've lost your mum, I hear? So this is the least I can do. Don't hesitate to knock for me if you need anything, understand?' And she strode off down the close towards the gate, her purple hijab fluttering behind her.

With curtains up in the windows and containers of home-cooked food in the fridge, the house was starting to feel more and more like a real home.

But now, Dad wanted to have one of our 'talks' and Khadijah Jones' macaroni pie was starting to churn in my stomach. I had been dreading this conversation for weeks and, now that Umar and Jamal had left the table, it didn't look like I was going to be able to avoid it. Is there ever a good time to tell your superambitious self-made father that you just aren't sure about all the superambitious plans you made last year? That you regret applying to study Law? That you just don't know what you want to do with your life anymore? No, there isn't.

I knew that plenty of the guys I went to school with would be taking a gap year after our A levels. It was almost an obligatory rite of passage. But those guys had parents who could afford to indulge them and would be totally cool about paying thousands of pounds for their kids to go backpacking in India or something.

That is not my dad.

Dad is the kind of father who will look through the uni prospectus before you do and put a star next to the courses he is prepared to pay for. According to him, my options were Law, Engineering, Computer Science, Economics and anything in the medical department.

I made a big show of collecting the plates and taking them to the kitchen. As I passed him on my way to the kitchen, Dad put his hand out and touched my arm. I looked down at him, trying to keep my expression neutral. It wasn't easy.

'Son,' he said, 'I've been on this earth a long time and I know when someone is trying to avoid an issue. So I suggest you put those plates in the kitchen and come and sit yourself down and tell me what is really on your mind.'

I swallowed and nodded. 'Sure, Dad. Just give me a minute.'

While in the kitchen, I mentally prepared what I was going to say, *Dad, I would like to take a gap year to consider my options in light of our new circumstances*. No mention of not being sure about studying Law. No mention about not being sure about what I want to do with my life. No mention of the fact that I felt the boys needed me at home because Dad was just too wrapped up in his own problems to really be there for them.

When I was sitting in front of him in the living room, facing his armchair, my delivery was smooth and even. But he didn't buy it. He peered at me over his glasses, a suspicious expression on his face.

'What do you mean "in light of our new circumstances"?'

I squirmed in my seat. *Please, Dad, don't make me do this.*

'Are you talking about the move, son?'

That was an easy exit so I nodded vigorously.

'Well, I don't see why that should make you change your plans. We already looked at the possibility of you living in halls of residence anyway...'

I bit my lip. 'That's not it, Dad...' I faltered. 'It's just that... with Mum being gone...and Umar... J...'

Dad looked at me sharply. 'What's that got to do with it?'

I became exasperated then. Why was he pretending that he didn't know what I was talking about? 'Dad!' I raised my voice, just slightly, just enough to let him know that I didn't want to play this game of Let's Pretend Mum's Still Here. Not anymore. 'Dad, Mum's dead. And I just don't think I could cope with studying Law right now. Plus it wouldn't feel right to go off to uni and leave you all...'

'Ali, you don't have to worry about us, we're fine!'

'Dad, please! Don't talk as if Mum's death hasn't affected us. Umar is angry, J is confused and I... I...' I tried to keep my voice level. 'I'm still hurting, Dad. I'm still grieving. Can't you understand that?'

69

But Dad's face remained a mask. 'Son, life goes on – we belong to Allah and we will return to Him, all of us. Your mother – may Allah have mercy on her – would have wanted you to continue with your studies and that is what you will do. You're so close now; I won't have you giving up.'

'But, Dad...'

No buts, Ali! I have said my piece. If you can't make sensible decisions, you will have to allow others to make them for you; it's as simple as that.'

'So that's it then, is it?' I flared again. 'You aren't even going to take my opinion into account?'

'Son, one day you will thank me for this. Remember, I am your father: no one wants more for you than I do.'

'Not even me?'

'That's right, son, not even you.'

***

I had to get out of that house. I pushed my feet into my running shoes and grabbed my iPod. I needed to run, to feel the wind in my face, to flood my ears with Mishari Rashid, to let the rhythm of running calm my jangled nerves.

When I got to the gate at the bottom of our road, I turned left, towards Brockwell Park, where I played basketball with the brothers. As I ran, I tried to empty my head. I didn't want to think about my conversation with Dad. I didn't want to think about the prospect of going off to uni to bury myself in legal textbooks, of leaving Umar and Jamal. I didn't want to think about how my whole attitude to everything had changed. What would Mum have thought? I guess that is a mercy for the dead: they don't have to watch the living falling apart as they grieve.

By the time I reached the top of the hill, it was starting to get dark. I prayed three *raka'at* under an enormous oak tree then began to jog back home.

Reaching our street, I keyed in the code to open the gate and began to walk up the hill. It wasn't bad at all, this place. Seville Close was clean, the gardens well kept and all the houses were in good condition: respectable.

As I looked back down the road before heading for our front door, I could just make out the figure of a girl walking up to the last house on the close. She was wearing a hijab and black *abaya* and, just before she turned into a driveway, I caught a glimpse of her face. My heart did a little flip. That was Zayd's sister, I was sure of it.

Then the realisation dawned on me: Zayd and his sister were my new neighbours.

14

It was him, I knew it. I would have recognised him anywhere. What was he doing on our street? Then, I remembered the moving van I had seen parked by number 7 and everything fell into place.

Mr Light Eyes was my neighbour.

Instinctively, I looked over at the sketch I had propped up on my desk, still piled high with A level textbooks, the sketch of his hands that I had drawn off by heart, literally.

Too close, I thought. *Too close for comfort.*

But, to my frustration, that thought didn't stop me dreaming about him that night.

* * *

I don't know how many times I fell asleep as the double-decker bus crawled along the High Road, choked with Monday morning traffic.

Four of us – Abdullah, Taymeeyah, Malik and I – were on our way to the Islamic centre in Streatham. The community had finally got itself together and put on a summer programme for the kids and I wasn't wasting any time: those kids were going to be the first to sign up for summer school.

Don't get me wrong now. It's not that I didn't enjoy the rugrats' company; it's just that I wanted them to get out more. It wasn't healthy, staying indoors all day, only playing with each other, fighting over the computer. I'd always wanted them to get out more – especially Abdullah. Abdullah, my sweet, loving, tender-hearted brother who was born deaf, needed this more than any of them. He needed to be around other kids his own age. And they needed to be around him, to get to know him, to learn that the fact someone can't hear you doesn't mean that they can't understand you, that they can't be your friend. Abdullah needed to get out there and so did the other two. It was breaking my heart to see them preferring computer games and TV to reading books and playing outside. Even their Qur'an and Islamic Studies had taken a back seat to those games, something Mum was always ranting on about. I told her to just take away the computer, let them go cold turkey, but she just looked at me like I'd gone crazy.

'Then what will we do with them?' she wanted to know. 'They're driving me crazy as it is.'

So I knew exactly what kind of summer holiday they could look forward to, especially with Mum in her *iddah* and on anti-depressants again. I overheard her talking on the phone to one of the sisters, Umm Laila, saying something about him not coming back, about needing to move on. But the waiting period after a divorce is three months and a lot can happen in that time. I walked away then. No way was I getting pulled into any of that drama.

All of which had made me even more determined to get my brothers and sisters into that summer school. I didn't want them soaking up all the bad vibes in the house.

'You guys excited?' I said brightly as we walked towards the Islamic centre. Abdullah was walking in front of us and I held Malik and Taymeeyah's hands.

'Stop sucking your thumb, Tay,' I said, nudging her with my elbow. She grinned up at me, flashing her big gap.

'But it tastes so *good*!' she giggled, batting her eyelashes at me.

'Yeah, that's because you flavoured it with bogey,' growled Malik.

'No, I didn't!' retorted Taymeeyah, whirling to face him. 'I pick my nose with *this* finger, not my thumb!'

'Arghh, Taymeeyah, TMI!' I laughed. 'No picking noses and no bogey business, all right?'

Abdullah had turned around and was looking at me, all the confidence gone from his face. 'Ams, do we *have* to go summer school?' he signed with his chubby little hands. 'Can't we just stay home with you and Mum or go park or something?'

'No,' I signed back, putting on my no-nonsense face. 'This summer's going to be different. You guys are going to do new things, meet new people.' Then I made my face bright and signed, 'Don't worry, yeah, trust me, it'll be fun!'

Abdullah looked up at me, doubt all over his face. Poor kid, he was finding it hard to trust anyone. That was problematic. I needed Abdullah onside. Without him, the whole thing could end in disaster. Like the time me and Rania took the kids to an Eid party in West London. Don't get me started on the tears, the yelling, the meltdown and then, the grand climax: the hide and seek that lasted three hours because Abdullah wanted everyone to just *leave him alone*. I stopped walking and knelt down in front of him.

'Hey, listen,' I said out loud, taking his face in my hands so that he would look at me and read my lips. 'I know you're nervous – that's cool. I would be, too. But I've got this, OK? You're going to be fine, I promise. Just relax, yeah? It'll be fine.'

Slowly, slowly, I saw him relax and his face lost that pinched, worried look. He believed me. Now I had to make sure that these people took good care of my babies.

I wasn't worried about the girls' side; Rania was volunteering to run the arts classes and she had roped me in to accompany them on the trips. It was the boys' side that I was worried about. Abdullah was ten, when they started having separate sessions for boys and girls, so I was hoping that, for once, the brothers had got their act together to cater for the boys.

When we got to the centre, it was clear that we were the first ones there. There was a big pile of boxes by the door and we could hear the sound of scraping chair legs coming from inside. A girl's face peered out of one of the windows, and then it was covered by a bright poster advertising the summer school.

Not bad, I thought, as we all stood there, reading the poster. Malik put his arms up to me and I picked him up so that he could read it too.

Well, they were certainly aiming high – Qur'an challenges, quizzes, football, art, you name it, they were hoping to offer it.

A young Asian brother with a wispy beard and a tracksuit top over his *thobe* came out of the front door and gave a little jump when he saw us.

AMIRAH ♀

'Oh, *As-salamu 'alaykum*, sister,' he said, his eyes sliding away from my face to the kids. 'Are you guys here for the summer programme?'

'Yeah, that's right...' *What else would we be doing there?*

'You guys are early,' he blushed furiously. 'Would you mind giving us 15 more minutes to set up?'

I looked around at the car park. There was nowhere to sit and I didn't want the kids to start getting restless. I turned to him and saw that he was having the same thoughts as I was: there was no way we were waiting outside.

'What am I talking about? Sorry, sister, please, come in. The sisters are setting up in that room over there.' He ushered us in. 'Just give me two minutes, yeah? I'll get one of the brothers to bring the registration forms over.'

The room that the sisters were in looked bright and welcoming. We greeted each other with *salam*s and smiles and then they got back to writing a big 'Welcome' sign on the blackboard.

When Taymeeyah and Malik wandered over to them to see what they were doing, they laughed, said how cute they both were and invited them to colour with them.

I began to relax.

Just then, there was a knock on the door. I heard a brother with a rather posh accent say '*As-salamu 'alaykum*, sister, I've got the forms.' And then, the door opened and there he was, as real as anything, in front of me.

It was Mr Light Eyes.

♀ AMIRAH

15

It was her. It was really her. I couldn't believe it. She looked even more amazing than the last time I had seen her, My mind was a blur of confused questions. What was she doing here? Did she remember me? I needed to keep it together get a hold of myself. Be polite, not too friendly. Try not to drop the forms I was meant to be giving her. *God, she's pretty*, I thought. *Astaghfirullah*.

16

I saw his eyes flash for a second as he did a double take. He recognised me, there was no doubt about it. He remembered me. I smiled inwardly. Definitely something naughty about that feeling you get when you become aware of how much power you have as a woman. Of course, it can be a very destructive power, which is why we hijab up, lower the gaze and all that. But I hadn't done anything wrong. I was just me, covered as always, behaving myself as usual. And yet... I'd had an effect on him.

Very naughty feeling indeed.

Of course, I then did what any self-respecting girl would have done: I acted like I had never seen him before in my life, let alone dreamt about him off and on for the past week.

'Yes, brother?' I said, my voice as cool and detached as could be.

He was taken aback, I could see it. His face coloured up just a little and he blinked a few times – so cute! – before holding out the forms.

'Umm, I think you're supposed to fill these in.'

'You think?'

He coughed and ran his fingers through hair that wasn't there. 'Uh, no, you need to fill those out for each of the children.'

'Ah, ok,' I nodded. Inside, I was dying of laughter, but I kept my straight face. His voice and demeanour were so *proper*! I thought of making him scramble for a pen but then I stopped myself. *Enough, Amirah, behave.* I had a pen anyway so I quickly began filling in the forms while he waited outside.

When I had finished, I went out to hand the forms to him. There were the hands, just as I remembered them. And, as he reached out, his shirt sleeve rode up and I caught a glimpse of a tattoo on his forearm.

Ohh, I thought to myself, *so someone has a PAST...*

'*Jazakallah khayran*, sister,' he said, reading through what I had written. 'So... Abdullah is it?' He looked up and saw Abdullah standing next to me, almost hiding behind my *abaya*. 'Hey, Abdullah, *as-salamu 'alaykum.*'

'He's deaf,' I said, suddenly gripped by anxiety. 'On the form, it said that there would be provision for children with impaired hearing...' All the giddiness of our exchange melted away and I remembered that I was about to leave Abdullah with a bunch of strange brothers for the first time in his life. Would they know how to handle him? Would they even be able to communicate with him? Be patient with him? Was I crazy putting him in this programme?

'Yes, that's right, there is.' He looked embarrassed for a minute. 'Does he sign or read lips or write notes or ...'

'All of the above,' I said proudly.

I was the one who had insisted that Abdullah learn to lip read even though he was a fantastic signer. Mum had never been good at sign language and still relied more on speaking slowly and writing notes, if things got too hectic. I had taught the others how to sign but they still got lazy sometimes.

But I could feel Abdullah shaking at my side so I turned away from Ali and knelt in front of him. I touched his chin and his big brown eyes met mine.

'Abdullah,' I said, signing at the same time, to make sure he got me. 'You are going to be OK. Don't be afraid. Remember Allah? He'll look after you, OK? And this nice brother here, Brother Ali, he's going to look after you, too, OK? Will you give it a try, please, just for today?'

He nodded and I smiled and pinched his dumpling cheek. 'That's my boy.'

I straightened up, suddenly embarrassed that Mr Light Eyes had seen me in such a private moment with Abdullah. I avoided looking at him and stepped aside as he came forward to kneel in front of Abdullah.

And his voice changed, became warmer, softer. 'Abdullah, you see that brother over there? His name is Brother Omar and he really needs some extra hands to help him set up because he's running super late. Do you think we could go over and give him a hand?'

To my amazement, I saw that he was signing! A bit rusty, true, and some of the signs and words didn't quite match, but he was signing, that was for sure. And Abdullah understood him, which was the main thing.

I couldn't help myself. 'So *you* are the provision for deaf children? Where... how did you learn sign language?'

He ducked his head, all modest. 'I took classes while I was in Senior School. We were twinned with a school for the deaf in Mexico and got to do some volunteer work out there, alhamdulillah.' Again, he ran his perfect hands over his head and looked around him. 'To be honest, it feels like a lifetime ago.'

'Mashallah,' I smiled. 'That's beautiful. It must have been so amazing... Mexico... I've always dreamt of going there.'

He looked up, his eyes bright. 'Really? Can you speak Spanish?'

I giggled, in spite of myself. '*Un poquito* – I took extra classes at school. But I'd love to learn properly one day.'

'*Usted sera capaz de hablar español un día*, Inshallah...'

I almost fainted with pleasure at the sound of his voice and his gorgeous Spanish accent but then the Asian brother came out of the other hall and cleared his throat. 'You got those forms, Ali?'

Ali looked over at him, clearly embarrassed. 'Yeah, just finding out how best to communicate with little Abdullah here. He reads lips and signs, mashallah.'

Then he smiled again and flashed me a look that said 'I'll take it from here.' I stepped back and watched as Abdullah walked off with him towards where Brother Omar was taping large sheets of paper to the floor.

Not bad, I thought once again. *Not bad at all...*

And, this time, I wasn't talking about his hotness.

No siree.

17

I have to admit, I was all over the place after Amirah left. The only thing that kept me focused was the fact that Abdullah wouldn't leave my side. It was as if the bond that he had with his sister had been magically passed on to me. He was like my little shadow.

When the rest of the kids arrived I realised how accurate my initial misgivings about coming here were. I could feel my confidence – whatever was left of it – seeping out of me as I watched the boys troop into the centre. Their faces were hard, their mannerisms aggressive, their language like the language of the thugs and rappers they were clearly trying to emulate.

I was totally taken aback. Was this the state of the Muslim youth? I found myself thanking Allah that Dad had decided to put Jamal in a maths enrichment programme at a local private school. This was no place for my little brother.

Usamah must have seen my horrified expression. 'Don't judge them too harshly, akh,' he murmured as he passed by on his way to a group of older boys. 'A lot of these young brothers come from broken homes, no dad at home, gangs and drugs all around them. We should be grateful they're here with us, instead of out on the streets. Try to put aside your prejudices and just be there for them. They need you to be a big brother to them, not just another adult criticising them, making them feel worthless.'

I felt ashamed of myself then. This was the essence of working for the sake of Allah: giving of yourself for others, for the greater good, not looking for personal gratification or worldly reward. I had been reading about these ideas in the sayings of the Prophet. It took a room full of disaffected Muslim youth to show me the significance of them.

Something about that day, the way Amirah knew my name without me telling her, the challenging look on the boys' faces, the trusting look in little Abdullah's eyes, made me think that this was only the beginning of a new journey for me.

And only Allah knew where that journey was taking me.

18

I felt surprisingly calm as I hopped onto the bus to Croydon. I was sure that I had made the right decision, that Abdullah would be fine – that Ali would look after him.

He was a sweetie. Really, he was. Not many brothers could have – or would have – done what he did, getting onto Abdullah's level, drawing him out in that way. It was as if he really cared. And, if he had been faking it, Abdullah would have sussed him out straight away. Kids like him are amazingly intuitive. They just *know* when someone is genuine. They can smell fakeness a mile away. But Abdullah hadn't turned away from Ali and clung to me; he had responded to his invitation and followed him, leaving me standing there, looking after him anxiously, my heart in my mouth.

Abdullah had trusted him. I felt sure that I could, too.

Time to focus on me now, I thought, as I made my way to Croydon Library for an art class.

I had always enjoyed drawing and art lessons but I really caught the bug at my new school in my GCSE year. Between school trips to the National Gallery and lessons with Ms Fergus, my art teacher, I learned to appreciate art in its many forms and it turned out that I had a way with paints, pastels and charcoal. I tell you, when I stepped into that art room, it was love at first sight. And it only became stronger when I started to go out and look at other artists' work. Yup, this hijabi, inner city Muslim girl was in her element among the ballet dancers of Degas, the landscapes of Monet and the abstracts of Kandinsky.

What stops me from turning my back on it is the thought of my art teacher, Ms Fergus, and how she had behaved when she saw my final piece of coursework.

You know, she stood there, in silence, for what felt like ages, looking at it. I tried to read her face; I had poured my heart and soul into that painting, all the tears, all the pain, the feelings of bitterness and regret, all went into that piece. Had it come through at all? Or was it just pretentious rubbish?

'Amirah,' she had said at last, her voice hoarse. 'I... I don't know what to say...'

I bowed my head, trying to blink back my tears. 'It's OK, Miss. I understand.'

Next thing I knew, she was hugging me, rubbing my back. I just stood there like an idiot. I just didn't know what to do. I mean, it's not every day that you have a teacher go to pieces on you.

'Amirah... it's beautiful... no, not beautiful... raw, real, powerful. That's what it is: powerful.' She turned to look at it again then reached for my hand. 'You have a gift, Amirah, you really do. And I don't say that lightly. I hope you will be allowed to use that gift. It would be a crime to hide it from the world.' She grabbed a tissue from her pocket and blew her nose. Small patches of red stood out on her cheeks and I wondered what it was like to have a face that broadcast all your emotions to the world.

'Promise me you won't give up on your art, Amirah,' she

said then, quite fiercely. 'Promise me.'

I knew what she was talking about. It was because I was a Muslim girl, a Muslim girl who had opted for a practical but boring degree course – Business Administration – rather than pursuing art as a career. If she had been talking to Caitlin or Imogen, she wouldn't have needed to say anything. She would simply have nodded in approval as they applied for degree courses at Central Saint Martins, waiting patiently for invitations to their shows in trendy galleries in Brick Lane and Shoreditch. After all, they had parents who appreciated art and would support them. Most Muslim girls came from families where the arts were still viewed with suspicion or, sometimes, open hostility. And no one's parents were going to support their girls when they thought they would be going to college or university to draw naked people and hang around with crazy artists with tattoos and expensive drug habits.

So, studying Business Administration was my cop-out, in a way. I didn't have the luxury of doing something I loved; I had to do something practical, something I could use later on in life, something that would pay the bills. I just hoped I would get the grades I needed to secure my place. The subjects I had taken with that degree in mind, Business Studies and Economics, had been much harder than I thought they would be. Add to that the fact that I spent all my spare time in the art room, instead of reading those boring textbooks, and I had reason to make strong prayer.

Mum had laughed at me when I first started going to galleries and art markets, dragging my new BFF Rania with me. 'Where you getting all these posh ideas from, eh?' she would tease. I never answered her. I knew she wouldn't understand. Instead, I relied on Auntie Azra to encourage me and, sometimes, drive us out to Abbey Mill to see the artisans at work and try our hand at pottery and basket weaving. Another world, I tell you.

Of course it had to be Auntie Azra who would take us. No one else in the community really did stuff like that. As far as they were concerned, that stuff was for non-Muslims or, to be more specific, white people. As if a brown girl like me can't appreciate the work of the French impressionists!

I guess those things – that world – is too removed from most people's day to day reality. Life is tough for most people. Art is for the select few, those who have the time and energy to appreciate it. You can't appreciate beauty if you are running on empty, struggling to survive.

All the more reason to choose a different type of life.

* * *

By the time I got to Croydon Library, there was a group of young people standing at the main desk, filling in application forms. They looked like your typical arty types – all jeans, beaten-up trainers and wannabe dreadlocks. I glanced down at my own outfit: my favourite khaki linen *abaya* with the front pocket and Palestinian kefiyyeh around my neck, regulation black hijab and my red Converse trainers. Yeah, avant-garde enough. I didn't quite fit in, of course, but then I wasn't here to fit in. I was here to do some serious creating.

If there's one thing I've learnt in my short time on earth, it is that you don't have to look, behave or think like everyone else to achieve. Just be sincere, work hard and Allah will take care of the rest.

AMIRAH ♀

After we'd filled in the forms, we all filed into the function room where the course was being held. It was breathtaking. Light streamed in through the tall windows that looked out over Croydon and the surrounding area. Each chair faced an easel with a pile of papers clipped to it. I fingered the sheets. *Thick, good quality rag paper, no doubt*, I smiled to myself. *I'm going to enjoy this.*

I looked around before choosing a seat next to a petite blonde with wild, frizzy hair and silver nose ring. We exchanged smiles as we sat down.

'Welcome, everybody,' said the woman who was now standing in front of the wall of windows. She was a tall black woman with piercing green eyes and a bright African print wrap wound around her head. 'Can you all take a seat? There, that's it.' She smiled, a brilliant smile that seemed to light up the whole room. 'My name is Collette Lee, I will be your tutor on this course. Let me tell you a little bit about myself: I am an artist by profession and I also teach art classes and do art therapy with children with special needs here in Croydon and in other boroughs.' As she spoke, her hands danced in the air, her silver rings flashing.

'As you know, you've all signed up for an advanced drawing class so I'd just like to confirm that all of you have taken art lessons before, at school or at college...'

I was mesmerised by her hands. They flew through the air, sweeping and fluttering, as she spoke of the artistic influences we would be drawing on. And I couldn't help thinking that her hands were signer's hands. That type of movement, that type of expression, just wasn't common among people who had the luxury of hearing and speech.

I made up my mind to ask her about her art therapy work

and whether she knew sign language once the class was over.

Just before the class broke up, she clapped her hands together to get our attention.

'Before I forget,' she said, 'Croydon Council is hosting an art competition and inviting artists between the ages of 12 and 18 to submit their work.'

'What's the theme?' my blonde neighbour wanted to know.

'The theme,' Collette said drily, 'is "Play". To be honest, it's not a very inspiring theme – probably the MP's idea – but I suppose it's what you make of it, isn't it. I'm sure that the fact that it is sponsored by a major sportswear brand had something to do with it, too.' She cracked an ironic smile.

As for me, I was not impressed. So what if the sponsor was a giant shoe company? How did they expect us to create cutting edge pieces of art with such a lame theme? I mentally scratched the competition off my To Do list and started gathering my things. I had better things to do with my pastels than some GCSE-style assignment.

Until I slipped up and let my mind wander to the sketch book that was lying on my bed. And the picture of those basketball-playing hands.

Play, huh?

Well, why not?

* * *

I took the bus home, all the while thinking of what I was going to do to the sketch on my bed. I could hardly wait to get home and get started and, as the bus rolled down the main road, I got up, eager to get off. I was also thinking of the brief conversation I had had with Collette about working with deaf children. As I'd suspected, she did know some sign language and she promised to tell me more about her work after the next session. My insides bubbled with excitement as I crossed the road.

That was when I saw a police car slow down and, its indicators flashing, turn into our driveway.

Surprised and curious, I stopped and stared as the police officer got out and walked over to the intercom. My eyes immediately went to the back seat and I saw the young black boy huddled against the window.

He looked about 14 years old and his eyes were red and raw. There was something familiar about him but I just couldn't put my finger on it.

Before I could figure out who he reminded me of, the car had swept past me in through the gates and up the driveway. I shook my head. Boys were getting up to all sorts these days.

90

19

Umar tried to stand tall, a sullen look on his face, as if he didn't care. But I knew it was just a front. One of his eyes was partly closed and a bruise was forming on his left cheek. Dad went to help him as he limped in beside the police officer, holding his arm, but Umar pushed him away with whatever strength he had. Dad had to make do with standing by him as the policeman lectured him.

'Found him in a scrap with some boys on the High Street… seemed to be a postcode thing. You lot from around here?'

Dad shook his head and cleared his throat. 'Hertfordshire,' he rasped.

The policeman raised his eyebrows. 'Long way from home, aren't you?'

Dad shifted, uncomfortable with the policeman's prying. 'Yes, officer, we are. Now, please could you tell me what happened? And what you will be doing with the boys who assaulted my son?'

The officer cocked his head and looked over at Umar. 'Well, sir, not much we can do with these boys, unfortunately. Eyewitnesses seldom come forward anyway. Best to teach your boy how to handle himself and avoid them.'

'I *can* handle myself,' growled Umar.

'Hmm,' said Dad, 'that's why you've got yourself a black eye, is it?'

Umar scowled and turned away.

'You'll have to keep a better eye on him, sir,' the other officer was saying. 'There is a lot of gang activity in this area – and getting into a fight with one of them could be fatal. Your boy needs to keep his head down and stay out of trouble.'

'Of course, officer,' Dad said, struggling to keep his voice calm.

The policeman said goodbye and closed the door behind him. Dad turned to Umar. 'What happened to you, son? Where were you?'

'It wasn't my fault, Dad!'

'Yes, I know, but tell me what happened!'

'These boys...' Umar started breathing fast and I realised, with a jolt, that he was on the verge of bursting into tears. 'These boys came up to me on the High Street – I was going to get something to eat – and they asked me where I was from, where my endz were... then they started taking the mick out of my accent, told me I shouldn't be there, that this was their territory... I told them to leave me alone, but then they started pushing me around.' He wiped his nose on his sleeve. 'I just tried to defend myself, Dad, like you taught me to. But then the police came and the boys all ran away ... It wasn't my fault, Dad, honest...' He blinked and sniffled, trying to keep the pain out of his voice. I knew better than to go to him when he was like that. He would have pushed me away, for sure.

I longed for Mum then. She would have gone up to him and held him and he would have let her, crying on her shoulder, letting her stroke his hair and soothe him until all the tears and the pain were gone.

How I missed her.

Dad was clearly uncomfortable. He didn't know what to say or do. In the end, he put his hand on Umar's sleeve and patted him.

'It's OK, son, I know it wasn't your fault. You've just got to be more careful. These streets can be dangerous...'

Umar looked up at Dad. 'When are we going back home, Dad? I hate this place! We don't belong here, we belong at home, in Hertfordshire. Before we came, you said there was a chance we could go back before the end of the summer, but you haven't mentioned anything since. Why is it taking so long to get everything sorted out so that we can go home?'

At that, Dad sighed and wiped his face with his hand and said, in a tired, tired voice, 'Boys, we need to talk.'

I felt a chill run through me, as if my blood had turned to ice.

93

We called Jamal from upstairs and he joined us in the living room. And it occurred to me that we hadn't sat down for a family discussion since before Mum died.

'*Bismillah*,' he muttered, before saying, 'boys, I have something to tell you. I didn't tell you before because I had hoped that I would be able to sort things out, to avoid... to avoid this.'

Jamal's eyes were wide and fearful. I put my arm around him. At least I knew that he wouldn't push me away. 'What is it, Dad? What's happened?'

'It's the house, boys. The house and the business. They're gone.'

'Gone? *Gone*? What do you mean "gone"?' I couldn't believe what I was hearing.

'That's exactly what I mean, Ali. The house and the

business… I've had to put them up for sale. I'm sorry.'

Sorry?

I had no words to describe the sense of anger, of betrayal, of *grief*.

No words.

But Umar had enough words for both of us, for all of us. He started shouting, crying, saying it wasn't fair, that Dad had promised we would be going back, that the move to London was just temporary. Dad tried to calm him down, to explain that he had tried everything, that he was applying for jobs all over, outside London, that this was fate, that we had to accept it, but Umar wasn't having it. He sprang up out of his chair and rushed to the door, slamming it on his way out. I heard his footsteps, heavy, on the stairs and then another slamming door.

94

I looked away from the door, avoiding Dad's gaze.

I didn't know what to think, what to say. I wanted to man up, to rise to the challenge, like I had when Dad first told me about moving to South London for the summer, but this time I couldn't find the strength.

Now it seemed that all we had ever known was well and truly gone forever. The house, Dad's business, and the family we once were. It was at times like this that I felt the need to pray, to wash with water and put my head to floor – and *pray*.

Allah had willed this chain of events, after all. My job was to trust that there was good in it somewhere and that He would bring us through it, just like He had brought us through everything else.

* * *

I went and looked in on Umar after I'd prayed. He was lying on his bed, looking up at the ceiling, with his headphones on. Seeking refuge in his music, as I had done so many times.

I sat on the side of his bed. His eyes slid towards me then he looked away again.

'I've got a new Qur'an CD,' I said, gently. 'Totally relaxes me. Let me know if you want to borrow it, yeah?'

Umar gave me a look.

I held my hands up in surrender. 'No pressure, man!'

He didn't say anything for a long time. When he finally spoke, his voice was hoarse. 'When you were my age, Ali, did anyone try to tell you to stop listening to music and listen to Qur'an instead? Did anyone tell you to stop playing in that band of yours and join a Muslim youth group? Did anyone tell you to take out your earring and put on a *kufi*? Did they?'

'Hey, Mum went crazy when I got my ear pierced!' I was trying to lighten the oppressive atmosphere in the room, but Umar just looked at me, unblinking.

'Did they, Ali?'

'No, Umar,' I sighed. 'No, they didn't.'

'I thought not,' he said sourly, and turned to look out of the window.

I swallowed hard. I had always known that Umar nursed this resentment, this feeling that he got the short end of the stick. 'It's different, bro,' I said, my voice soft. 'We know better now. I was wrong, Umar. Don't envy me...'

'But I do, Ali, that's what you don't understand. It's like you got everything: the great school, the girls, the fun times... And Mum. You got Mum, too.'

My breath caught in my throat and I felt tears well up in my eyes instantly. Umar had hardly mentioned Mum since she died. At times, I wondered whether he would ever mention her again. 'No, Umar,' I said, shaking my head. 'That's where you're wrong. You were the apple of her eye. You were the one...'

But Umar's eyes were red now and he clenched his fists. 'Then why'd she have to go and get sick, huh? Why'd she have to leave me?' Next thing I knew, he was crying like a baby, rubbing at his eyes with balled fists, just like he used to when he was little.

'Hey, Umar,' I said softly, 'it was Allah's will that Mum got sick. *Inna lillahi*, remember? We belong to Allah and we will all return to Him. We can't be angry with Mum about that... and we can't be angry with Allah, either.'

'Well, *I am*,' he said firmly, his eyes fixed on the ceiling. 'And nothing you can say is going to change that.' He shrugged my hand off and pushed me away from him.

My heart was heavy as I left the room. Why couldn't I get through to Umar?

I didn't know how to help him heal, not without Islam. Because, without my faith in Allah, none of it made any sense to me.

***

My gran, Nana Jordan, rang to speak to us later that night.

'I miss you, Nana,' I said, suddenly wishing I was a little boy again, sitting at her kitchen table, stuffing myself with her delicious beef stew with fried dumplings. Then there would be apple crumble for afters, with ice cream, cream – or both. Tears stung my eyes at the memory; apple crumble had been Mum's favourite dessert. She'd promised to teach me her secret recipe but, when she was well, I had always had something else on and, when she became sick, there simply was no time. There were so many other things that needed to be done...

'I miss you, too, darling,' Nana was saying. 'Just how long am I going to have to wait before I am blessed with a visit from my grandsons, eh? Doesn't that religion of yours say anything about the rights of grandparents?'

I chuckled. Nana was always trying to shame us into things by quoting Islam – even though she was a staunch Christian. 'Yes, it does, Nan. It's called "upholding the ties of kinship".'

'Yes, that sounds right,' she clucked. 'So let's see some upholding around here, shall we? How about I meet you boys in London next weekend? We can go out, see the sights, have lunch... sound good?'

'That sounds great, Nana. Just great.'

'And so where is my baby, Umar. Can I speak to him?'

I took a deep breath. 'To tell you the truth, Nan, he's not doing so well. This area is quite rough and... he's been getting into a bit of trouble.'

'What kind of trouble, Ali?' Nana asked, her voice rising, tense.

'Some of the kids around here... nothing major... but worrying.' Then I checked over my shoulder to make sure no one was in earshot. 'To be honest, Nan, I wish we could get him out of here. Out of all of us, he is the one I'm most worried about. Do you think you could...?'

'Ali, look. There is nothing I would like more than to have Umar up here with me, to get him ready for the new school year. I've tried, you know that. I even suggested to your father that he send him to stay with me for a few weeks but he wouldn't have it. Said he didn't want to divide the family, that he had everything under control.'

'Well, he doesn't,' I said grimly. 'I don't think Dad realises the extent of our problems out here.' I heard the door close behind me and I swung round to see Dad crossing the corridor to go into the kitchen. 'Listen, Nana, let's talk next week when you come, OK?'

'OK, darling, I'll see you then.'

20

I couldn't stop fidgeting after I saw the police car pull up outside Ali's house. My mind was buzzing with questions: why were the police there? What had Ali's brother done?

I didn't have to wait for long to find out. Zayd went over there and found out that the middle boy, Umar, had been in a fight with some boys from the estate nearby.

'He really doesn't know who he's messing with,' was Zayd's comment. 'The boys round here don't like strangers. If you come on to their turf, they can get really crazy.'

'Doesn't he *know* that he needs to watch his back around here?' I couldn't believe it. The boy looked about 14, too old to be that naive.

'Well, they're not from the city, innit. Things are different out in the countryside. He's going to have to adjust fast...'

I shuddered to think of the police turning up at our doorstep but then again, it was hardly likely, was it? Zayd had been on the straight and narrow for as long as I could remember. He had never been one of those boys out on the road, even while all his friends were getting into trouble for postcode-related beef and petty crime. They were mosque boys, too, brought up coming to *jum'ah* in *thobes* and *kufis*, hanging with the brothers from age seven. But that hadn't been enough to keep them out of trouble, not with the mean streets of South London all around them. So, one by one, they fell away, coming to the *masjid* less and less. They started changing: their dress, the way they spoke, what they spoke about. I know it hurt Zayd to see his childhood friends turn gangster on him. He had never been into all that.

'Keep your head down and stick to your *deen*,' Uncle Faisal, Abdullah's dad, had told him. And Zayd had listened. He had done well at school and set his sights on uni. When the offer to study in Saudi Arabia came up, he was ready.

I was proud of him. He was one of the few good examples for the younger boys coming up in the community. Aside from the fact that he was a bit over-the-top when it came to certain things, I knew that I wouldn't exchange him for any of the other boys his age. My Haram Police Officer was here to stay.

By now, Taymeeyah, Abdullah and Malik were clamouring to be taken to the park.

'Come on, sis,' Zayd said, pulling at my arm. 'Let's take them to the park, just like old times.'

How could I say no?

* * *

What a blessing to have a gorgeous park literally minutes from your door! As I watched the rugrats take over the pavement with their bikes and scooters, I smiled and took a deep breath.

I watched Zayd as he ran ahead to help Malik get his scooter straightened up. Poor kid was always getting it twisted up and ending up hanging off the kerb. Zayd waited for me to catch up with him.

I grabbed his arm and squeezed it. He laughed, clearly a little embarrassed at my public display of affection.

'Hey, what's up, Ams?' he chuckled, trying to untangle himself.

'Nothing,' I smiled up at him. 'I'm just really proud of you, that's all.'

'Aww, sis, what's this all about? You going soft on me or what?' He punched me lightly on my shoulder and I returned the favour.

'Nah, not soft. I'm just glad that you're my brother, that's all. I'm glad that Abdullah and Malik have you as a role model...'

If I didn't know better, I would have said that Zayd was blushing. But, of course, he got all serious on me and said, 'Mum and the kids need me to be strong for them. Even you do. I know Allah will question me about you guys so I have to up my game, you know that.'

'Yeah, I know...'

'That reminds me – I wanted to chat to you about something.'

'Yeah? What's that?'

He coughed then and looked ahead of us, to where the kids were turning into the small iron gateway of the park. 'Well, you know my friend from Saudi, Hassan? The one I studied with?'

'Umm, yeah, I think so...' Zayd had actually mentioned him a lot while he was in Saudi. He had spent some time in the UK, but his family were in Madinah. Apparently, they had become really close and Zayd had been accepted by Hassan's father as part of the family, staying over at weekends and having barbeques with them in the desert. 'What about him?'

'Well, I spoke to him the other day on Skype; he graduated, mashallah.'

I felt a twinge of guilt when Zayd said that. I was the reason he had had to abandon his studies. I always wondered whether he resented me for that, whether he held it against me. Of course, he put it down to destiny and never mentioned his feelings about his studies to me. But now that his best friend had graduated he *had* to have been feeling *something*.

'Mashallah,' I said, my voice small. 'Good for him.'

'Well, he actually got in touch to tell me that he's looking to get married...'

'And?'

He stopped walking then and turned to face me. 'I suggested you, Amirah.'

I will never forget his face when he said that: vulnerable, full of hope. If I had been able to pull myself together, I would have. Unfortunately, Zayd had just said the wrong thing to the wrong girl.

'You did *what*?' I couldn't help the look of horror on my face. 'What on earth did you go and do a thing like that for?'

'Because I know he will make a really good husband, he's got knowledge, he's solid, hard-working...'

'Whoa, hold up. Wait just one minute. What makes you think I'm interested in marriage at all?' I shuddered. Not interested was an understatement. Allergic would have been a better word.

Zayd shot me a look. 'Well, you're not a kid any more, Amirah.' He had called me Amirah instead of Ams. He was definitely serious then. 'You know as well as I do that, as a Muslim, it's better and safer to marry while you're still young...'

♀ AMIRAH

I started laughing then because I knew that if I didn't, I would end up crying. He wasn't going to do that religious blackmail stuff on me, not now. 'Oh no, you don't, Zayd,' I said, holding up my hand. 'Don't go quoting Qur'an and *Sunnah* to me on this. I've read the books, I know my rights. I'm not interested, not interested *at all*. I'm sure your friend is great and everything but marriage isn't part of my plans, certainly not now. I'm going to university, inshallah, then I'm up out of here. I don't want to marry your friend from Madinah. I don't want to marry anyone. And if you can't understand why I feel that way, you don't know the first thing about me!' I turned away from his shocked expression, his gentle words that were meant to soften me up, his reminders that were meant to bring me back into line.

Not this time, bro, not ever.

21

I didn't see Amirah again for what felt like forever. Her brother, Zayd, started bringing the kids to the Islamic Centre for summer school in the mornings, taking them home again afterwards. Usamah had recruited him, too, and so, three afternoons a week, he was volunteering to coach the boys and get them ready for a football festival at the end of the month.

* * *

One day, Amirah's brothers and sister were dropped off at the summer school by someone I hadn't seen before. They were with another brother, Abu Hassan, someone we had seen at the school a few times, dropping his kids off, picking them up.

I couldn't put my finger on it, but something about the man with Amirah's brothers and sister felt off. The rough way he spoke to the kids, the way he didn't make eye contact as he gave *salam*, the way he ignored Abdullah when speaking, all of it gave me a bad feeling.

Abu Hassan smiled as he shook my hand. 'Mashallah, bro,' he said in his soft voice. 'May Allah bless you guys for what you're doing for these boys. They really need it, y'know.

There's just too much madness out there...'

The other brother stepped forward, a look of concern on his face. 'But akhi, I have to tell you, your *deen* programme is weak.'

I was taken aback. 'What do you mean, brother?'

'I mean all this stuff – sports and that – is great, but you need more *deen* in there. Why don't you have any classes for the boys, something that will really benefit them?

'These kids are too *jahil*, man, too ignorant. If you see how they behave when they come in the *masjid* – no *adab* at all. The other day, I had to cuss two of them who were going on – I told them sit down and read some Qur'an or get out!'

I glanced at Usamah and I could see that he was feeling the same way I did about the brother. But he didn't say anything.

'Yeah, akh, you're probably right,' Usamah said at last. 'We're trying, y'know. That's all we can do.' Then his face lit up. 'Hey, how about you come in and give classes to the boys. We sure could use some older brothers on board.'

The brother smiled and rubbed his beard again. 'Yeah, well, I would, y'know, it's just that I've got a lot on, with family and that. But I'll see what I can do, yeah?' And he gave *salam* and left.

As they walked away, Usamah kissed his teeth. 'I can't stand brothers like that, man. All talk, no action. All they want to do is criticise but the minute you ask them to help out, they've got so many other things to do. Man, that makes me mad!' He was getting angrier now, I could see it. He turned to face me. 'Man, that makes me *mad*! These kids don't need lectures! They don't need some brother getting up in their face! They need role models, people who care about them. People who'll give them *salam*, give them some time, even when they're not doing what they should, even when they're slacking. *Especially* when they're slacking.'

He started to walk back inside, shaking his head. 'All brothers like that do is chase people away from the religion, I swear. Don't let that brother near me again, OK? Coz I don't think I'll be able to hold back.'

Just then, Zayd appeared, carrying some shopping bags. The boys were going to be making lunch that day. 'What's up, Usamah?' he asked.

'It's that brother,' Usamah said and pointed at the man walking away. 'He was just here, telling us how our programme is too weak, that there ain't enough *deen*. Then I ask him if he'll help out and he comes up with some tired line about having too much on with work and all that. That's just some weak rap, man.'

106   Zayd tried to diffuse the situation. 'Maybe he does have a lot on his plate, bro. We've got to make excuses for each other, y'know...'

'Excuses!' Usamah exploded. 'How am I supposed to make excuses for a brother who won't help out but wants to lecture us about not having enough *deen*? I mean, what is that?'

Zayd backed up then, shocked by Usamah's outburst. I could see his jaw clench. 'That's my mum's husband,' he said shortly. 'And Malik's dad. At least he is dropping them off here.'

Then it was Usamah's turn to back up. He wiped his hand over his mouth and looked crushed. 'Yo, I'm sorry, man,' he said in a low voice. 'I didn't mean to disrespect your family. It's just that...'

Zayd held up his hand. 'No need, bro. It is what it is.' He

clearly didn't want to go into any more detail.

***

Later on, after the *salah*, while everyone was eating their lunch, I asked Zayd about the summer scheme. It was being run by a bunch of brothers that were way too young to have kids of their own.

'It just doesn't make sense to me,' I said, looking out over the field where the boys were spread out in clusters. 'It doesn't make sense to me that their parents aren't more involved. These are their kids. Don't they feel a sense of responsibility towards them?'

Zayd looked out over the football field and sighed. 'I don't know, bro. I really don't. It's been like this ever since we were kids. I've thought about it a lot over the years – maybe it's because of the way they grew up, maybe it's because they didn't have any good examples... But you know, after a while, you get tired of trying to understand it. It is what it is. I can't defend it; I've just got to do what I can to help my community, with or without their help.'

I looked at him with new respect. And I realised then that I barely knew anything about him, that he was still a mystery to me, in spite of everything.

'Was your dad... ?'

He cut me straight away. 'My dad wasn't Muslim. And he didn't stick around, anyway. In a way, I'm glad he didn't interfere. My mum raised us as Muslims, mashallah. If he'd wanted to be involved, it might have made things difficult...' He looked away and it was clear from his body language that he didn't want to say more on the subject.

107

I tried another tack. 'I heard you studied Islam at university in Saudi, bro. What was that like?'

He took a deep breath and shook his head. Smiling, he turned to me and said, 'Those were the best years of my life, bro, I'm not going to lie to you. Of course, I was raised a Muslim, y'know, and I knew things in theory: Qur'an, *Sunnah*, halal, haram. But studying it properly, studying it with the scholars, made me see it in a different light. We're blessed, bro, we are blessed with a beautiful *deen*, an amazing legacy.' Then his voice changed and he looked out at the boys again. 'We just don't appreciate it.'

The sincerity in his voice touched me. I knew exactly what he was talking about. Hadn't I been one of those careless Muslims for a large part of my life? 'You're right, bro. It's just so easy to take the blessing of *iman* for granted, especially when you didn't choose it; your parents did.'

108

'That's what I'm saying, bro,' he answered. 'That's why it's so important for us to connect with the *deen* for ourselves. We all just need to return to what really matters, innit?'

'So what happened with the studies, man? Did you graduate?'

A cloud passed over his face then and the seriousness returned. 'No. Family stuff,' he said shortly, getting up and dusting off his jeans. 'Had some family stuff to sort out. Yo, catch you later, inshallah. I'm going to make sure the bus is here.'

I could have kicked myself. He'd just started to relax with me and I had to go and mess it up with my questions. Zayd was a private guy, I could tell that. And hadn't Usamah already told me that he didn't like people talking about his family?

I should have listened to him.

But, to be honest, I couldn't help it. I thought about his sister – Amirah – all the time. Almost subconsciously, I looked out for her every morning. Every day, I expected to see her coming in from the car park, holding Taymeeyah and Malik's hands, signing '*salam*' to Abdullah. But she didn't come. Instead, Zayd brought them when he came in to work and, without knowing it, he kept me in check. I felt shy to think about her while he was around – which seems crazy.

Maybe it was Allah's way of keeping me sane. I don't think I could have dealt with seeing her every day and keeping up my guard. Something about her tugged at me in a way I couldn't explain.

It wasn't a physical thing, not really. Well, there was that, but there was more than that. She intrigued me. I just wanted to get to know her better, wished I could find out what made her tick, how to get her to laugh.

109

But I was good. I kept myself in check. I resisted the urge to get her number from the forms and call her or text her. It was the least I could do, especially when she probably never gave me a second thought.

No, for sure, it was better that way.

22

'*As-salamu 'alaykum*, baby girl!'

Rania's chirpy voice invaded my ear space. A phone call. At 8 a.m. It could only have been her, on one of her spontaneous drives through the neighbourhood.

'*Wa'alaykum as-salam*,' I groaned, throwing the duvet back. It had been a hot night and my neck and pillow were damp with sweat. A shower was in order.

'Let's roll!' There she was, still harassing me.

'Leave me, man, Rani!' I scowled. 'You know I haven't even left my bed!'

'Well, you'd better get your backside up because I'm outside!'

'Huh?' I ran to the window and peered out. She wasn't lying. There was Auntie Azra's car, right outside my house. Rania waved at me from the driver's seat, a stupid big grin all over her face. She knew I would have to come out now.

With a groan, I grabbed a scarf and wrapped it around my head, pulling Mum's prayer garment off the coat hook. I was just stepping outside; no need to go to all the trouble of putting on an *abaya*. Let alone having a shower.

As I opened the door, Mum called out, 'Is that you, Ams? Where are you going?'

'Rania's here, Mum,' I said, biting my lip. The silence was deafening but I took it as her consent anyway. A few years ago, she would have told me that I wasn't allowed to see her, that she shouldn't come round. But I was 18 now, and she had given up on trying to keep Rania and I apart.

Mum isn't one of those mothers who hates all her kids' friends. It was just Auntie Azra's family she had a problem with, something to do with stuff that happened between them way back, when we lived in Stockwell. All I remember is, one minute, Mum and Auntie Azra were best friends and, the next, they were barely speaking to each other, even at the *masjid*.

I think it may have had something to do with Malik's dad. When they got back together after the first divorce, he'd said, 'That sister is *fitnah*. I don't want to see her around here anymore.'

And, with that, a 12 year friendship was changed forever. Auntie Azra never set foot in our house again.

I stepped outside and, for a moment, I was dazzled by the strong sunlight. I shaded my eyes and turned to the car. The window was open now and there was Rania, her sunglasses perched on top of her scarf, two lollipops in her hand.

'One for me, one for you,' she grinned as she opened the car door.

And that was when I saw him coming around the corner.

My heart stopped beating and everything around us seemed to freeze. I couldn't hear what Rania was saying, just a rushing in my ears and a sudden panic rising in my throat. I hadn't seen him in weeks – and I had been quite happy that way. Now, here he was, strolling down our street, looking as good as good could be, bouncing his basketball, making me weak at the knees without even trying.

The rushing in my ears stopped in time for me to hear Rania say my name. 'Ams?' She was looking at me, mystified. Then, she followed my gaze.

At that moment, our eyes met and I saw his face light up with that gorgeous smile of his. He stopped short.

'Hey... umm... Amirah, *as-salamu 'alaykum...*' he said. Then he did this blushing thing, looking all confused, and I realised that he was embarrassed. And then it was my turn to be embarrassed, standing there in my mum's prayer garment and a gypsy scarf around my face. Shame!

'Oh, hey, *wa'alaykum as-salam*,' I replied, my mind working furiously: how on earth did he know my name anyway? 'Rani? This is Ali...'

Rania shot me a look and gave *salam* to Ali, trying not to stare.

'How have you been?'

'Alhamdulillah, good. Ummm, I wanted to thank you for taking care of Abdullah at the summer programme. He's really been enjoying it, mashallah...'

'Aww, that's great. He's a great kid, he really is.' His eyes darted nervously towards our front door, the upstairs windows. I knew just who he was looking out for. It would have been cruel to keep him there and risk getting caught by Zayd. 'Umm, OK, see you around. Got a basketball game...'

'OK, inshallah,' I said. 'Take care.' And I said the last bit in sign language.

He grinned in appreciation, signing 'You too.'

Then he was gone. I willed myself not to look at him as he loped down the drive. That really was the word for it: loping. Like a wild cat, maybe a leopard or a cheetah, strong and elegant.

♀ AMIRAH

'Wowee,' Rania breathed next to me. 'Where did *that* piece of fineness come from?' And then she caught herself, 'I mean, mashallah, is that your new neighbour?'

We looked at each other then and, at exactly the same time, we started giggling uncontrollably. I had to drag Rania into the back garden, near the kitchen, just in case he heard us and thought we were a pair of complete nutters.

'So?' Rania demanded, as soon as she got her breath back. 'Who is he and why haven't you told us about him?'

I tried to act like I wasn't fussed. 'No reason, Rani. I mean, he's just a guy, a guy who happens to live down my road, OK?'

'Wrong!' she crowed, rolling her eyes. 'Duh! That is one fine-looking Muslim brother right there – a real Mottie! And he looks like he's got it going on. Come on, spill, what are the stats? Age? Education? Marital status?'

'I don't know, Rani, seriously! And I don't even care, you know that...'

'SPILL!'

'OK, *OK*! Look, I've only met him, like, once! He seems nice, polite, a bit posh though. Sounds like he went to a private school or something...'

'So, when did you get to speak to him?'

'He volunteers at the summer school – he's Abdullah's group leader.'

Rania's eyes grew wide and she touched her heart, a look of reverence on her face. 'Ohh...' she breathed. 'Mashallah – he volunteers?' That was enough to convince her of his worth, without a doubt. 'That's amazing... So, what do you think of him, huh? Is he a potential candidate, huh? Does he qualify? Huh? Huh?'

I swatted her with my *abaya*. 'Get a hold of yourself, woman!' I huffed. 'I've hardly said five words to the guy!' But I could feel heat rising to my face again and a smile tugged at my lips when I thought of the painting I was working on upstairs, alone, where no one but Allah could see me. But Rania's eyes were too sharp. She had me sussed.

'Wait a minute,' she said, narrowing her eyes. 'Let me just get this straight: so you have a total Mottie living on your road. You've *spoken* to him. You've left *Abdullah* with him. And you've not told us anything about him? For sure, there's something there! *For sure!*'

I gave her my haughtiest look. 'Not at all, Sherlock. For once, you have it completely wrong. For a start, he plays basketball with Zayd; he's one of his friends! And you know what that means, don't you...'

'Oh, oh, oh!' Rania gasped, fanning herself. 'I do believe Miss Ice Maiden has a crush on her brother's friend! OMG, wait until I tell the girls about this!'

'Don't you dare breathe a word,' I gasped. 'Not one word!'

'Uh-uh, sisters' honour! You can't keep stuff like this from us!' And she whipped out her phone to text the girls.

Just then, I heard someone clear his throat inside the kitchen.

Zayd.

I looked up and saw, to my horror, that the kitchen window had been open the whole time while we were talking all our foolishness. And, of all the people that had to be standing in the kitchen, it just had to be Zayd.

I could have died, right there on the spot.

114

23

'D'you want to explain to me what that was all about just now?' Zayd's face wasn't angry, as I had expected it to be. More than anything, he appeared worried, anxious.

'Zayd...I...' I knew I had to choose my words carefully. 'I'm sorry. We were just kidding around, honest. You know what we're like sometimes...'

Zayd looked at me hard. 'Ams, you know I only want the best for you, right? And that I've got your back, no matter what. But I need to know: is there anything going on between you and Ali Jordan?'

What a question. Was there anything going on between me and Ali – Jordan? Of course not. Like I told Rania, I'd barely spoken to him. And that was the way I wanted it to stay.

It was safer that way.

I shook my head. 'No, Zayd, there's nothing going on.'

He looked like he was mulling that over. Then his eyebrow went up and he peered into my face. 'OK, then, tell me this: do you have any feelings for the brother?'

'*Zayd*!'

But he wasn't backing down. 'Well?'

115

'OK, Zee, look. I'll admit that he seems like a nice guy. And he's not so bad looking either.' Zayd's eyes started twitching and I laughed. 'Yes, yes, I know I should be lowering my gaze but I took my one look, all right? Relax!'

Zayd gave a grudging smile. I was too smart for him now.

I continued. 'But, listen, all joking aside, I know my limits. And I haven't done anything wrong, nor am I intending to...'

'But you admit that you've been checking him out?' Zayd's eyes were still bugging and I could tell he was trying to hold it down.

'Zayd,' I laughed again, 'please! D'you think it's only guys that check girls out and talk about which ones are fit and which ones aren't? Us girls notice too, trust me.' Then I looked at him slyly. 'And I don't mind telling you that you don't do too badly in the Mottie ratings...'

'*Astaghfirullah*, Amirah!' he cried, shocked. 'I hope you haven't been allowing your friends to discuss me!'

I laughed again at his appalled expression. 'Relax, bro, relax! We haven't shared our trademarked 'Mottie Scale' on the Internet – yet!'

'All right, all right, you can give it a rest now.' I had managed to soften him. 'But don't think I haven't noticed that you haven't answered my question.'

My eyes were wide. 'What question?'

'Oh, forget it,' he huffed, waving his hand at me.

I let out a tiny sigh of relief. I had narrowly avoided a potentially embarrassing conversation – confession – and Zayd wasn't mad at me. Result!

I turned to leave.

'Oh, Ams,' Zayd called after me. 'My friend, Hassan, the one I told you about? He called me the other day...'

My heart sank. Why was he telling me this? 'Yeah?' I squeaked. Sound normal, Amirah, I told myself. Sound normal.

'Yeah, well, he's coming to London...'

'Coming to London?'

'He's got some work to do for his dad's company at their UK office so he asked me to help him out, show him around and that. I thought... I thought maybe you two could have a sit down, y'know, get to know each other a bit...'

I had no words, just anger that he could be so presumptuous, so dismissive of my feelings when I had already made them crystal clear. He must have seen the look on my face because he took my hand and said gently, 'Ams, I know you. I know you're fighting this. Please, don't. Just be open. Remember the *hadith*: if someone comes to you with good *deen* and character...?'

I shook my head then, tears forming in my eyes. 'No, Zayd,' I said, my voice shaking. 'Don't go there. Don't try and use the *deen* to browbeat me. You of all people should know why I feel the way I do.'

He let go of my hand then, exasperated. 'Come on, Ams,' he said, his voice rising slightly. 'You can't keep doing this. Someone tries to give you some advice, tries to remind you about Allah, and you say he's 'browbeating' you, 'blackmailing' you, 'guilt tripping' you. It ain't blackmail, sis, it's the truth from your Lord!'

Then I really started crying. The guilt. I couldn't stand it: knowing that I felt one way when Islam said I should feel another. Of course, I knew that marriage is *Sunnah* and that every Muslim should be striving for it, but I told him, 'I'm sorry, Zayd, it's just too hard for me... I can't do it. You'll just

AMIRAH ♀

have to accept that.' And I ran out of the room, up the stairs, to bury my face in my pillow.

***

Later that evening, Mum came up to see me. By that time, I had recovered from my outburst and was busy working on my painting. I had told Colette that I would have it ready for Monday as the competition entry deadline was Friday. I was looking forward to getting her feedback although, secretly, I suspected that this was going to be one of my best pieces.

'*As-salamu 'alaykum*, Ams,' Mum said, glancing over my shoulder. 'Oh, that looks nice. Very realistic.'

I looked up at her and smiled. 'Thanks, Mum.' It was rare for Mum to comment on my work, even if all she said was that it looked 'nice'. 'I'm entering it for a competition down in Croydon, inshallah.'

'Oh, that's nice,' replied Mum, absently fingering my hair. A trim was long overdue.

'I heard you and Zayd arguing earlier,' she said, gathering my hair up and spreading her fingers over my scalp from the nape of my neck. I didn't say anything but closed my eyes and let her give me a head massage, something she hadn't done for months. 'You know he only wants what is best for you, Amirah.'

I sighed and pulled away. Turning to face her, I said, 'I know what's best for me, Mum. It's my life, remember?'

Mum smiled then, a pitying look in her eyes. 'Amirah, as I always taught you: Allah knows best. You're only 18, y'know. You need to learn to trust Him and stop fighting, hmm?'

☿ AMIRAH

I pressed my lips together then, clenching my fists. And, in my head, I said bitterly, *What, like you did, Mum? No, sorry, the last thing I want to do is live by the lessons you taught me.*

24

That morning, as I made my way over to the basketball court, my mind was racing. So, I had finally seen her again. I had *spoken* to her. Not that I made a great impression or anything – stammering and stuttering like a lunatic! But it was a start. A shaky start to an unknown something, true. But a start.

I was glad that Zayd was nowhere to be seen when I got to the basketball courts. I didn't think I would be able to hold it down around him, not after I had just spoken to her. I felt sure he would be able to see it in my eyes or smell it on me or something.

As usual, Usamah gave me a big man hug and *salam*s when I got to the court and we played a quick game, hard and fast, just the way I liked it. My intention was always clear: this was a distraction, something to take my mind off unhelpful desires, something to give me an outlet. Fasting during a British summer took more willpower than I could muster, what with sunrise being around 4 a.m. and sunset after 8 p.m.. Basketball was my only alternative.

By the end of the game, I felt cleansed. Amirah didn't flash into my head every few minutes; it was all I could do to get my breath back. And that was when my phone rang with an unfamiliar number.

It was Pablo, my best friend from Hertfordshire.

It hadn't been easy and I had changed my mind about it a dozen times but, in the end, I sent him a message on Facebook with my new number late the previous night. He must have called me as soon as he saw my message.

'Al!' He sounded exactly the same as I remembered. 'What's up? Where have you been, mate?'

I sat down on the bleachers and, fighting to get my breath back, I told him about the house, about moving to South London. He read between the lines, just like I knew he would, and I didn't have to mention Mum, or Dad's business.

'So, how are they treating you down there?'

I paused, looking over at the brothers shooting hoops, thinking about everything that had happened – that was still happening – and said, 'Not too badly, mate. We're getting there...'

121

He said nothing, waiting for me to continue, but I really didn't know what to say. My frame of reference was now so different to his: if I mentioned the summer school, the picture in his mind would be so alien to the reality; if I mentioned a girl, he would jump to totally the wrong conclusion. Better to play it safe. 'So, how is everyone? How are the guys? You seen anyone lately?' I could just hear his mum in the background, her enunciated vowels, her carefully modulated tones. And Vivaldi. That was Vivaldi playing. Pablo's mother's favourite.

'Yeah, I caught up with some of them last weekend. We went to this amazing party up in Oxford. First class, man, totally.' A pause, then, 'Amy was there.'

Amy?

'Cool.' I didn't know what else to say.

Pablo coughed, my lukewarm response obviously making

him unsure of himself. 'So... aren't you going to ask about her? She asks about you, mate, every time I see her.'

I shifted, my palms wet all of a sudden. 'Pablo, you know that Amy and I broke up before the exams.'

'That's not what she said... she asked me to give you a message if I spoke to you: to tell you that she misses you. That you should get in touch.'

The conversation ended soon after that. I was shaken, to tell the truth.

Pablo had been my best friend at senior school – we were close, did everything together. Hearing him talk brought back memories of all our crazy adventures, all the wild things we had done together: my old life.

Now that I was living in South London, trying to practise my *deen*, with other brothers who were all on the same journey, I could see how astray I had been for so many years, how oblivious.

I had been far away, so much further than either Mum or Dad could have known. For a while, I didn't even call myself Muslim – I wasn't absolutely sure that I believed anymore. Allah was a distant concept for me, a being I couldn't relate to, much less understand. And school made me ask so many questions, questions I didn't have the answers to, questions I was afraid to ask at home. So I floated away into philosophical debates, rugby and house parties, schoolboy pranks and puppy love. I was a boy with a Muslim name, lost in the world.

Of course, when the world came crashing down around me, when Mum succumbed to the cancer, nothing could ever be as distant as it was before. I had confronted death – my fantasy life had to end and real life had to begin. Because, as it says in the Qur'an, 'Every soul shall taste death', and that is the one reality than no philosopher can deny.

But I wasn't so sure about London either.

Now that Hertfordshire was really behind us – something I was still struggling to accept – nothing was clear. What would Umar's future be? And what about Jamal? Every day, I saw the kids Jamal's age in our youth group, and I got upset. Their attitudes, their manners, their aspirations (or lack thereof) – was this what lay ahead for my little brother?

Was running with gangs and getting arrested what lay ahead for Umar? A thought that occurred to me when I caught sight of Mahmoud coming around the corner. He looked pretty awful, to tell you the truth. Mahmoud was a reckless guy, and he partied hard, but I had never seen him looking so rough.

He greeted us, listless, rubbing his stubbly chin. 'What's up, guys? How's it going?' he croaked.

Usamah burst out laughing. 'You sure you should be here, akh? You look like you should still be in your coffin, staying out of daylight!'

'Nah, didn't you know? Mahmoud is the Daywalker!' We roughed him up until he starting grinning and a load seemed to lift from his shoulders.

'Did you go out on a bender last night?' I quipped, as I jogged around the court.

Mahmoud groaned and mumbled something about Edgware Road and shisha.

I laughed. 'Definitely a bender, Muslim style.'

If Mahmoud had been out the night before I wasn't surprised that he was having a bad morning. I had been out with him and his mates, just the once.

Mahmoud's friends had been loud, they'd revved the car

a thousand times every time they passed a pretty girl on our way to Edgware Road.

I remembered this girl, Zizou, and her friends coming over to our table to chat and laugh and flick their hair about. One of them had taken a bit of a shine to me but Mahmoud told her that I was a good Muslim boy who did not need to be corrupted by girls like her.

I remembered the argument about whether shisha was haram (they decided that it wasn't), and whether smoking cigarettes was worse (they decided that it was).

When I turned down the shisha pipe Mahmoud had said, 'hey, don't be such a neek, man. You can still have fun without being a total ho, like me.'

But that hadn't stopped him from dropping me at the gates of Seville Close at one o'clock in the morning, reeking of tobacco and shisha. Needless to say, Dad hadn't been impressed the next morning.

'You better slow down, Mahmoud,' Usamah said, 'the fast life's got a way of catching up to you, if you know what I mean.'

Mahmoud glanced at me guiltily. 'Yeah, I know, no need for a lecture, bro.' Then his face changed and he bit his lip. 'Ummm, dude, what would you do if… if a girl… if a girl told you she was… y'know… expecting?'

Usamah's eyes narrowed. 'Expecting what? A birthday present?'

'No… expecting a baby.'

'Whose baby?'

'Your baby, man, what do you think?'

Usamah started laughing then. 'Bro, that could never ever happen. You know why? I keep myself tight, you know what

I'm saying? I ain't got time for no *zinah* in my life.'

I peered at Mahmoud. 'Why do you ask, Mahmoud?' My curiosity got the better of me.

That was when Mahmoud clammed up. 'Nothing, man, nothing. Just giving Usamah a taste of his own medicine, innit?'

And he was off to shoot hoops with some other guys who had just arrived.

After he'd left Usamah said in a low voice, without looking at me, 'a brother's got to be careful, y'know. One false move, one moment of weakness, and you could be living with the consequences for the rest of your life. Keeping your chastity ain't no joke but guys like to think that the rules don't apply to them. But when they spill their seed and ruin a sister's life, and have a child that they won't raise, they wonder why there ain't no *barakah* in their affairs. Brothers got to fear Allah and stay strong.'

125

'And fast,' I murmured, lost in my own thoughts. 'Just like the Prophet said.'

'Or get married,' chuckled Usamah. 'Whichever's easier.'

'Well,' I said, getting up from the bleachers, 'I know which one I'd prefer!' And I went to join the basketball game that was just starting up.

25

Between looking after Mum and the kids at home, art school and hanging out with the girls, I made myself too busy to think of Mr Light Eyes. My conversation with Zayd had pretty much put the fear of God into me: if I wasn't ready to have a meeting with Hassan, why on earth was I even thinking about my Mottie neighbour who probably just saw me as his friend's little sister anyway?

Madness, clearly.

So, life went on, pretty much as it had done before. OK, so my heart skipped a beat when I stepped outside my front door, because of the slim chance that I might bump into him. But I didn't see him for ages. Either our schedules were completely different or he was deliberately avoiding me.

So it was easy for me to pretend that he didn't exist. I had also managed to convince Rania not to say anything about him to the girls so I could avoid their teasing – a mammoth task, I assure you.

When I got to Rania's house, everyone was helping Auntie Azra prepare for her Urban Muslim Princess event. We'd always helped her with preparations for the various functions and fundraisers she was involved with as an event co-ordinator, but even I could see that this Urban Muslim

Princess show was going to be bigger and better than any she had done before.

Today, it was a real family affair: not only were all her daughters' friends there (i.e. us), but Auntie Azra's sister, Caroline, was there too, helping out. 'You've got some amazing sponsors this year, Auntie,' I said, eyeing the make-up samples, glossy magazines and gift vouchers for the goodie bags we were packing.

'Yes, we've had fantastic support this year, mashallah. And Caroline got some of her clients to chip in, too. Yasmin, I understand your brother's bike club, Deen Riders, has pledged the proceeds of their next rally to our cause?'

Yasmin nodded. 'Yeah, the Deen Riders are trying to get more involved in charity work and I mentioned our event to my brother...'

'I'm sure they didn't need much convincing, what with all the yummy stuff you make for them, mashallah!' Yasmin beamed and ducked her head.

Auntie Azra sat down at the table, a wistful smile on her face.

Rania looked over at her. 'What're you thinking about, Mum?'

Auntie Azra smiled at her. 'Oh, just thinking of how proud your father would be of us, *rahimahullah*.'

Rania gave her mum a hug. 'Daddy always knew you could do it, Mum. He always knew the business would be a success.'

Auntie Caroline laughed. 'He was the one who pushed you into it!'

Auntie Azra smiled and nodded. 'He told me I was wasting my time, twiddling my thumbs at home when you lot finally went off to school.' She took a sip of her coffee.

'He was a good man, sis,' sighed Auntie Caroline. 'No doubt about that. They don't make them like that anymore.'

Auntie Azra turned to face her girls. 'He always believed in me, your father did. Even though I didn't go to college or uni, he always encouraged me to pursue my goals.'

'Did you really never go to uni, Auntie?' I still couldn't believe it, after all these years. Auntie just seemed so confident, so knowledgeable about all sorts of things. It didn't make sense that she had left school with just a handful of GCSEs.

'Only much later on, when my kids had gone to school,' she said. 'I just read a lot of books and became a self-taught expert on kids, homemaking and homeschooling.'

Auntie Caroline laughed. 'You did everything the wrong way round, didn't you, sis?'

'It was the right way for *us*,' Auntie Azra said primly.

'Well, I know my nieces won't be making the same mistake, will you, girls?' Auntie Caroline arched her eyebrows at Rania. 'These girls are too young to be thinking about marriage. They haven't even got their exam results yet! They'll have plenty of time to think about marriage when they're older.'

Auntie Azra shrugged her shoulders. 'It's different for us, Caroline. Muslims are not allowed to date, you know that. The only sanctioned relationship between a boy and a girl is within marriage.'

'So, are you saying that love isn't "halal", then?'

Auntie Azra smiled. 'Of course love is halal, Caroline, don't be silly. But, in our religion, halal love is between a husband and wife, no exceptions. And if a young person feels that they are physically and emotionally ready to be in a relationship, Islam encourages them to do it the right way, with honour. Why do we see nothing wrong with 13-year-olds having sex – which they do – but have such a problem with the idea of an 18 or 19-year-old getting married? I know which one I would choose for my girls!'

Auntie Caroline huffed. 'Well, I still think they're too young. They should be thinking about their education, building their careers, not getting tied down.'

'My point exactly,' I added.

'OK, let's change the subject, shall we, before Amirah goes on another anti-marriage rant.' Samia gave me the side eye. ' I swear, you've become a total fascist, d'you know that? Anyway,' she turned to Auntie Caroline, 'I don't see why I can't do both. Getting married doesn't mean the end of your life. It's just the start of a new journey, one I'd like to take with my husband at my side. I still intend to study and I'll still be able to work if I want to.'

Then Yasmin said, 'In the Asian community, getting married early isn't always an option, really. If you don't have a degree and if the man isn't financially secure, nobody's interested. You'll struggle to find a good match, that's what all my aunties say.'

'I think 20 plus is a good age, personally,' was Rania's response. 'Maybe while you're at uni, or just after you graduate. But I'd prefer to marry someone older, someone more settled. He needs to have everything in place, as far as I'm concerned. I'm not into the starving young couple thing!'

We all laughed and Auntie Azra turned to me. 'What about you, Amirah? What do you think is a good age to get married?'

I wrinkled up my nose. 'Ummm, how about never?' Everyone groaned and rolled their eyes at me.

But Rania wouldn't let it go. 'But *what if*, Amirah, *what if* you met The One: the perfect guy for you? The one who ticked all the boxes, who really got you, who was everything you dreamed of? Good *deen*, good character, *and* a total Mottie? What then, eh?'

I drew myself up and arched my eyebrows. 'Well, if I met The One, I wouldn't hesitate for a moment. I would marry him straight away and go backpacking across the world, praying on the beach and sleeping under the stars. We'd be broke, but we'd have each other and that would be enough. We'd take each day as it came, building our future together and I would love him fearlessly and with all my heart. *That* is what I would do!'

The whole room erupted into screams and whoops and squeals of delight.

'OMG!' crowed Samia. 'The ice maiden has melted! She has succumbed!'

Yasmin literally had tears in her eyes as she sighed, 'That is just sooooo romantic, Amirah! Who would have thought?'

'Aha!' I said then, holding up my hand. 'There is only one problem with this scenario: that guy you asked about, Mr Perfect? The One? Well, I hate to break it to you, ladies, but he *doesn't exist*!'

Everyone booed and started pelting me with whatever they could find: bits of tissue, rolled up socks, elastic bands. I ducked them all, grinning. I just couldn't resist winding them up. And indulging in my own secret fantasy at the same time. Only Allah knew how true everything I had just said was. Only He knew.

But then Rani blew my cover. 'Ummm, maybe you'd like to tell us about a certain brother from Saudi Arabia who is interested in our local ice maiden?'

More screams and dropped jaws. I shot her a dirty look and folded my arms, my lips pressed tightly together.

Rania decided to do the honours, 'Oh, only that Zayd's got this friend that he knows from uni in Saudi and he's interested in getting married and wants to meet Miss Madam here...'

'And I'm like "Whatever, dude, in your dreams!"'

'Amirah, I can't believe you kept that quiet!' Samia said, grabbing me by the arm. 'Remember the pact we made last year? We swore to tell each other any and all details about all things romance and marriage related. You are in serious breach of your contract, girl, so you'd better start talking!'

I shuddered. 'Ugh, do I have to?'

Rania came and put her arm around my shoulder. 'We're sisters, Ams, and sisters share things. Anyway, you need us to help you make the right decisions; you know you can't be trusted to take care of things like this since you're basically an anti-marriage extremist.'

'In total contradiction to the *Sunnah* of the Prophet, I might add,' remarked Samia drily. I scowled and stuck my tongue out at her.

'Enough,' I growled. 'Zayd beat you to it with the religious lecture, believe me.'

Then Yasmin got all serious. 'OK, joking aside, Ams. What's the deal with this Saudi brother?'

I sighed and said, in my most unexcited voice, 'Well, for a start, he's not Saudi. He's actually born in the UK. He just went to Saudi to study at the university there. I think he has some family there or something. He's a friend of my brother's. Basically, Zayd told him about me and, because he likes Zayd and trusts him, he wants to have a meeting when he comes to London...'

'Where does he live, Madinah?' was Samia's question.

'Yeah, I think so,' I replied, realising only then that I hardly knew anything about Hassan, apart from the fact that he was living in Saudi, had graduated from an Islamic university and was Zayd's friend. Nothing about his personality, his interests, plans for the future, what he was looking for in a wife...

That's because you're not interested, remember?

'Subhanallah, a student of knowledge? Living in Madinah? Amirah, you'd be crazy not to give this brother a chance.' Her face went all dreamy. 'To be able to make *umrah*, hajj... to pray in the Prophet's mosque every day,' she sighed. 'Bliss, man. Bliss...'

'It does sound kinda nice when you put it that way.' I had to admit, it did sound tempting. But I had other plans, remember? Plans that definitely did not involve getting married and moving away to a foreign country.

'Then I think you know what you need to do, Ams.' Rania took charge. 'You will agree to meet him when he comes to London. It's only fair to give him a chance, isn't it? Who knows, he could totally sweep you off your feet!'

They all started laughing again and I joined in. What was the point of getting all huffy with them? They didn't understand, not really. For them, it was a no-brainer: give it a go; if it doesn't work out, you just keep on going. But I had already lived through that mindset – Mum's mindset – and I knew how difficult it could be to pick yourself up and start moving forward with your life.

No, better not to tempt fate. Better to stay safe. Better to concentrate on filling those goodie bags.

♀ AMIRAH

The next day, at the library, Collette had good news.

'Amirah, your painting was shortlisted! I'm so pleased for you!' she gushed. 'The judges picked your painting out of hundreds of others – a real honour. You should be proud of yourself!'

Mashallah, I said inwardly. *Cultivate humility always.* But I beamed all the same. I was really pleased with that painting and, to have it displayed with the other finalists was fantastic – a first for me. In other art competitions while I was at school, I had never been quite good enough, had never been in the running for any prizes.

'I've started painting with my brother, Abdullah,' I said, all of a sudden overcome with shyness. 'He's deaf – but he's 133 been responding really well.'

'I work with deaf children all the time,' Collette enthused. 'It does wonders for their self-confidence and ability to communicate.' Then she looked at me, her head on one side. 'Why don't you come down one day and see how I work? Maybe you'll get some ideas for your work with your brother.'

I couldn't think of anything I'd love more.

26

The summer flew by, each day melting into the other, establishing a routine that seemed to have always been there. It was as if we had always lived on Seville Close, as if I had always been working with tough youth, praying at the *masjid*, trying to memorise the Qur'an, dreaming about a girl I dared not speak to. It was as if Jamal had always been my shadow, as if Umar had always been AWOL, hiding behind his walls.

One day, I walked into Jamal's room to find him crying softly to himself. As soon as he saw me, he sniffed and tried to hide his face, wiping the tears from his cheeks with his too-long sleeves.

'Hey... Jamal? What's up?' I tried to get him to look at me, but he kept his face turned away. 'Has something happened, Jay? Talk to me.'

Eventually, he spoke. 'I miss Mum, Ali. I miss her so much...' And then he started crying for real and it occurred to me then that he had hardly cried when she died. He'd just stopped talking for a while and clung to me like I was his only lifeline. I searched desperately for something to say to ease the pain. I knew just what he was feeling. I had been there – I was still there: missing her, mourning for her, hurting. I knew that there were no words, really, that could ease the pain. So I just held him and let him cry it all out.

When he was done and all that he had left were sniffles, I made him look at me. 'Jamal,' I said, 'I'm sorry I haven't been there for you. We haven't gone out together, just the two of us, in ages – and I miss that. Tell you what, let's do something together, today. What would you like to do? Just name it.'

He chewed his bottom lip and thought for a moment. Then he looked up at me and said, 'Mum used to take me to the library. We'd go to the kids' section and spend hours there, reading to each other. Mum always chose the picture books – she said she missed out on them when she was a kid and wanted to catch up on all the latest ones.' His voice became wistful. 'Then, afterwards, we would choose our books – 15 books each! – and then go for a hot chocolate. That was our special routine, our special time, just Mum and me.'

'You want to go to the library, Jay?' I asked softly. 'No 135 problem. Nana's meant to be coming to see us tomorrow so we can go today. Just make your bed and we'll hop on the bus to Croydon. I heard that the library there is great. I think you'll like it.' I smiled at him and ruffled his hair. The look of relief and hope on his face almost broke my heart. *O Allah*, I made *du'a. Help me to take care of my responsibilities towards Jamal in the best way. And protect and guide him always.*

And that was how we ended up on the Number 250 bus to Croydon. That was how I got to see Croydon Town Centre for the first time. That was how I found myself face to face with a piece of me on the wall of a cafe.

It was crazy.

One moment, we were enjoying the buzz and unique look of the Croydon Library building – the high ceilings, the dedicated children's library area, the three floors of books,

books, books – and the next, I was staring at a painting that was so realistic, so familiar that, for a moment, I wondered whether my eyes were playing tricks on me.

Hanging on the walls of the library cafe were several pieces of art, all linked by a sporting theme of some sort. Sketches, abstract paintings, portraits. But there was one piece, a larger than life painting of a pair of hands holding a ball of fire, about to shoot it into a basketball hoop, that made me stop short.

I recognise those hands.

At first, I thought I must be dreaming, seeing things. I rubbed my eyes and stepped closer.

The shape of the fingers, the nails, the way the veins stood out on the inside of the wrist, were all as familiar to me as my own face. I turned my left hand over and looked down. There was the birthmark, below my knuckle, just as it was in the painting.

No, there was no doubt about it: those were my hands.

Totally confused – and pretty weirded out – I looked down at the name that had been scratched into the paint in the corner of the canvas.

Amirah Wyatt.

Zayd Wyatt's sister. My neighbour.

My composure fell away like the flimsiest house of cards. Wild thoughts raced through my mind.

To have drawn my hands in such minute detail, leaving nothing out, meant that either she had a photographic memory or... or she had made a point of noticing every little detail about my hands.

I smiled then, giddy with hope, with the threat of possibility.

136

She *did* remember me. She *was* thinking of me. Maybe...
Maybe...

* * *

The following Monday, at summer school, I made a point
of catching Zayd alone. I wanted to test the waters, to see
whether she had mentioned me to him at all.

'Umm, Zayd,' I began, trying to sound all casual. 'Your
sister's into art, right?'

Immediately, I saw his defences go up and he looked at
me, barely disguising his suspicion. His reply was guarded.
'Yeah... kind of. She's been taking classes down at the Croydon
Library. Just won a prize of some kind. Why d'you ask?'

'Oh, no reason... was just wondering. I... I saw one of
her paintings hanging up at Croydon library and thought I'd
ask...' I trailed off, withering under his stern gaze.

'Yeah, well you asked, didn't you? And you got your
answer. Anything else?'

I shook my head vigorously. 'No, nothing, bro... nothing
at all.'

He nodded curtly and walked off. I let out a sigh of relief.
I had been afraid that he was going to jump me right then and
there.

Usamah had already warned me about asking about
Zayd's sister – I don't know why I hadn't listened. Zayd was
definitely unimpressed by my line of questioning.

It was clear that, whatever was going through Amirah's
head, she was keeping it to herself.

Perhaps I should have done the same.

* * *

137

Later that night, I typed her name into Facebook.

Up came her public photo feed, full of images of various buildings in London, food, and different shop displays. But the latest photo in the feed was a picture of her painting of my hands. The caption read: Prize winner, mashallah! Underneath it, all her friends and followers had left congratulatory comments and lots of <3 and xxx.

I hesitated – *Is this halal*? – but only for a moment; I quickly typed my own comment: A mirror image, mashallah. Real skill. Mr Lightfoot.

Then I clicked the tab shut, closed the laptop and found that I was shaking.

What did it all mean?

And why did I feel so happy?

27

Mr Lightfoot.

It was him. I just knew it was. He'd been on my page. He'd seen the picture. And, if his message was anything to go by, he knew those were his hands.

'The plot thickens,' Rania would say.

'OMG,' Yasmin would say.

I didn't know what to say. Much better to ignore my racing heart and that feeling in the pit of my stomach.

Much better to pay attention to preparing for my art therapy class with Collette.

***

Collette's class was a real eye opener. There were children there with different forms of disability: deafness, blindness, autism. We introduced them to a variety of different materials – paint, clay, fabric – and then just helped them create what they wanted to create. The two blind children absolutely loved the clay and it was a real treat to see them 'seeing' what they wanted to create with their fingertips. I felt totally comfortable using sign language with one little boy. He wanted to create a picture to express how he felt when his dog died that weekend.

At one point, Collette came up behind me and stood there while I helped a little girl with autism create a village out of different materials. She said nothing for a while, then put her hand on my shoulder and said, 'You are a natural, Amirah. I'm very impressed...' And then she was gone to help with the clay sculptures.

I left the class walking on sunshine, even though the weather forecast had predicted summer showers. I felt so good; I'd been involved in creating pieces of art with the most wonderful children. I couldn't help thinking to myself that more people needed to come out of their comfort zone and spend time with children with special needs.

As I left Brixton station, I looked up at the sky and noticed the huge, dark clouds that were gathering beyond the church. Not wanting to get caught in the rain and have to go through the process of blow-drying my hair again, I decided to pick up a small umbrella from the newsagent.

And, right on cue, while I was on the bus to Herne Hill, the rain started coming down, pelting the windows like hailstones, blurring the world outside. By the time I got to the bus stop outside Seville Close, the streets were flooded. I shook my head: UK summers really were something else.

As I crossed the road through the rain, trying to keep my backpack from getting wet, as well as keeping the umbrella over my hijabed-up head, I noticed two people standing at the entrance to the compound. My heart began to thud as I recognised the tall, lean figure and the little cutie at his side: it was Ali and his little brother, Jamal.

When he turned towards the street, he saw me coming towards them and that smile appeared again, like the sun

140

breaking through the thick rain clouds.

All of a sudden, I felt a wave of shyness wash over me. My cheeks burned and my palms grew moist. I knew that he knew about the picture. Not only that, I knew that he knew that I knew that he knew. That was awkward and I felt a bit foolish for thinking that I would be able to keep the painting.

Now, here he was, in the flesh, and I wanted to disappear into the hedge that lined the fence.

But he didn't do anything out of the ordinary. Just greeted me with *salam*, with the same manners as usual: shy but friendly, open but respectful.

And dripping wet.

'What's going on?' I asked, staring at the two of them hunched outside the gate. 'Isn't the gate working?'

Ali ducked his head, clearly embarrassed. 'They changed the code, remember? I forgot to make a note of the new one and now we can't get in. We tried ringing all the bells – doesn't look like anyone's home.'

'Never fear,' I grinned, 'Amirah is here. I stored the new code in my phone.' And I handed the umbrella to Ali while I fished around in my bag for my phone.

The umbrella wasn't a big one and we all ended up being in much closer proximity to each other than we had ever been before. I caught a whiff of spicy cologne and coffee, and my breath caught.

Rania is never going to believe this! I thought as I keyed in the code.

Ali pushed open the gate and let me and Jamal go through, handing me the umbrella. Our fingers almost touched, *almost*. But, alhamdulillah, they didn't. That might have sent me over the edge completely. I struggled to keep my face normal when, really, I felt giddy and just wanted to grin like a mad woman. I wanted to look into his eyes and see what secrets were hidden there. I wanted to ask him what kind of coffee he liked. I wanted to share his coffee. And pancakes. And eggs. And toast.

Stop, Amirah. Just stop, OK? Do yourself a favour and control yourself.

We walked quickly up the hill through the rain, not saying anything, Jamal and I sharing the umbrella. I didn't trust myself to be able to hold it down. I don't think Ali did, either. I mean, surely he wanted to ask about the painting, right? And, if he did, wouldn't I just die of embarrassment? Discussing the painting would mean getting personal. And that wasn't safe territory. I knew that.

And yet, a part of me wished he *would* ask me. The daring part that wanted to see what would happen, that wanted to see how he felt about it, whether he felt anything at all. That part that wanted more food for dreams. More fuel for my fantasy.

The naughty part.

But I had her well trained by now, so I didn't speak to Ali again as we hurried along, Jamal and I under the umbrella, Ali getting soaked beside us.

I was able to be more relaxed with his little brother. 'Abdullah's been asking after you, Jamal. Said you promised to help him with his maths in exchange for teaching you sign language.'

Jamal nodded, his face bright. 'Yes, Ali's been prepping me. Just teaching me the basics. I'm a bit worried that I won't be able to teach Abdullah properly if he can't hear me and I can't sign properly.' He bit his lip. 'That's what's been holding me back.'

I smiled at him – what a sweetie! 'You don't have to worry about that, Jamal. Abdullah can read lips, too. Just make a date and come over, OK? I'll stick around if you need any extra help with him.'

He looked more relaxed.

'And I'll make you my trademark brownies, too.'

Then he grinned and put his hand out to me. 'It's a deal!'

I shook his hand and saluted, then glanced up to see Ali looking at the two of us with this soppy smile on his face. The rain was starting to ease up. 'I suppose you'll be wanting some brownies too, right?' I said with a smirk.

'Well, a guy can dream, can't he?'

'Well, there's no law against it, that's true.' We both fell silent as we reached my front door.

'You guys take the umbrella, OK?' I said, handing it to Jamal this time. 'You need it more than I do.'

'OK, so you're talented, caring *and* generous?' Ali remarked, out of the blue. 'Isn't there anything you can't do?'

'Umm, yeah...' I felt my cheeks start to burn. 'I can't take a compliment,' I said, then dashed indoors to hide under my duvet. Now I could grin all I wanted.

Minutes later, I was on the phone to Rania: 'Girl, you will never believe what just happened...'

143

28

It was my third time out with Yusuf and the other Deen Riders. Despite my initial misgivings and the fact that I had been absolutely terrified the first couple of times I rode on one of their huge bikes, I couldn't deny the thrill I got from it. The power of the machine, the landscape rushing past, the speed. I was definitely hooked.

144 Usamah had laughed at me when I dismounted after that first ride, legs shaking, eyes watering, a crazy grin plastered all over my face. 'That's some good stuff, huh? Get your blood pumping, get some colour in those cheeks!' All the brothers laughed, but in a really great, welcoming way. I had looked out over the field, to the woods and to the red roofs of London beyond and felt my chest expand with so much gratitude. So this is what it felt like to conquer your fears. Definitely a feeling I could get used to.

I knew then that I would be back to ride with the brothers again.

Now we were in a lay-by on one of the long, winding country roads out past Croydon. In front of us was a spectacular view of the green fields of Surrey. Behind us, there was a meadow framed by woods. The horses were startled at first by the sound of all the bikes and they galloped to the other end of the field. But once we had cut the bike motors, they calmed down and went back to grazing.

I took off the helmet that Yusuf had lent me and took a deep breath. How I had missed the country air. The great, old trees and rolling patches of green reminded me of home. *Hertfordshire will always be home*, I thought to myself. *No matter what.*

Then Yusuf put his helmet down and reached into his backpack. 'Brothers, some goodies from my sister's kitchen...' And he held up a large yellow cake box.

Immediately, the brothers crowded round. It was clear that they were not strangers to Yusuf's sister Yasmin's skills in the baking department. And there was a cheer when Yusuf opened the box to reveal a selection of delicious-looking muffins. The smell was mouth-watering.

Yusuf held the box out to me. 'Since you're the guest, bro...'

I didn't need asking twice. I took one of the muffins that was closest to me, took a bite and was blown away by the taste. 'OK, this is my new favourite,' I joked. 'Any wife of mine needs to know how to make these, inshallah. That will have to be top of the list!'

The others laughed and Yusuf smiled at me. 'You thinking of getting married, are you?'

I grinned at him. 'Seems like that's the only thing some brothers talk about – as for me, I'm only 18! Well, about to turn 19. But still, I don't think I'm ready to get married. I haven't even got my degree yet!'

Yusuf chuckled and nodded at one of the other brothers, a short, stocky guy with a ginger beard and bald head. 'Yo, Dav, come and tell my boy, Ali, about your little halal love story!'

Dav turned red and threw one of his riding gloves at Yusuf. 'How many times have I told you to mind your own business, bro? I'm going to have to teach you a lesson one of these days...'

Yusuf threw the glove back. 'Nah, don't be like that! I just want you to tell Ali here your thoughts on early marriage, innit.'

Dav came over, brushing the muffin crumbs from his beard. 'You thinking of taking the plunge, are you?'

I shook my head vigorously. 'No, no, I was just telling Yusuf that I'm not settled yet. Not settled enough to provide for a wife and all that stuff – I only start uni next month.' The thought of going off to university made me feel queasy all of a sudden and I didn't trust myself to speak.

Dav said, 'Yeah, I understand what you're saying. I mean, we're always told that marriage is something you do when you've achieved your other milestones like education, a good job, a house in the suburbs, and all that. But when I was about your age – maybe even younger – I was just learning about Islam. My girlfriend of the time was, too. When I took my *shahadah*, I knew I'd have to break it off with her but it was so hard...'

'He loved her, you see,' commented Yusuf, ducking another one of Dav's riding gloves.

'Anyway, she ended up becoming Muslim, too, and we both decided that we wanted to get married straight away, not wait until we were 'financially secure', as my mum and dad kept saying. So we got married at 18, and we're still together, ten years and four kids later, mashallah.'

'You were *18* when you got married?' I was incredulous.

146

I could only imagine what Dad would say if I tried to spring that on him.

Dav smiled at what were clearly fond memories. 'Yeah, we both were. We didn't live together straight away, though, because we were both studying while living at home and our parents were dead against it. But after about six months, I got a part-time job and we were able to get a little one bedroom flat together and start living as man and wife.' He sighed then, a wistful look on his face. 'The best years of my life, I tell you.'

I frowned. 'But wasn't it tough? I mean, how did you manage to make ends meet? Do the whole *providing* thing?'

'Well, my wife wasn't one of those women who wanted the high life; she was never like that. We both had to make sacrifices but, mashallah, they were worth it. It's something special to struggle through those early years together, when you're both still strong and have loads of energy and your *iman* is high. And you're both still learning, y'know? That's one of the best bits about it: you're still learning about yourselves, each other, Islam, and the ways of the world. And you're like best friends, really. Companions on a journey...'

147

Yusuf nudged me and winked. 'Told you it was a halal love story. So, has he managed to convince you yet?'

I smiled and said nothing but, inside, I was trembling. The relationship Dav described struck me as so beautiful, so perfect, that I couldn't speak.

Of course, it is obvious who I was thinking about. Our chance encounter in the rain a few days before had only made it even harder to forget about her. I still wasn't sure that I should have thrown in those compliments at the end, but I couldn't help myself. I just hoped she didn't think I was a total loser after that. But as I thought of Dav and his 'halal love story', I smiled to myself. Maybe getting married young wasn't such a bad idea, after all. Especially to the right girl.

* * *

When we got back to the cafe Yusuf remembered the donation that the Deen Riders had to send to Sister Azra for her fundraiser. The sun was going down and, in a few moments, it would be time to pray. Already, some of the brothers were freshening up in the cafe toilets, making *wudu*.

'Listen, Yusuf,' I said, 'let me take the donation to the hall tomorrow. It's really close to where I live and I don't mind at all.'

'Really, bro? That would be such a help. *Jazakallah khayran*.'

'No problem,' I shrugged. 'I owe you one anyway.'

Yusuf reached into his backpack and pulled out an envelope. 'Please make sure it gets to Sister Azra safely, yeah? And do you think you could do me a personal favour? I wanted to get some flowers for Yasmin – my sister – just to say "well done". Do you think you could get some for me from the florist in Herne Hill? I know it's lame to not get them myself and everything but...'

I smiled. 'No problem at all, bro. I'll do that for you. Your sister is lucky to have a big brother like you.'

He smiled, 'I'm the lucky one, alhamdulillah. And she's going to make some brother very happy one day.'

'I've no doubt about that,' I nodded, thinking how different Yusuf and Zayd were about their sisters: one wouldn't even mention his, the other talked about his all the time!

Then Yusuf stopped smiling and looked at me intently. 'Well, maybe you should give it some thought, bro. I like you, y'know? You're a good brother. You just let me know if you'd like me to help set up a meeting or something.'

I laughed, taken aback by his candour. But I didn't want to offend him. 'Yeah, sure, bro, *Jazakallah khayran.*'

After the Maghrib *salah*, which we prayed on the tarmac, I caught Yusuf looking at me again, a thoughtful look on his face. I frowned and thought maybe I shouldn't have spoken so freely about his sister like that.

I quickly gave *salam* and hopped onto the back of Dav's bike. And though I was still high on the adrenaline of the day's events, I couldn't help the feeling that kept nagging at me, that I had put a foot wrong somehow.

29

My bags were packed with the stuff we were going to need for the show. Now I had to get myself ready.

Just as I slipped the silver baby-doll dress over my head, I heard a knock at the door.

'Ams, can I come in?' It was Mum.

She stepped into my bedroom and I swear it felt so strange to see her there. She smiled when she saw me standing in front of the mirror, a smile that was in a weird way both shy and proud. But I could see that today was one of her good days and I was glad.

'I thought you might like some help with your hair,' she said, holding up a set of ceramic straighteners. I smiled back at her, relieved. She remembered. She remembered that I was rubbish at straightening my own hair.

'Looks like it's going to be quite a night for you girls, eh?' Mum said, as she clamped a section of my hair between the heated pads and began to pull it gently away from my head.

I nodded. 'Yeah, Auntie Azra said the tickets are pretty much sold out.' I half turned to face her, flinching as I felt the heat of the straighteners come dangerously close to my ear. 'Why don't you come, Mum?'

Mum looked away, a frown on her face. 'Well, you know

me and Auntie Azra aren't that close anymore... And these events are not really my thing.'

I didn't say anything. It still upset me that Mum had let Abu Malik come between her and her oldest friend.

Mum finished doing my hair and I was soon swinging it around like a Pantene model on steroids. My dress fit me just as it should and, after I had slipped on a stack of silver bangles and some drop earrings, and put on my strappy silver sandals, I looked at myself in the mirror, grinning. This was a different Amirah: a gorgeous being who held nothing but love, hope and *iman* in her heart; owner of a glowing future; heiress to success and happiness. A *princess*.

Taymeeyah squealed in delight when she saw me coming down the stairs, all dressed up, with Mum behind me.

'You look just like a pwincess, doesn't she, Ummi?' she lisped, pouting so that I could put some strawberry lip gloss on her rosebud lips.

Mum smiled and nodded. 'Mashallah, your sister does look lovely.'

'Beautiful!' signed Abdullah, a big, fat grin on his face. Malik looked up from the computer screen, flashed me his missing teeth and turned back to his latest online game craze.

'Thanks, guys,' I smiled. 'You know who got the good genes now, don't you!' We laughed together and I went to get my new *abaya* and scarf from the peg by the door.

Just then, Zayd stepped out of his room behind the stairs. The look on his face when he saw me going towards the door, hijabless and dressed to the nines, was priceless.

'What's going on here, then?' he asked, looking from me to Mum, to Abdullah and to little Taymeeyah, who was still staring at my dress.

'Amirah's going to a big, fancy party, Ibi,' she chirped. 'And it's not even Eid!' She laughed at her own joke and danced off to the kitchen with Mum, no doubt to fix yet another bowl of her favourite cereal.

A look of comprehension lit up Zayd's face and he smiled and nodded. 'Ahhh, this is that Muslim Princess thing you told me about, yeah? Safe...' Then he frowned and put his hands on his hips. 'Oi, you sure there aren't going to be any guys at this party?' I could tell that he was only half joking.

'Oh, no, Zayd, Auntie Azra thought that, now that we've finished school, we can start having some *real* fun. I think Rania mentioned something about Chippendales...'

He grinned sheepishly. 'All right, all right, no need to get sarcastic on me, yeah? I was just checking, doing my duty and all that.'

152 'Yeah, I know, bruv, but sometimes there's, like, no need? I don't need you to be my in-house Haram Police, yeah? I got this. You know, at some point, you are actually going to have to trust me and let go.'

I saw his face go all funny then. I should have ignored it. I should have walked away, towards the door, put my *abaya* on and gone out of the door. Instead, I looked into his eyes, the way I always did when I wanted to probe him. He took the bait.

'I know that, sis,' he said, all quiet and serious. 'It's just that sometimes... sometimes I worry that you'll slip again, y'know?'

I shook my head. 'Zee, that was, like, a lifetime ago. You're still stressing about that? I thought we had moved past it.'

He frowned. 'We can never be too sure of ourselves, sis,

you know that. The believer is always vigilant coz *shaytan* is always ready to trip us up. And... when I see you like this, all dressed up, doing your thing, it reminds me of how easy it is to get fooled by the *dunyah,* this world, and fall into old habits...'

I groaned inwardly. *Astaghfirullah*, but I really wasn't in the mood for one of Zayd's *khutbah*s, not tonight when all I wanted to do was have a little fun with my friends – halal fun, at that! I looked down at my phone. I was running late!

'OK, I'm out of here before the Haram Police arrive with an arrest warrant!' I laughed, skipping to get my *abaya* and hijab before he could quote me a particularly apt fatwa.

30

When I stepped into the hall where the Urban Muslim Princess show was to take place, my heart skipped a beat. It was like a dream, a dream I had had since I was a little girl. You know those proms you see in American movies – all mood lighting, ball gowns and glittering disco balls. This hall was like that – but better.

There was a red carpet down the centre of the hall. One of the younger girls was scattering white rose petals over it. The tables were covered with crisp white tablecloths and red sashes were tied on the backs of the chairs. Tea lights and flowers floated in glass bowls, twinkling, their reflections dancing in the water.

The ceiling above was covered in paper chains, paper flowers and balloons.

The air in the hall was scented with *bukhoor* and Maher Zain *nasheed*s played in the background. Until our shrieks and laughter drowned it out.

'*As-salamu 'alaykum*, babes, you look gorgeous!'

'OMG, can you believe this?'

'Mashallah, this is amazing!'

'Seriously, Rania, may Allah reward your mum for her awesomeness!'

♀ AMIRAH

I craned my neck to catch a glimpse of Auntie Azra in an elegant black *abaya* with fluttering sleeves. She was in 'Event Manager' mode now, I could see: her phone was jammed against her ear and she was telling Maryam and her friends where to put the goodie bags. Then she looked over at us.

'Oh, Amirah, there you are! You've still got your hijab on. Please, honey, could you go out and get some more donations that have come in? The brother from Deen Riders is waiting outside and I've got too much going on here...'

'Sure, Auntie,' I called out. I made my way to the back of the hall, where the double doors were. Kicking aside a balloon, I pushed the door open and stepped out into the corridor.

At the other end of the corridor, by the entrance, a brother in a leather jacket was standing with his back to me. He held a motorcycle helmet under one arm and an absolutely beautiful bouquet of flowers under the other.

'*As-salamu 'alaykum*?' I called out, my voice echoing in the empty space.

The brother turned around.

It was *him*.

My heart literally stopped, I was so surprised to see him. What was he doing here, looking so delicious, tonight of all nights?

His face lit up in that cute way of his and he smiled when he gave *salam*, shy but a bit more confident than before. 'Hey, *wa'alaykum as-salam*, Amirah. How are you?'

I smiled too. I just couldn't help myself. 'Yeah, I'm good. What's going on?'

He seemed to remember what he was there to do and held out the flowers.

I gave him a questioning look. 'What am I supposed to

AMIRAH ♀

do with these?'

'Umm, they're for you...' he stammered, rubbing his hands on his jeans. 'For you... you sisters...'

I smiled to myself as I screamed inwardly. I wasn't falling for that! This was some serious halal chirpsing going on. Flowers! Swoon. I mean, really. Totally dead.

'*Jazakallah khayran*, I'm sure *the sisters* will think they're beautiful...'

He was really embarrassed now, I could tell.

'Well, I hope tonight goes well for all of you...' Then he reached into his back pocket. 'Here's the donation from the Deen Riders charity rally. The brother in charge, Yusuf, apologised that he couldn't bring it himself...'

Oh, that's quite all right, I thought to myself. To him I said, 'Please thank the brother for us. May Allah reward all of you.'

Just then, I heard Rania's voice behind me. 'Amirah, come on!'

'I've got to go,' I said, not wanting to tear myself away but knowing that I had to. 'See you around...'

Another smile, a *salam*, a wave and he was gone and I was running back towards the double doors, my heart racing, almost tripping over my *abaya*, the flowers heavy and wonderful in my arms.

Rania was at the door and she took one look at the flowers and then at my face and squealed and hugged me. 'Ohhhh, I can't believe this is happening!'

Neither could I. But there was no time for believing or thinking or talking. We had a show to put on. And, as sisters began to come in through the double doors, holding their goodie bags, their eyes bright as they looked around the beautiful hall, I felt like I was covered in diamond sparkles from head to toe.

The sparkles shone as I changed out of my *abaya*. They lit up my face as I did my make-up for the show. They danced and shimmered as I strutted down the catwalk.

I wasn't awkward, sarcastic Amirah Wyatt from Seville Close.

I was Princess Amirah, beautiful, kind and generous, sharing my sparkles with everyone in the crowd. When I got to the end of the runway wearing my last outfit, I turned and blew the diamond sparkles to everyone in the crowd. The sisters cheered and drummed the tables as I sashayed off the stage, triumphant at last. Rania had tears in her eyes as she hugged me.

'You were amazing out there, girl,' she sniffed. 'Making me tear up here and everything...'

Alhamdulillah, I thought while I got changed in the dressing room. *Alhamdulillah*. I looked at myself in the mirror and for once, *for once*, I actually liked what I saw.

Definitely a gold star night.

Definitely.

* * *

I was still floating when I joined the others at our table for the three course dinner. There they were, my girls - Samia and Yasmin and, of course, Rania. And other girls were there, too, girls we knew from school, from the *masjid*: Asiyah and Rabia, Tasnim, Fatima and Hadiyah – we had laughed together, cried together, prayed together and played together;

we were like a family.

Where would we all be in a year's time? Who would be at college? Who would have gone to uni? Who would be married? As I looked around at all my friends – smiling, laughing, looking gorgeous, happy – I wanted to hold that moment and never let it go.

One of the girls held up a delicate vol-au-vent. 'Bet you'll be doing the catering next year, Yasmin!'

Yasmin ducked her head. 'Oh, I could never pull off something like this...'

'You never give yourself enough credit, Yaz,' I said to her, quietly so that the others wouldn't hear. 'You need to believe in yourself, babe, like we all do.'

'You think so?'

'I know so,' I smiled, thinking that I would start to make more of an effort with Yasmin, help her to see her potential, maybe even put in a good word for her with Zayd...

But I should have kept my arrogance in check.

The next few minutes rushed by in a blur.

First, Auntie Azra came to our table, holding the flowers, my flowers. I stood up and reached out to take them from her, but she turned away from me and towards Yasmin, sitting small and quiet in her chair.

'Mashallah, Yasmin,' she beamed. 'These are for you!' She was waving the little card that had been taped to the cellophane wrapped around the bouquet.

The card that I had foolishly neglected to open.

My mouth went dry and I sat down abruptly.

I glanced up and saw that everyone was admiring the flowers. Everyone but Rania who was looking right at me, confused.

158

♀ AMIRAH

'I swear, when I get married, I want my husband to bring me flowers like this every single day!' one of the girls was saying.

Yasmin blushed and a little smile came to her lips. 'It's nothing, girls, really. Just my brother getting ahead of himself.'

'What's all this about then, Yaz?' Rania tried to sound normal.

'Nothing, nothing.' Yasmin's trademark modesty. 'Yusuf's just been telling me about this brother that he's become quite close to through his Deen Riders club. Said he's really nice, mashallah; different.'

'Really?' Samia's eyes were wide. 'So, who is the mystery brother? Come on, tell us! You can't leave us in suspense like this!'

Yasmin frowned for a moment, thinking, then her face lit up and she looked over at me. 'I think he lives near you, Ams. 159 Umm, I think his name's Ali? Yes, that's right: Ali Jordan.'

I could have died, right there.

31

When I got home, I was still grinning. Amirah had looked so beautiful, I could only imagine how stunning she would have been after taking off her hijab and *abaya* in that all female hall.

Thoughts it wasn't healthy to entertain but thoughts I was having nonetheless.

That had to be one of the best things about being married: the laws of hijab no longer applied. You could check out your wife 24 hours a day if you wanted to, no problem.

I was still thinking about Amirah when I opened the front door – to find Dad standing there, his face tense and drawn.

'*As-salamu 'alaykum*, Dad,' I said, stepping inside. 'What's the matter?'

'It's your brother, Ali.'

'Who, Umar? Jamal?'

'Umar. He's not home yet. He's not answering his phone. I've got a bad feeling...'

'I'm going to look for him,' I said, turning to walk out of the door again. Dad grabbed my arm.

'Wait, Ali. We've no idea where he went, or when. Where will you look for him?'

'Everywhere,' I said simply, and began to walk away. Dad

could stay home to wait for him, just in case he came back while I was out looking for him. Jamal needed him at home as well.

'Just call me if he turns up, ok, Dad?'

As I walked down towards the entrance gate, I racked my brain, trying to think where Umar could be. Who did he know in South London? Where had he been? It occurred to me that I didn't even know who he had been spending his days with. I mentally kicked myself. Umar was my responsibility. I had promised Mum I would look after him – and now look what had happened.

Instinctively, my footsteps took me towards number 7, where Zayd and Amirah lived. I rang the bell and waited. After what seemed like forever, Amirah's little brother, Abdullah, opened the door. I had grown to love that little guy; out of all the summer school boys, he was definitely my favourite.

I signed a greeting. 'How are you, Abdullah? Is your brother at home?'

Abdullah nodded vigorously and dashed off to call Zayd who appeared a few moments later. '*As-salamu 'alaykum*, bro, what's up? Everything OK?'

'No, not really,' I replied. 'Have you seen my brother at all? The middle one, Umar?'

'You mean the angry one?'

'Yeah, I suppose you could call him that. It's just that he's not home yet – and that's not like him at all. He doesn't even know anyone around here. I want to look for him but I just don't know where to start...'

Before I could finish my sentence, Zayd was shrugging on a tracksuit top. 'I'll come and help you look. Come on, let's go.' He turned and called into the house, 'Mum! I'm off to

161

help the brother, Ali, from next door, yeah? Don't know what time I'll be back – hopefully not too late...'

He turned to me. 'Let's go.'

I tried to hide my surprise at his willingness to help me, no questions asked.

As we strode towards the entrance gates, Zayd took out his phone and called a few people, asking if they had seen Umar – 'Fourteen years old, skinny, green eyes, screw-face'. Nobody had. 'We should try the stations in the area first,' he said shortly.

I simply followed his lead, making *du'a* the whole time, scanning the streets for any sign of him – bus shelters, shops, under the bridge. No sign of an angry 14-year-old anywhere.

We got to the station. Zayd went to the ticket officer behind the thick glass screen. 'My friend's looking for his little brother. Tall, skinny, mixed-race boy. Green eyes. Did he come through this station?'

The man gave him a blank stare.

'Look, this ain't no joke, yeah. We think he may have run away from home...'

'Do I look like a human CCTV camera to you, son?' was the ticket officer's response. 'I have hundreds of people coming through this station every day. Do you really expect me to remember every one of them?'

I could see that Zayd was beginning to get frustrated so I stepped to the glass window to try some good old private school charm. 'Please, sir, try to think. It's really important.'

But the officer took no notice. He was already turning to do something else. 'Go to the police, fellas. They'll know what to do.'

'Come on,' barked Zayd, jerking his head towards

the street outside. 'We're wasting our time here. Let's keep moving.'

We walked back up the road to the High Street, checking inside shops, asking shopkeepers. No one knew anything.

I began shivering.

This was my fault. I hadn't kept a close enough eye on him. I hadn't been there for him. Now, he could be anywhere: shacked up in some flat, sleeping rough in the park, lying bleeding in a gutter, at the bottom of the Thames. My imagination began to go into overdrive, thinking of all the terrible things that could happen to a young man out on his own at night in a big city like London.

We sat down in a bus shelter and I called home. Still no word.

I couldn't speak to Zayd, couldn't tell him how worried I was. If Usamah had been with me, I know I would have been more open, but I was still wary of Zayd's moods.

Yet, to my surprise, he was the one who started speaking and, when he did, his voice was full of feeling. 'Don't worry, bro. I know you're killing yourself, imagining all the things that could have happened to him but don't. He'll be all right, inshallah. Just keep making *du'a*. You have to believe that Allah will take care of them.'

'You sound like you've been through this before,' I said, forgetting all about respecting his privacy and all that.

'I have,' he said in a low voice. 'I have. And I know how it feels: like your whole world is upside down and nothing makes sense and it's all your fault.' He looked out into the street and was silent as a bus stopped in front of us, creaking and shuddering. As the bus pulled away again, he looked over at me and, for what felt like the first time, I met his gaze. I'd always been too intimidated before; intimidated and guilty. But I had nothing to feel guilty about now, nothing to be ashamed of.

You'd be surprised by how much you can tell about a person by looking into his or her eyes. When I looked into Zayd's, I didn't see the hard, prickly character I had experienced before. I saw worry, a sincere concern for me and my predicament. And I saw something else, something I couldn't put my finger on.

Then he looked down. 'I know what it's like, bro, trust me. I know what it's like to have such an important person in your life disappear. You blame yourself. You think you'll never forgive yourself if something happens to them. But you can't lose sight of the fact that Allah is All Mighty, All Powerful. The Best of Planners. You have to hold on to that and trust that He will bring you through, no matter what. His promise is true, Ali, remember that.'

Zayd obviously had no idea of the effect his words were having on me. So much of what he said applied to me, to our family, to losing Mum, to having to give up our old lives. And it was true: He *had* brought us through. We were still standing.

And at once I was filled with a sense of hope and optimism. When I examined my heart, my gut, I did not believe that Umar had been harmed. Allah would keep him safe, I was sure of it.

Just then, my phone rang. It was Umar.

'Umar!' I answered the phone immediately. 'Where are you, man? We've been worried sick! Are you ok?' The questions tumbled over each other, not making sense.

Umar's voice was distant when he answered me. 'I'm at

Nana's, Ali. I'll be staying here for a while, OK? Just tell Dad for me.'

'Why'd you have to disappear like that, eh? Dad was about to lose his mind. You'd better call the house and explain yourself because...'

But he interrupted me. 'No, Ali, I don't want to speak to Dad. I know just what he'll say and, to be honest, I don't want to hear it right now. Just let him know that I'm safe, OK? Take care, bro. Bye.'

'*As-salamu 'alaykum...*' My voice trailed away. I couldn't get over my mixed feelings as I told Zayd that Umar was safe with my grandmother. On the one hand, I was relieved that he was safe. I knew how much Umar had been dying to stay with Nana, and how much he had been missing home. It made complete sense. I mentally kicked myself again, for not figuring it out sooner. But he had sounded strange, distant. And what was all that about not coming back? I was sure that Dad would have something to say about it all.

And he did.

'Umar is with your grandmother?' Dad repeated, a frown on his face. 'This is disastrous. Really disastrous.' He must have sensed that I did not know what on earth he was talking about because he looked up at me and said, 'Do you know what my mother said to me once? She said she could accept me becoming Muslim if that was what I had to do, but she would pray till her dying day that her grandchildren would return to Christianity. Umar running away to stay with her is just sending her the wrong message entirely.'

'And what message is that?'

'Come on, Ali, isn't it obvious? Your brother doesn't want Islam. That's why he is up in Hertfordshire with Nana instead of here, with us.'

I was so shocked by Dad's lack of understanding of Umar and his situation, what he was struggling with, that I couldn't speak. I just couldn't.

At last, I looked up at him. 'Dad,' I said hoarsely, 'it would help if you just tried, for once, to listen. If you just tried to put your own ideas aside and really *listen*.' And, with that, I turned and left him standing in the middle of the hallway, a look of bewilderment on his face.

32

I couldn't get home fast enough. After Yasmin dropped her bombshell, I excused myself, saying that I need to go to the bathroom, powder my nose or something. But instead I slipped out into the car park, lugging my bag full of shoes, clothes, make-up and accessories behind me.

I had to get out of there. I had to get home.

How could I have been so stupid? So naive? What on earth had made me think that Mr Light Eyes saw me as anything other than his slightly crazy neighbour? What had made me even imagine that he kind of liked me, that there was something there? My mind ran through all the signs I had thought were so crystal clear: our conversations, that smile, his comment on my page, that time in the rain... Maybe he was just like too many other guys: a big fat flirt.

Stupid, stupid, stupid.

I started walking towards the main road, stumbling under the weight of the heavy bag, the hem of the *abayah* I was wearing catching on my heels. Ordinarily, I would never have taken a cab on my own but tonight it didn't seem like I had any other choice. Also, I had felt the first drops of rain as I left the hall and I wasn't keen on getting caught in a summer downpour. Thankfully, the cab office was around the corner

AMIRAH ♀

so I didn't have to walk far.

In the cab on the way home, I thought of the bright lights of the stage, everyone smiling, happy, the smell of those flowers and my reflection in the mirror, a beautiful princess in one of Rania's gorgeous outfits, and thought bitterly, That is why this world is an illusion: here today, gone tomorrow. And then the tears started.

My phone vibrated. A text. I knew it would be Rania, asking if I was OK. I wasn't in the mood to lie so I sent a message: 'Gone home. Chat tomorrow.'

Almost immediately, the phone rang, as I expected it to. But I switched off the ringer and shoved the handset deep into the bottom of my bag. Being out on my own, I wasn't about to turn the phone off completely, but I certainly didn't want to hear the calls that were bound to come through. All I wanted was to get into bed and sleep for the rest of the summer, until it was time for our A level results to come out and my life could begin again. By then I would have forgotten all about this silly crush, Ali and Yasmin would probably be engaged or something, and I would be off to uni to live the life that was waiting for me.

But obviously a summer-long sleep was not going to happen. I was going to have to get over this heartbreak the old fashioned way: with time, tears and lots of chocolate.

I was actually looking forward to getting home. My eyes were dry now and I had rehearsed my lines for when anyone asked me about the event. I even had a special smile in store for Taymeeyah, just in case she had waited up for me.

'Next year,' I thought to myself as I walked quickly up the drive, 'I'll take her with me. She'll love it.' As I turned my key in the door, I smiled, thinking of my little sister's starry eyes and lisping compliments.

But the smile froze on my face when I stepped in the front door and came face to face with the last person in the world I wanted to see, standing in the kitchen as if he owned the place.

'Hey, beautiful,' he smiled in that wolfish way of his, as if he had every right to be there. 'You're a bit late, aren't you?'

'What are you doing here?' I hissed, ignoring his smile and the way his eyes flickered downwards from my face to take in the rest of me.

His smile widened and I was suddenly afraid, so afraid that I could hardly breath. 'Ah, mashallah, your mum and I made up, innit? So we're one big, happy family again, right?'

He stepped towards me and I stepped back, my bag bumping into the front door that had closed behind me. 'Where's Mum now?' I asked, trying to keep the tremor out of my voice.

His eyes flicked upwards, and he jerked his head towards the stairs. 'Sleeping.'

'Zayd?' I clutched the bag in front of me, peering down the darkened corridor, hoping that I would see the sliver of light from under his door, that, at any moment, he would push his door open and come and rescue me. But the corridor was dark and Abu Malik was closer now, so close I could smell the perfumed oil he loved: Egyptian musk. I felt a rush of nausea as he reached out to touch my arm. I jerked away and he stepped back, chuckling.

'Wow, you're uptight, innit? Aren't you pleased to see your old Amu back in the house? I thought we could spend some time catching up...'

I shoved my bag towards him before yanking the front

door open while he stood there, laughing at me.

I heard the rain before I felt it but I didn't care about getting wet anymore. I just wanted to get away from there. I walked through the rain, hunched over, my arms crossed in front of my chest, hands in my armpits. It was the only way I could keep myself from shivering uncontrollably. I didn't care about the water that had soaked into my hijab and the slosh-sloshing of my *abaya* against my shoes. I knew I looked like a tramp but, what made it worse was that I felt like a tramp. A dirty little tramp with loads of dirty little secrets hidden in her dirty *abaya*.

Later that night, after sneaking into the house and up to my bedroom, I pulled the chest of drawers up against the door and took off my soaking clothes.

On my bed, rolled up under the covers, I used my fists to muffle the sound of my crying.

170

33

For the rest of the weekend, after Umar had gone, I bristled with nervous energy. I kept finding excuses to go out of the house, to walk down the drive, all the time hoping I would 'bump into' Amirah. The sparks from our meeting at the charity event kept me buzzing: there was *definitely* something there.

But every time I left the house, I saw every neighbour but her. It was as if she had disappeared.

Until Sunday night.

I had popped into the local express supermarket to grab some things for Jamal's lunch the next day when I heard a familiar voice in the aisle behind me. I would have recognised it anywhere.

She was with her little sister and Abdullah and they seemed to be arguing about something. Stuck in the middle of the disagreement between her siblings, Amirah's head was down, her long eyelashes sweeping her cheeks, a hint of a smile touching her lips.

I was torn between keeping quiet and simply listening to her voice, and letting her know I was there.

The part of me that wanted her to look up and see me, that wanted to see that smile of hers widen when she saw me, that wanted to get just one more look at that cute dimple, won over.

I cleared my throat. 'Amirah?'

Her head jerked up when she heard my voice and her eyes widened but, to my surprise, a smile didn't light up her face; instead, her face seemed to close, to darken somehow.

'Oh. It's you.'

Not the reaction I had been hoping for. She seemed almost embarrassed as she muttered *salam* then quickly looked away from me towards her sister who was tugging at her *abaya*, pulling her towards something on the other end of the aisle. Only Abdullah acknowledged me with his amazing smile and a warm hug. I hugged him back, baffled by Amirah's behaviour. We had shared a moment just a few days before, I had been dying to see her all weekend and here she was, pretending I didn't even exist. I mean, she totally blanked me! And now she was about to go to the checkout without saying a word to me.

I tried calling out to her again, a little less sure of myself this time. OK, a lot less sure of myself.

She glanced back at me, a troubled look on her face. 'You could have told me, you know.'

'I'm sorry... told you what?'

'That the flowers you brought were for Yasmin. I'm just saying... it would have made things a lot clearer.' Then she turned away. Taymeeyah pulled at her hand.

'Come on Ams,' she said in a loud whisper, 'let's go. Ummi said we shouldn't talk to boys.'

Before I could explain why I was there with the flowers for Yasmin, she was gone, leaving me standing there in the middle of the supermarket, utterly confused.

172

I couldn't even remember what I had come in for in the first place.

***

I had to wait until the following Friday before I heard about Amirah again. I was on my way out to get some jerk chicken from the food trailer that parked outside after the *jum'ah* prayer, when Zayd called out to me. 'Hey, Ali, there's someone I'd like you to meet. This is my best buddy, Hassan. We studied together at the university in Saudi. Hassan, this is my neighbour, Ali.'

When we shook hands, Hassan's grip was firm and confident. He flashed a smile at me.

'Good to meet you, akhi,' he said in a deep voice. 173 *'Barakallahu feek.'* His Arabic accent was pitch perfect, too.

After they walked away Usamah came over and dropped the bombshell.

'You see that brother, Hassan? Word on the street is that he's looking to marry Zayd's sister...'

The world stopped turning.

'Zayd's sister?' I heard myself say. 'Amirah?'

'Yup,' said Usamah, looking at me sideways. 'And, from what I hear, Zayd's all for it.'

So that explained her sudden coldness: she was interested in someone else.

And, with that realisation, all my hopes and carefully crafted dreams began to crumble, one piece of wishful thinking at a time.

34

It didn't take me long to succumb to the pressure from all sides and agree to at least meet Hassan, Zayd's friend. After my majorly embarrassing misreading of the situation with Ali on the night of the Urban Muslim Princess show, I decided it was time to stop dreaming and forget about Mr Light Eyes.

The girls had managed to convince me that I had nothing to lose by meeting Hassan and, to tell the truth, I was more than a little curious about him after all this time. And what he would make of me.

But it all happened so fast. One minute, I was reluctantly agreeing to give Hassan a chance, to meet him, and the next, Zayd was getting ready to go and pick him up.

Friday soon came around: the day of the meeting. Mum was so excited she could hardly function. She kept breaking into giggles and squeezing my arm, all while trying to keep an eye on her roast lamb. Abu Malik had gone to the *masjid*. I had made it quite clear to everyone that I wanted Zayd to act as my *wali*. I had started keeping my prayer garment on while Abu Malik was around and would never be alone in a room with him. Mum commented on my 'full-time hijab', but didn't ask why. She could never see anything she didn't want to see. But as for me, I would be vigilant, and keep him at arm's length.

♀ AMIRAH

I got to speak to Mum about the situation the morning after the show, when I realised that Abu Malik was back in the house and that their divorce was now invalid.

Trying to keep my voice steady, I asked her, 'How long will he be here for this time?'

She shot me a look. 'What kind of question is that, Amirah? I don't know, do I? We're trying to work things out... for you kids. I don't want to go through another divorce, really I don't. I will do whatever I can to make this marriage work, inshallah. Just make *du'a* for us, ok?' Her voice was jangling with that fake kind of cheerfulness that jarred my nerves.

I looked at her as she fiddled with a bottle of nail polish. I felt a surge of pity well up inside me. 'Mum,' I said, 'why do you always let them come back?'

She blinked at me a few times, smiled, then frowned. After a few moments, she looked me straight in the eye and said, 'Because I don't want to be alone, Amirah.'

Then it was my turn to frown. 'You've never been alone, Mum. We've always been right here with you.'

'But you're my kids, Ams, it's not the same. Maybe you'll understand one day. I'm the kind of woman who needs a man around. That's who I am.'

'Even if they treat you like dirt?'

Mum's face changed and she pulled away from me, straightening her back. 'You haven't had to make the choices I have, Amirah. I pray that you never do. But if you do ever find yourself in my position, I hope that you won't judge yourself as harshly as you judge me.' And she swept out of the room.

I blinked, stung by her words, upset by the grain of truth that they contained.

* * *

The kids were super excited at the prospect of meeting Hassan. To them, he was a double hero: their big brother's friend from university and someone hoping to marry their sister. They dashed around the house, trying to make themselves useful, but just getting under everybody's feet. In the end, I chucked them all out into the garden.

'I need to tidy up, you guys!' I said. 'And you're not helping!'

'Oh, Amirah, we'll help,' cried Taymeeyah. 'Honest, we will.' She looked up at me with her best puppy dog expression and I stopped being angry and pinched her cheek.

'No, sweetie,' I smiled. 'I need you to look after Malik, OK? Keep him out of trouble. Make sure he stays in the garden and doesn't make his *thobe* dirty.'

Mum had insisted that they dress their *jum'ah* best for Brother Hassan's visit.

And that had been another issue with Zayd.

'You're going to wear a niqab, right?' he had said that morning.

I'd stared at him, horrified. 'Why would I want to do that, Zayd?' I asked, feeling unease creep up my skin like a rash. 'I don't normally cover my face, do I? So, he should see me as I normally am.'

Zayd was trying hard to be patient with me, I could see that. 'Because, my darling sister-who-has-to-question-everything, he's just come from Saudi. He won't be expecting to see your face in the first meeting. If you guys get along and he wants to take it further, then he may ask to see your face the next time. Wouldn't you prefer it that way?'

I sighed, knowing that there was no use arguing. 'Fine, Zayd, fine. It just seems silly to hide my face from him in a sit-down, when I show my face every time I step out of my freakin' front door!'

Zayd raised his eyebrow at me. 'Well, maybe that's something you should reconsider, eh? The niqab would protect you from a lot of things, y'know, a lot of *fitnah*...'

I threw my hands up in mock horror. 'Yes, Zayd, I know: the hordes of lecherous men out there, ready to jump me at any minute!' I shook my head and looked at his reflection in the mirror. The expression on his face was one of profound pity. I couldn't help it: I burst out laughing and, eventually, he did, too, shaking his head as he left the room.

I looked at my reflection in the mirror and felt a little shiver. Excitement? Apprehension? Maybe a bit of both?

What if he liked me? I mean, really liked me, enough to want to get married? What would I do then? Would it make me feel how I'd always wanted to feel: special, loved, cherished, that someone wanted me for me? Did I dare to imagine?

A moment later, my eyes flew open and I gave myself a little slap. 'Amirah!' I said sharply to the girl in the mirror with the stupid, dreamy expression and the head full of cotton wool. 'Wake up! Let's get one thing straight: this is merely a formality, OK? Just something to do so that you can say you tried, and get Zayd off your case for a few more years. You've got your plan, remember? Stick to it.'

* * *

After Zayd left to meet Hassan at the underground station in Brixton, time seemed to slow down. Agonising minute after agonising minute crawled by, with both Mum and I checking the wall clock constantly. They were at *jumu'ah*, said Zayd's text. They'd be here soon.

In the end, I couldn't take the ticking clock, Mum's pacing up and down and Taymeeyah's endless questions: 'Does he have any sisters? Does he have any sisters my age? Will he bring his sisters? Can we go and see his sisters in Saudi?'

And, of course: 'Are you going to marry him, Ams? What will you wear to the wedding? What will I wear to the wedding? Will we get to sing and play the duff? Can I invite my friends to the wedding?'

'Enough, Tay! Mum, tell her please: I'm not marrying anyone...'

'Yet,' said Mum, trying to soothe Taymeeyah. 'Amirah hasn't even met him, Tay. You'll have to save your questions till after she meets him.'

'*Allahu akbar*!' I cried, flinging myself out of my chair. 'I'm going to my room, Mum. Call me when they get here, please.'

Once in my room, I picked up my Qur'an and started to read. It seemed like the right thing to do to get my nerves under control and get some perspective.

Just as I finished reading the first *juz'*, I heard Zayd's voice downstairs, followed by another, much deeper one. My mouth immediately went dry.

He was here. In my house. Downstairs. Waiting to meet me.

O Allah, bless and protect me. Guide me to make the right decisions.

I stood up to put on the niqab that Zayd had bought me a few months before. It had never been worn and a fine crease ran down the middle of the black chiffon. I adjusted it

178

to make sure no fabric touched my eyes, tugging it down until it felt comfortable. I looked at my reflection one last time: I was a figure dressed in black from head to toe. Obscured. Nothing to distinguish me from any other sister.

I took a deep breath – and went downstairs to where Zayd and Hassan were waiting.

35

She was probably in the meeting with him already. Talking about getting married – to him. While I'm left feeling wretched, angry, jealous. I thought there was something there, a spark, something. Was it all just wishful thinking? Was she just messing with my head?

Wild, reckless thoughts danced around inside my head: I should go there, right now, and demand to speak to her, tell her to forget this Hassan guy, that I'm the one for her.

But what business is it of mine? It's not like I've even said anything to her. It's not like I have anything to offer her. I don't even know what I'm doing with my life anymore. All I can see in front of me is a load of questions, unanswered questions at that. I ached for Mum. I wondered what her advice would have been. What would she have told me to do?

But of course, I knew. She would tell me search my heart, be true to myself.

Thoughts of Mum and Amirah gave me the strength to ask Dad about marriage. Knowing Amirah would consider Hassan meant she might consider me.

'Dad, you don't still think that early marriage is a bad idea, do you? I mean, I remember hearing you rant about it to Mum once.'

Dad shook his head, smiling. 'Oh yes, your mother was always talking about marrying you boys off, the earlier, the better. Not on my tab I used to tell her.' He laughed, as he often did when he remembered Mum these days.

I wiped my sweaty palms on my jeans. 'But you don't still feel that way about it, do you, Dad?'

Dad looked at me seriously. 'Your job right now is to put all thoughts of girls to the side and concentrate on your education. You're off to university next month, son. You don't have time to think about any desires you might be having.'

I stared at him. 'You think the only reason I might want to get married is because I can't control myself?'

'Well, what else would it be, Ali?'

I was starting to get agitated. 'So you're telling me that, if I met someone, and I genuinely thought she was special, and that I wanted to be with her in a halal way, you wouldn't support me? Is that what you're saying?'

'Oh, Ali, what rubbish! Trust me, you may think a girl is special, but you will meet plenty more like her when the time is right. And the time is not right, Ali, that's for sure.'

'Is that what your dad told you when you insisted on marrying Mum, even though you were still at university? Or is that what Nanni told Mum?' I shook my head. 'Isn't it amazing how quickly adults forget what it was like to be young?'

Dad swallowed hard. 'That was different, Ali...'

I laughed bitterly. 'What made me think I could expect support from my father to do something pleasing to Allah?'

'Ali! That is out of order!'

But I was already walking away, asking Allah for guidance:

181

♂ ALI

Allah, show me the way forward. I thought my life was perfect when Mum was alive. But You knew better. You took her back to teach me the reality of this life. To guide me back to the Straight Way. It was a price I didn't want to pay – an almost unbearably high price – but we don't get to choose our tests. Everything is encompassed by Your Wisdom. You alone know the reason for everything.

When I was at my lowest point, your Word brought me comfort. Your Word guided me. Guide me once more.

Guide me.

do with these?'

'Umm, they're for you...' he stammered, rubbing his hands on his jeans. 'For you... you sisters...'

I smiled to myself as I screamed inwardly. I wasn't falling for that! This was some serious halal chirpsing going on. Flowers! Swoon. I mean, really. Totally dead.

'*Jazakallah khayran*, I'm sure *the sisters* will think they're beautiful...'

He was really embarrassed now, I could tell.

'Well, I hope tonight goes well for all of you...' Then he reached into his back pocket. 'Here's the donation from the Deen Riders charity rally. The brother in charge, Yusuf, apologised that he couldn't bring it himself...'

Oh, that's quite all right, I thought to myself. To him I said, 'Please thank the brother for us. May Allah reward all of you.'

Just then, I heard Rania's voice behind me. 'Amirah, come on!'

'I've got to go,' I said, not wanting to tear myself away but knowing that I had to. 'See you around...'

Another smile, a *salam*, a wave and he was gone and I was running back towards the double doors, my heart racing, almost tripping over my *abaya*, the flowers heavy and wonderful in my arms.

Rania was at the door and she took one look at the flowers and then at my face and squealed and hugged me. 'Ohhhh, I can't believe this is happening!'

Neither could I. But there was no time for believing or thinking or talking. We had a show to put on. And, as sisters began to come in through the double doors, holding their goodie bags, their eyes bright as they looked around the

156

36

o a room where your future husband
you to come in? Too weird. No one
that moment, no matter how many
o matter how many talks you've
f this strict, Islamic way of finding

What do you say? No one had
iner details of the 'sit-down' – that
al suitor – to me. I didn't want to
l, but then I didn't fancy playing
f you get what I mean.
ly thing that made sense, under
u 'alaykum...'

esponded, Hassan flashing a big
fect teeth and a mole on his left
ut not too long – the beard of
lis eyes crinkled at the corners
s were pristine.

ppearance. Skin problems. Dirt
white *thobe*. But the only thing
with was his black ankle socks
r Timberlands for him, clearly.

183

I had to stop myself from staring. He was attractive, no doubt about that, much better-looking than I had expected.

I told my heart to be still.

I sat down on the sofa closest to the door. Mum came in with a tray of drinks and Hassan thanked her and told her that his mother sent her *salam*s and a gift. He took a blue velvet box out of his bag and passed it to Zayd to hand it to Mum. Her face shone as she opened it and lifted out the Arabic perfume oil inside.

'Oh, mashallah!' she beamed. 'Your mother is too kind, *Allahumma baarik*.'

Hassan flashed a megawatt smile my way. 'She sent one for you, too, Amirah...'

Zayd looked over at me as if to say, 'I *told* you.'

I smiled under my niqab, tugging it down slightly. '*Jazakallah khayran*,' I said, clearing my throat. 'That was really thoughtful of her.'

'I've told her a lot about you, mashallah... from what Zayd has told me, of course.'

He smiled again and I felt my heart flip, ever so slightly. Now I couldn't deny it: I was intrigued. I wanted to be right in the middle of our conversation, past all the awkward small talk, after the others had given us a bit of privacy. I wanted to see how he played this game. Was he a talker? A listener? Would he have a sense of humour or be super-serious? Would he be keen to hear what I was looking for in a husband, what I wanted out of life? What were his hopes and dreams? What were the deal-breakers for him?

I felt my thumb begin to twitch and realised that I had been sitting on the end of my seat, my hands pressed tightly together, my shoulders hunched. The conversation had moved

catch a glimpse of Auntie Azra in an
 fluttering sleeves. She was in 'Event
 could see: her phone was jammed
 was telling Maryam and her friends
 bags. Then she looked over at us.
 you are! You've still got your hijab on.
 go out and get some more donations
 rother from Deen Riders is waiting
 uch going on here...'
 out. I made my way to the back of
 loors were. Kicking aside a balloon,
 d stepped out into the corridor.
 corridor, by the entrance, a brother
 ling with his back to me. He held a
 e arm and an absolutely beautiful
 e other.
 I called out, my voice echoing in
 nd.
 ed, I was so surprised to see him.
 oking so delicious, tonight of all
 e way of his and he smiled when
 ore confident than before. 'Hey,
 . How are you?'
 't help myself. 'Yeah, I'm good.
 hat he was there to do and held
 ook. 'What am I supposed to

on. Hassan was telling Zayd about his father's business, some new contracts they were here to sign, what had happened to all of their university friends.

I shifted in my seat and coughed lightly. Had he forgotten that I was still in the room? They both turned my way and Hassan smiled apologetically.

'I'm so sorry, sister, it's just that I haven't seen your brother in years. We've missed him in Saudi, subhanallah...'

So he didn't really want to speak to me.

Fine.

Absolutely fine by me.

I inclined my head. 'Please, don't let me get in the way of your catching up session. I need to help Mum with the dinner anyway.' I got up. 'Brother Hassan, it was nice to meet you. *Jazakallah khayran* for the gifts...'

I left the room without waiting for a response. As soon as the door closed behind me, I ripped the niqab up off my face. I heard a tearing sound but I ignored it.

Mum appeared in front of me. 'Well, he's lovely, isn't he, mashallah? What I always imagined a student of knowledge would be like.' Her eyes grew soft as she put her hand on my arm. 'I think you two would make a lovely couple, inshallah.'

I forced myself to smile up at her. If she wanted to see this as a fulfilment of all her wishes for me, who was I to burst her bubble? 'Let me help you get the dinner served, yeah?'

And I did. I cut up vegetables for the salad, dressing it with vinaigrette. I cut up Mum's spicy roast lamb, dished up the macaroni cheese and sent it through with the peas and carrots. But I didn't go back into that room.

I'd tried: I'd shown up, been polite, had actually allowed myself to get a bit excited. But there had been no need. He had obviously been put off by something. Why else would he have practically ignored me and spent the whole time talking to Zayd?

I hadn't wanted him. Not at all. But somewhere, deep inside, a little hope had flickered. I had hoped that maybe, just maybe, he would have wanted to find out more, to get to know me a little bit, maybe take things further, even if that wasn't what I wanted.

Stupid, I know. But that's girls for you.

* * *

Later that night, after I'd cleaned up in the kitchen, I crept back into the living room. Mum and the kids had crashed. Zayd was on his way back from the station. It was hard to believe that, a few hours earlier, Hassan had been sitting in this very chair, giving Mum a gift. That I had allowed myself to hope that he might like me. I took a deep, shaky breath.

It's for the best, Ams. Remember the plan, I sat thinking. *Next week, the A level results will be out and all this will be behind you. Once you're safely in uni, you'll be on your way and no one will be bugging you about sit-downs anymore.*

Just then, I heard Zayd's key in the door. I turned towards the door. How had he felt about the disastrous meeting? He had pinned so many hopes on it going well; I almost felt sorrier for him than for myself.

'Mashallah, Ams, that was great!'

'Huh?'

'You know? The meeting?'

I shook my head, confused. 'What are you on about, Zee?

The meeting was terrible! He hardly even spoke to me!'

Zayd put his arm around me and laughed. 'Nah, sis, that's just how mans roll, innit! He was well pleased with the meeting! Kept saying how he's going to talk to his mum, tell his dad and that.'

I frowned and turned to look into Zayd's face, convinced he was taking me for a ride. 'Zayd, tell me the truth: what did he really say?'

'He said you seem like a nice sister, a good sister. He got on really well with the kids, the family and that. And, of course, he's like my brother, innit? His family treated me like their own son. If it wasn't for them, I would have gone hungry more than once!'

I interrupted, 'And if it wasn't for me, you would have graduated by now.' That old guilt, gnawing away at me.

He went all serious then. 'Sis, you've got to put your trust in Allah. He wants what is best for you. When Mum told me that you had run away, I was ready to dash everything and come. But Hassan reminded me to pray *istikhara* first. And I did – and Allah brought me back to do what I needed to do here, OK? Don't ever think that I blame you for that, yeah? That was all part of Allah's plan. And, who knows, maybe you marrying Hassan is part of that plan, too.' He squeezed my shoulder. 'He wants to have another meeting, next week. And he'd like to see your face this time.'

37

'Ali, you know that you are always welcome here. And your father is, too, if he would stop being so stubborn and hard-headed.' Nana's voice was calm on the other end of the phone. I was calling her to ask if we could come up to see Umar. I had to go to my old school to pick up my A level results and I didn't want to come back to London without seeing my brother. I also wanted to speak to her about my options for the year ahead. I figured I could use some advice – and someone to back me up when it was time to talk to Dad about it.

After weeks of applications, Dad had finally heard back from a company in Bedford that was keen to work with him. But the prospect of leaving London and living closer to Nana hadn't softened his stance towards Umar. 'I'm not going,' Dad said when I told him what I wanted to do. 'When Umar is ready, he will call us.'

I pulled myself up and looked squarely at Dad. 'Well, you can wait in the car then, if you think that's best. I want to see Umar and, if you don't want to take us, Jamal and I will get a coach.'

Dad rubbed his temples and closed his eyes for a long time. When at last he opened them, he looked at me. 'You're right, son, we should go. I don't know what I was thinking.

We'll go first thing Friday morning, inshallah.'

I nodded and turned to leave. His voice calling my name made me stop and turn back. 'Sometimes, Ali,' he murmured, a faraway look in his eyes, 'I wonder how I would manage without you. May Allah bless you, son, you've definitely inherited your mother's strength.'

I felt a lump rise in my throat so I just nodded and turned to leave the kitchen before the tears could start falling.

***

Our visit to Nana's house was an unusually tense affair, mainly because Dad was being so hostile.

'You are pushing him too hard, Andrew,' Nana said. 'Expecting too much from him. You will end up pushing him away.'

'We brought Umar up as a Muslim, Mum,' growled Dad. 'It's not like this is all new to him.'

Nana's eyebrows were arched. 'Isn't it? I have to say that I have seen a marked change in you since Anisah fell ill. You can't tell me that you haven't changed as a Muslim. You remind me of when you first converted – that zeal, that dogmatism. Except that now you're expecting your teenage son to follow you blindly, without putting up a fight. Come on, Andrew, even you must see how unrealistic that is.'

Dad huffed. 'Well, why can't he, eh? Doesn't he trust me?'

'Some children are like that, son,' Nana said. 'You try your best for them but, in the end, they have to want it themselves. They have to make their own choices.'

'Well, Umar has always been the problem child.'

'No, Andrew, you have always treated him like one,' said Nana. 'There's no use denying it.'

Dad looked over at me. 'I've always been fair to you guys, haven't I?'

I shrugged and said nothing. I wasn't about to walk into a hornets' nest with my eyes wide open. Besides, Nana did have a point. Dad had always been extra hard on Umar. Mum was always going on at him about it.

As Nana and Dad carried on their back and forth, I went outside to Umar. I couldn't deny that he looked better: his skin had cleared and he seemed more relaxed. We sat down under the big oak tree at the bottom of the garden and, for a while, we just watched the bees and butterflies dancing between Nana's flower beds.

When at last he spoke, Umar said, 'When did it all start to make sense to you, Ali? When did it all seem real?'

'When did what seem real?'

'Islam.'

I was silent for a long time, then I turned to him. 'It seems like a lot of rules at first. Some of them, you understand. Others, you don't. But you trust that there's some kind of wisdom to it. And, one day, the penny drops. You understand what you were put on this earth to do, and it's not any of the things they tell you at school or on MTV. It's not to get a degree, or a good job or a fat crib or even fall in love. Allah created us to worship Him, pure and simple. And that puts everything in perspective, straight away. You're not searching anymore. Not really. And you're not trying to escape either, to lose yourself in thrills of different kinds. You're conscious.'

Two tears rolled down Umar's cheeks. 'How come I don't feel that, Ali? How come all I feel is anger? I don't feel any love, none at all.' More tears fell.

Slowly, I put my hand on his clenched fist – and he didn't pull away this time. He let me rest my hand on his as he cried.

When the tears seemed to have dried up, I looked at the hand I was holding. 'Have you ever really spoken to Allah about how you feel?'

Umar shook his head, chewing his bottom lip.

'Try it,' I said. 'He will respond. Trust me, Umar, I would give anything to spare you this uncertainty – but I can't make your journey for you. But I want you to know,' I said, and, by then, I was sniffling too, 'that I'm right here with you. I won't ever give up on you, OK? I promise.'

He let me put my arm over his shoulder and there we were, two wounded boys on the way to healing, holding each other under an oak tree.

38

I woke up on Friday morning with a bubbling feeling in my stomach. I rolled over, dragging the duvet over my head. What was it about this time?

Then, I remembered. A level results were out that day. My future would be decided that day.

I grabbed my phone and switched it on. Rania had got there first with a text: *Salam. Meet u @ skool @10.*

I couldn't bear the thought of breakfast, I was so excited. Mum smiled at me when I came downstairs from my shower, glowing, scrubbed up, my hair still damp.

'Someone's excited, mashallah,' she winked conspiratorially. 'Bet you're still flying high from your second meeting with Hassan the other night, huh?'

My heart lurched at the thought but I kept my composure. 'Mum,' I said gently, 'we get our A level results today. Remember?'

She frowned slightly then smiled. 'Oh, I'm sure you've done well, sweetie, you always were clever, mashallah.' Then she squeezed my arm. 'And now this situation with Hassan is moving forward – well, it looks like it's all coming together, doesn't it?'

She was talking about my second meeting with Hassan,

the one during which he got to see my face and actually spoke to me. It had been nerve-wracking, definitely, but I was relieved to see him smile when I walked into the room. Zayd was under the impression that he was about to marry me off any minute – he was just waiting for the brother to get back to him.

As for me, I was keeping my mouth shut. Today was the day it would all be decided.

Of course, Rania demanded a blow-by-blow of the whole meeting.

I told her about how I'd sat across from him in the living room, trying to imagine myself waking up with him every morning. Cooking for him. Living with him. Getting to know his family. The picture was blurred and swam out of focus constantly. I tried hard to sharpen the edges, but found that I couldn't pin the images down.

'So, what, you weren't feeling him, or what?'

I sighed. 'I don't know, Rani. I feel like a bit of fraud, to be honest. I mean, he hasn't asked me about anything that I consider important, like, my views on things, what I like to do, my ambitions. I have a feeling that he has made a load of assumptions about me based on who Zayd is and on the fact that I was wearing a niqab when we first met...'

'You wore a niqab? You never told me that!'

'Yeah, well, let's put it down to peer pressure, shall we? Anyway, so we basically had this one-sided conversation during which he told me all about what he expects his wife to do, how he wants his children to be raised, textbook stuff, I suppose, but all the while assuming I agreed with everything he said!' I sighed. Completely against my will, my mind had drifted to the one conversation I had had with Ali, at the summer school. Now more than ever, I was aware that the two of us had clicked. And the more Hassan droned on and on about his perfect little Muslim wife, the more I longed to hear Ali speaking my language: spiritual connection, beauty, adventure, fun times. Everything that I longed for.

But Ali wasn't interested in me. His eyes had been on Yasmin all along. Mr Light Eyes was a dream – and Hassan was the reality.

So I had to make my move first. A place at university, even if it was to study boring Business Administration for the next three years, should be enough to cool Hassan's heels.

* * *

I decided to walk up the hill to school. I had missed my twice daily walks up and down that hill to school.

Just as I reached the top of the hill, I felt my phone vibrate. It was a text from Zayd. *Hope you get the results you want today. And may Allah bless them for you. Z*

I smiled, tears pricking my eyes for no good reason. I really loved that crazy brother of mine. Subhanallah.

When I got to the school gates, I saw Rania, Samia and Yasmin standing together, all waiting for me.

'Ah, there she is – finally!' cried Samia, pretending to faint.

'*Salam*,' I said, kissing Rania's cheek, hugging Yasmin.

Samia grabbed me by my hand. 'It gets rid of sins, remember?' She always said that when we forgot to shake instead of kissing air like a bunch of old Moroccan ladies.

Rania made us all hold hands. 'This is it, girls,' she said, looking each one of us in the eye. 'This is the beginning of a new chapter. You ready?'

'Ohhh, I can't believe school is really over!' cried Yasmin, her eyes welling up. 'What if we don't see each other again? We're all going off in different directions – what if this is the last time?'

'Don't be silly, Yasmin,' I said, nudging her. 'Have you forgotten about social media, and Skype and Instagram?'

'Oops, how could I forget?' Samia whipped out her iPhone. 'Come on girls, let's do a before and after shot. Squeeze up and let's do a hijabi smackdown.'

We all squeezed together, getting our faces into the frame. Samia took the picture on her phone and then we all argued over which filter to use. Once she had saved it, she messaged it to us.

'Now, you guys ready to meet the rest of your life?'

We all nodded, linked arms, and marched into the school building to look at the results board.

195

* * *

I blinked. Once. Twice. Three times.

No.

It couldn't be.

But it was.

Through my tears, I saw the little letters that spelled the end of all my plans.

D in Economics.

C in Business Studies.

I hadn't got the results I needed to get on to the Business

Administration course.

I had failed.

All I remember was the sense of shock working its way through me, tears flooding my eyes, reeling, stumbling past the other girls, rushing to get away, to leave it all behind, to escape and never come back again.

Then, there in front of me was Ms Fergus, her arms outstretched, a huge smile on her face. I didn't understand why she was smiling and I almost ran past her in my desperation to get out of there.

But she reached out and, grabbing my arm, pulled me back to the board, and made me look at it again.

Made me see my 'A' in Art.

Made every assumption I had made about myself and my future fall away.

My phone vibrated again. It was a message from Zayd.

'Hassan wants u 2 meet his mum. Wants 2 get married. Alhamdulillah!'

♀ AMIRAH

39

I couldn't go home after school. What would I tell Mum? How would she react as I tried to explain to her the massive gap between what I had expected and what I got and what it meant for my uni plans? What if she just brushed it aside and kept right on talking about Hassan and his proposal?

My heart sank. His proposal would seem all the more inviting now. After all, he hadn't asked about my exam results. He hadn't asked me about going to uni or working. He hadn't been interested in any of that. The little that he knew about me and what he had seen had been enough for him. My blood boiled. I now knew why our first meeting had bothered me so much: to Hassan, I was just a set of ticked boxes. Loads of others would be able to tick those same boxes.

'Too any expectations,' Zayd or Mum would have said.

'Too many romance novels,' Samia would have said.

'Too much ego,' Yasmin would have said.

'Hold out for what you want,' Auntie Azra would say. 'Don't sell yourself short.'

The thought of Auntie Azra gave me strength. That was where I wanted to be: in her living room, soaking up her love and support, trying to work out what my next move should be.

***

'You didn't need to run away like that, you know,' said Auntie Azra gently.

'I always run away, Auntie,' I sniffed, wiping my eyes with a raggedy piece of tissue. 'I always run away.'

She nodded and took a sip of her coffee. 'I know, sweetie. But you've got to stop doing it. It doesn't help, does it? When you come back, you've still got the same problems staring you in the face. And this life is a test, don't forget that. Remember the words of Allah: "Do they think they will be left to say 'We believe' and that they will not be tested?" This is the *Sunnah* of Allah. The *Sunnah* of life.'

I sighed then, a deep, trembling sigh that seemed to come from somewhere unbelievably deep inside. 'I'm sorry, Auntie. But I feel I've been tested so much already. I was looking forward to the ease. Doesn't Allah promise that there will be ease after difficulty?'

'Of course He does.' She looked at me, her head to one side. 'But what made you think going to university would bring you ease? Isn't it just another set of trials? University is no picnic, you know...'

'I know, I know.' I rubbed my eyes. How silly I sounded, how naive. 'I guess I preferred the idea of struggling to get a qualification, even if it was in something I wasn't crazy about, than struggling like... like...'

'Like...?' Auntie's voice was gentle.

'Like... like Mum.' There, I'd said it out loud: I didn't want my mum's life. I stole a look at Auntie Azra's face, expecting to see shock or disapproval there. But all I saw was a look of knowing compassion. 'The scrimping and saving. The council housing. The government benefits. Relying on men to determine your future...'

'I see,' she said shortly. 'So this is about not ending up like your mum?'

'If I'm honest, yes, it is. Well, partly, anyway...'

'Well, Aminah, I don't need to tell you that your mum has had it rough all her life. You know that already. But she's always tried her best to do what she believes to be right. She's fought to raise you kids properly, sometimes with no help at all.'

'You think I don't know that?' My voice rose suddenly. 'I've always been the one to pick up the pieces, haven't I?'

'You have been a rock, mashallah,' she soothed. 'We all know that and, more importantly, Allah knows. He does. Your mum's choices have resulted in her trials – just like your choices will result in yours. The only difference between those trials is how we respond to them.' She shrugged. 'That's what I've learned over the years. We always think someone else has it easier than us but, when you pull back the layers, you see that they are struggling too, just in their own, unique way.'

'But you, Auntie Azra, you don't seem to ever struggle, mashallah. You've got this perfect life where everything goes your way... that's what I want...' I looked down then. I had never expressed my deepest thoughts to Auntie Azra – or anyone else for that matter.

She looked at me then, a look of surprise on her face. 'You think I have a perfect life, Amirah?' Shaking her head, she turned to look at the mantelpiece where a large framed piece of Kashmiri carpet hung. 'Maybe I once thought I did, too. But then I lost my husband, Rania's father. Amirah, I loved that man so much – subhanallah – when Allah took him back, I lost the will to live for a while. I just couldn't conceive of life without him. But human beings are amazing like that.

We're resilient. And Allah tests us with the things we love so that we can return to Him and long for His love, not the love of His creation. That was when I realised that this life isn't meant to be perfect. It's a place for test and examination. The true happiness, the true bliss, will be in the afterlife, *Akhirah*. That's when I hope to taste pure happiness, with no loss, no tears, ever.'

I had never heard Auntie talk about Rania's dad. I kept quiet, thinking about her words.

'What you're experiencing right now, Amirah,' she said, turning back to me, 'is not the end of the world. It's not the end of your dreams, either. It's a temporary setback, one you will surmount. One you will get over and move on from, inshallah. Don't cry anymore. You need clear eyes to look to your future and decide what to do.'

I nodded, tears rolling down my cheeks. Everything she had said, all the things she was telling me, they were just what I needed to hear, right at that moment.

* * *

We spent the rest of the afternoon talking about what I really wanted to do with my life, in terms of study and work, and I ended up sharing just how much I loved art. I told her about my work with Abdullah, and Collette's art therapy course. We checked out courses online. I realised that there were other degree courses I could take with the grades I had – ones that would allow me to make my art into a viable career. Art and Design. Illustration. Graphic Design. Art Therapy. That last one really resonated with me and I made up my mind to talk to Collette about it at our next class.

I left Auntie Azra's house a different person.

I had hope again. All was not lost. This was all part of Allah's plan.

40

3 As.

   3 As.

'Mashallah, Ali, you did it!' Dad's smile had been huge, his eyes bright with tears. 'Your mother would be so proud of you, son, so proud.' And he'd hugged me, holding me to him for a long time. 'The world is your oyster now, inshallah.'

And I just felt amazing, absolutely amazing.

To think that, through all the upheaval and heartbreak, I had managed to step up at exam time and get my predicted grades! Mum would have been over the moon.

The drive home from Hertfordshire was like a warm, fuzzy dream. We talked about Mum and other trips we had taken as a family. We sang songs Mum had taught us for long car journeys. We remembered Mum together, openly, without reservation, for the very first time. And it was wonderful.

'Fancy a meal out, boys?' yawned Dad as he unlocked the door. 'Or should we order something?'

'I think it's going to be instant noodles and bed, Dad,' I replied. 'I'm exhausted!'

'Yes, it was quite draining, wasn't it,' said Dad ruefully. Then he grinned. 'Still, all's well that ends well. Oh, and you were right to insist that we go to see Umar. I feel so much better after seeing him, alhamdulillah.'

'You see,' I chided. 'You should listen to me more often.'

'Yes,' mused Dad, 'maybe I don't give you enough credit, eh?' He stood in front of the freezer, poked around inside, then turned to me. 'I feel bad, Ali. We should be celebrating tonight, shouldn't we?' His eyes went misty. 'Your mum was always the one to organise our family celebration dinners, wasn't she? I just turned up and waited to be told what we were celebrating!'

I smiled and opened my mouth to add my memories of our celebration dinners when the doorbell rang. Dad's eyebrows shot up. He still wasn't used to living so close to people. The constantly ringing doorbell set his nerves on edge.

'I'll get it, Dad,' I said, scooting to the front door. I didn't want anything spoiling his mood, not after the day we'd had.

I opened the door without looking through the little spyhole. I was sure it was Usamah – he was the only person who would turn up unannounced.

But it wasn't Usamah.

'Al... Ali?'

It was Amy.

Just the sight of her was difficult.

Of course I hadn't forgotten her, not a single inch of her, no matter how hard I'd tried. But now, here she was, in the flesh, at my front door, looking straight at me with those big blue eyes. The light above us was bright. It bounced off her hair and, for a moment, I was dazzled. I felt my senses betray me – the smell of her perfume, the memory of her skin, those eyes. Lowering my gaze was proving to be hard work.

A'udhu billahi min ash-Shaytan ir-Rajeem, I said to myself. Only Allah could protect me from myself, I knew that.

Dad's voice came from inside the kitchen, 'Who is it, Ali? It's late...' And then there he was behind me, staring at this golden-haired girl standing on his front doorstep.

'Amy?' He must have remembered her from a school show or something. 'Amy McIntyre? What are you doing here? Is something wrong?'

'No, Mr Jordan, I just came to speak to Ali.'

Dad gave me a look, then scanned the dark outside the house, the neighbour's house opposite. 'Well, you'd better come in, Amy. We can't have you standing there like that.' And he opened the living room door and then wedged it so that it stayed like that: open. I was grateful for that. I really didn't trust myself around her.

We didn't say anything for a few minutes.

Then, 'How are you doing, Ali?'

204   I remembered her voice so well – like liquid honey. It brought back so many memories of feelings, times and places I had tried hard to forget that, for a moment, I couldn't speak. I didn't know what to say, where to look, how to act.

'Amy...' My voice came out all croaky and I cleared my throat. 'What are you doing here?'

'I was talking to Pablo and he... he told me that you were in South London. He got me the address. And I came to see you...' She was looking right at me and I knew that I didn't have to ask her why she had come to see me. Her face, her voice, her body language all spoke louder than words. But she could see that she had rattled me. She looked down, embarrassed.

'Look, Ali, sorry for just turning up like this but I didn't know how else to reach you. Your old number isn't working anymore, you closed your Facebook page, you didn't leave me an address. None of the guys knew how to contact you – it's like you disappeared once school was over!'

'Yeah, I know,' I mumbled. 'Sorry about that... It was hard, you know, coming to terms with everything...'

'Yeah, I heard about your mum. I'm really sorry.' She bit her lip. 'But why didn't you talk to me, Ali? Why didn't you let me be there for you? I thought we had something special. I even thought...'

Don't, I thought. *Don't say the words...*

But she didn't. She knew better than to do that. 'I thought we had something special, you and I...'

I looked down. I couldn't lie to her. I had never been able to lie to her, not in all the years we had known each other, the time we had been together. 'We did, Amy, we did. It's just that a lot of things changed for me when Mum died. Too many things. And I couldn't make those changes without pulling 205 away from my old life.'

'Is that how you see me now, as part of your old life?'

The hurt in her voice seared my brain. Hadn't I promised her always and forever? What useless promises.

'No, Amy, it's not like that. It's just that Mum's death made a lot of things clear to me. One of them was the fact that I had to learn about Islam. I had to start practising my religion, the one my mum taught me. It was too hard to do that with everything that was going on so I had to get away. And now... I've got a new life, different priorities.' I shrugged. That was it in a nutshell: I had different priorities now.

'I know, Ali,' she said, looking down. 'I know that you've rediscovered your faith and I'm really happy for you.' She looked back up at me. 'I just wanted to know whether there was any space in your new life for me.'

My heart stopped beating for a moment and I looked at her in confusion. 'What do you mean?'

'I mean I'm willing to do whatever it takes to get you back. I'm even ready to convert, if it means we can be together...'

I laughed out loud. I just couldn't help it. This was Amy the beauty queen, Miss Popular herself, the fun-loving, outgoing envy of all my friends, offering to accept Islam, just to be with me? The whole idea was ludicrous.

Or was it?

'You can't convert just for me, Amy, I would never want you to do that. Islam isn't like that – something you can use just to get what you want. It's a genuine spiritual commitment, a way of life...'

She reached out and put her hand on my arm then, right where I had covered up my tattoo with my shirt. I flinched at her touch. 'Don't you want me, Ali?' she asked, her voice husky. 'Don't you miss what we used to have?'

I couldn't say anything. My only defence was to pull my arm away and look behind her – at my red Converse trainers standing by the door.

And, just then, the image of Amirah popped into my mind. In her hijab and *abaya*, her dark features and no-nonsense attitude, she was the complete opposite of Amy. And yet, there was something about her, something deep, something vulnerable under all that bravado, that made my heart soften when I thought of her.

No, Amy wasn't the one I wanted. She was too perfect to suit me anymore. I had once been a wealthy student at a private school, poised to go to university to study Law, earn loads of money, buy houses and cars, have a glamorous wife on my arm, but all of that was nothing to me now. I knew what I wanted to do with my life now – it had been becoming clearer and clearer with every passing day – and I knew that this was a distraction.

I was damaged – but damaged in a way Amy would never be able to understand. Of course, she would sympathise, but it wasn't sympathy that I needed. I needed healing. If once I had been that perfect golden boy, I was him no longer. I had sinned, I had erred, I had made *tawbah* and I had been through trials and come out of them with stronger *iman* and a clearer purpose. Somehow, I knew that Amirah had walked that same journey. She was my true partner, not Amy.

'I'm sorry, Amy, but this isn't going to work. We're too different, you and I. You've got your great life in Hertfordshire, where you belong. I'm sorry...'

I opened the door to let her out and she paused on the threshold and looked up at me.

'Are you sure this is what you want, Ali?'

I wasn't looking at her when I answered. I was looking out onto the driveway at a figure with a beard and a white *thobe*, a figure that had stopped short, made eye contact with me, glanced at Amy and shaken his head, hurrying past without saying a word.

Later, when I was brushing my teeth, I looked into the mirror – and saw the shocked, accusing eyes of Zayd staring back at me.

41

For what felt like the one hundredth time, I opened my phone up to look at the picture I had taken of Amirah's painting. My hand. *My* hand.

What were you thinking when you were painting this? What were you feeling? Did you ever think that I would see it? Will I ever know?

I slid the phone shut when I heard the doorbell ring. I was feeling irritated with myself. Since when did I sit staring at pictures of inanimate objects, having one-sided conversations with indifferent girls in my head?

Usamah had come over to taste my legendary pancakes.

'I'll be going back home soon, at the end of the month,' he said as he sat down.

I stared at him. 'What?'

'Yeah, my year is up. I gotta get back to school in New York, back to my family. They're fixing for me to be married after I finish college so they've got a few sisters lined up for me to meet when I get back.'

I leaned back against the stove, too stunned to speak. Usamah? Going back to the US? Getting married? 'Bro, do you really feel ready to get married? Like, really ready?'

Usamah chuckled. 'What would I be waiting around

for? You know my online business is doing well, better than I thought it would, so I got money coming in. My folks always said they would support me when I got married but I figure I won't be needing their help for much longer, inshallah, as long as things keep going good.' He shrugged. 'Besides, I ain't getting any younger, n'a mean? And lowering your gaze 24/7 gets real old, real quick.'

I laughed. 'I hear you, man, I hear you...' I thought for a moment, then said, 'So, these girls that your parents have lined up, do you know any of them?'

'Yeah, I remember some of them from back in the day at the *masjid* – all the girls liked me back then, man!'

'So, you got your eye on any one girl in particular?'

Usamah rubbed his beard and raised an eyebrow. 'Well, there is *one*... but I gotta meet her first, y'know, see if we still cool, get to know her for myself a little bit. I'm sure she's changed since we were kids and if you're gonna marry someone, you gotta be sure that she's the one.'

'Easier said than done, isn't it?'

'Yeah, it is, but my momma always said that, when you meet the girl you're meant to marry, you'll know.'

'That is so crazy!' I said, shaking my head. 'That's just what my mum used to say!'

Usamah took a gulp of orange juice. 'Moms know, man. They know. You better believe it.' Then he put the glass down on the table. 'So, you still feenin' on Zayd's sister?'

'*What*?' Usamah's candour knocked me off balance. Where was all that cultivated cool, all that studied nonchalance? Had I been that transparent? I tried to make a joke out of it, 'What're you talking about, man?'

Usamah chuckled and looked out of the window. 'That's

what I love about you, man: you've got all these fancy British manners – what do y'all call it again? Stiff upper lip?'

I nodded sheepishly.

'Yeah, you got all that stiff upper lip going on, but you're just as transparent as everybody else around here. You think I haven't seen how you look at her every time you meet? How you have to fight to lower your gaze? How you wanna talk about her all the time – even with Zayd? You don't do that about *anybody* else!'

I kept quiet. What would be gained by admitting my feelings? But one look at Usamah's face and I knew that I didn't have to admit anything – he already knew. I expected him to tease me, like Mahmoud would have, but he didn't. Instead, his expression grew serious and he fixed me with his gaze.

210   'You really like her, don't you, akh?'

I nodded. 'Yeah,' I breathed at last. 'I do...'

'OK, that's cool... Do you know what you like about her?'

I laughed. 'Everything, man! She's amazing: so talented, unique, interesting...'

Usamah frowned. 'Y'all been in contact, like, in private?'

'No, no... nothing like that. I... I've bumped into her a few times... at summer school, here on the close... nothing major. To be honest, I wasn't even sure she knew who I was until I saw her painting...'

'Her what?'

'This.' I grabbed my phone turning it around so that Usamah could see the picture that flashed up.

Both his eyebrows shot up this time. 'Woah. You sure those are your hands, though?'

I didn't say anything, just held both my hands up for

him to look at. He nodded, looking back and forth between the picture and my hands. 'Yup, looks like she got them memorised, bro.' Then he frowned. 'So she's never given you any other sign, any hint that she... well, likes you?'

'Well, I thought that she did... we bumped into each other a couple of times... but then she went all funny and started ignoring me. Then I heard about this Hassan dude... To be honest, Usamah, I don't know how she feels. But, at the end of the day, there isn't anything official between us, is there? And Zayd won't even give me the time of day, where she is concerned...' I frowned, thinking about how Amy and I must have looked, standing at my door together. Zayd didn't seem like the kind of guy to make too many excuses for you if he caught you in such a compromising position.

Usamah stared at me. 'You tried to speak to him about his sister? Even after I told you how he feels about that kind of thing?' He shook his head. 'Bro, you crazy.'

'What was I supposed to think? I see this painting and I'm thinking she must have mentioned something to Zayd. Boy, was I wrong! He almost ate me for breakfast!'

Usamah was quiet for a moment, looking at me. Then a wicked gleam appeared in his eye and he leaned forward in his seat. 'Yo, man, what if Zayd is your test?'

'Huh?'

'Well, you really like this girl, right? And Zayd's kind of acting like the gatekeeper, right? Maybe you need to face your fears and take him on. Make him listen to you.'

'You're saying I need to man up?'

He chuckled. 'I guess that's another way to say it. But, yo, don't be bothering him if you ain't serious!'

'Serious? What do you mean?'

'You see that brother, Hassan? He's a brother who's serious. He knows what he wants and he's going about it the halal way. Unlike some people...'

I held up my hands. 'Hey, I haven't done anything wrong! I've been really careful to keep my dealings with her strictly halal – I'm not interested in sinning here...'

'Then what *are* you interested in, Ali? Why've you got this picture in your phone? Why you still thinking about her? What's with this fixation?'

'Look, Usamah, I don't know why I can't stop thinking about her. OK, so, at first, it was a physical thing, I'll admit it...' I looked down at the mole on my left hand. 'But it's more than that now. I feel a connection there. I've seen little sparks of her personality and I can't help myself: I want to know more. What can I say? I guess I'm curious about her, you know?'

'Yup,' Usamah pressed his lips together. 'And curiosity killed the cat.'

But there was more than curiosity there. I felt drawn to Amirah, as if we were kindred spirits. Amirah had been playing on my mind like a soundtrack on repeat and it was only the *deen* that was keeping me from going up to her and asking her out. Sure, plenty of Muslim boys would do that – no regrets – but I wasn't about to compromise her principles or mine like that. How can you expect Allah to bless something if you don't fear Him while you're going after it?

'Yo, man, I ain't saying that you've been involved in anything haram. I ain't saying that. What I am saying is that you need to start thinking like a Muslim, like a *mu'min*. You know the deal: one track. If you're serious, then we talking marriage. Now, you've told me that you dig this girl, and that's real cute, but you haven't told me anything about her that makes me think 'wife material'. Is she wife material? Would you want to wake up with her every morning, for the rest of your life? Would you want her to be the mother of your kids? Those are the questions you gotta answer before you decide which way to go forward.'

I stayed silent for a moment, stirring the pancake batter. Did I see myself waking up with Amirah every morning? Definitely. I could definitely see that.

Would she make a good mother? I smiled as I thought of how tender she had been with Abdullah on that first day of summer school. She had seemed so loving, so maternal. Yes, I did think she would make a good mother.

'OK...' I said slowly, turning the idea over in my head. 'Suppose I did think she would make a good mother. What else should I consider?'

'*Deen*, of course. The Prophet *sallallahu alayhi wa sallam* said that a woman is married for four things: her beauty, her lineage, her wealth and her *deen* – you know which one to go for, right?'

I thought about that for a minute. 'Well, she's practising, I know that...'

'And it ain't about the hijab, bro. Don't let that fool you...'

'No, I know that she comes from a practising home.'

'Well, if you're serious, you would have to find out more about her from her friends, people she works with and all that. But on a real tip: how would your dad feel about all this? I mean, you're meant to be going to university in a couple of months, right?'

I shook my head. 'That's another problem,' I said. 'My priorities have changed so much. I mean, I don't even want to study Law anymore! I used to be attracted to the prestige – and the money. But now, I want different things. I want to make a difference in people's lives. I want to live each day. Being a lawyer isn't doing it for me.'

'Your dad...'

'Don't mention him, please. I haven't even plucked up the courage to tell him. But I have been doing some research, though. I spoke to my old school friend, Pablo, about spending a year working in Mexico. We volunteered at a school for the deaf there, while we were at school, and Pablo kept in contact with them. He put me in touch with the directors and they've said they will consider it. And my grandmother thinks it's a great idea.' I smiled. Nana had even agreed to loan me the money for the airfare.

'And there are Muslims in Mexico. I could work with them, as well...'

214

'Sounds like you got it all figured out.'

'Well, it's just a dream at the moment... something I would love to do. But I don't think my dad will go for it, to be honest. It will all sound crazy to him.'

'Hmmm, so what about you hooking up with Amirah then?'

I shuddered. 'That's where things could get really sticky. Dad's never been a fan of early marriage, especially not on his tab. And if I'm planning on living abroad... what about her plans for university and stuff?'

Usamah considered this. 'Well, you could definitely work something out with Amirah and her folks – maybe you could get engaged and she stay here? Or she could take a year out, too? You just need to start having this conversation.'

'OK. I'll do it.'

'*Bismillah*, bro, go for it. You ain't got nothing to lose and you've got everything to gain, you know what I mean?'

'Yeah, bro, I do.'

'Hey, what about if Amirah's family don't want her to marry some footloose kid living in the barrios of Mexico?'

I smiled to myself and watched as the butter sizzled in the pan. 'Something tells me Amirah would be just fine with that plan.'

42

Everyone in the house was ecstatic. Hassan's proposal had swept my disappointing exam results under the carpet and no one spoke about them.

Except my stepfather, of course. 'So, looks like you'll be sticking around, eh, Amirah? Got your little wake-up call, eh?' He waggled a finger at me. 'It doesn't pay to go thinking you're better than everyone else, yeah.'

He was silent for a moment, then he looked at me sideways. 'This brother, Hassan. He's quite sweet on you, isn't he?'

I swallowed hard and said nothing. What was he getting at? Why was he bringing Hassan into this?

'Tell me, Amirah, have you told him about your past. All those little secrets of yours? Hmm?'

I frowned and shook my head, backing away from him.

'Oh, no,' he smiled. 'Tsk, tsk. You really should come clean, don't you think? I mean, imagine if your student of knowledge husband found out later that you were really a dirty little...'

I had already pushed past him and was running down the stairs, covering my ears to block out his disgusting words. I didn't stop until I was out of the front door, the evening

216

♀ AMIRAH

air cool on my flushed face. I realised that my teeth were chattering.

How I hated him.

I don't know how long I stayed out there, sitting in the back garden, but it was long enough to overhear him talking to Zayd, in that fake 'serious and concerned' tone of voice.

'I think the brother has the right to know, Zayd,' he was saying. 'You would want to, if it was you.'

'Want to know what, exactly?' I heard the edge of irritation in Zayd's voice.

'That your sister's been around. You know? That she's got a *past*, innit?'

'What *is* it with you and my sister? This thing has nothing to do with you. I'm Amirah's guardian, not you, and I can take care of this. *Jazakallah khayran*.'

'I'm just trying to advise you, Zayd. Because if you don't tell him, someone else might.'

Later that night, Zayd came into my room, asking to speak to me.

'How do you feel about Hassan knowing stuff about your past, Ams? About the time you ran away?'

I felt my heartbeat quicken. 'Does he have to know, Zee?'

Zayd ran his hands over his head. 'I don't know, sis. I mean, he knows that something happened because I had to leave Saudi. But he doesn't know any details.' Zayd rubbed his eyes and sighed. 'You're my sister, Ams. I wouldn't want anything bad to happen to you. But he's my friend, y'know? I don't think it's right to be less than honest with him from the beginning. So that there are no surprises along the way... am I making any sense?'

I bit my lip. 'D-do you think it will change things? Like,

will it put him off?'

Zayd didn't look at me. 'Inshallah, it won't,' he said shortly. 'Do you want to tell him or shall I?'

'You tell him, Zee. I don't think I could do it...'

'I'll speak to him in the week, inshallah,' said Zayd. And I noticed that his footsteps were heavy as he left the room.

All I could do was sit and wait and pray.

***

I went to the *masjid* that weekend. There was a seminar entitled 'Trusting in Allah' and I thought that was something I needed to understand a lot better.

All the girls were there, as well as the usual *masjid* aunties. One of the girls, Sumayyah, was one of the first of us teenagers to get married, the previous year, and now she had a gorgeous four-month-old little boy, Yasir, whom I had unofficially adopted. He had grown even cuter and more edible since the last time I had seen him and I spent most of the first session cuddling him and playing peekaboo.

'Hmm, are you here to seek knowledge or babysit?' asked Samia, giving me a look.

I stuck my tongue out at her. 'Preferably both. It's a very useful skill, my dear, so don't be a hater.'

'You may need those skills sooner than you think, huh?' Rania nudged me. 'What's the deal with the brother, Hassan?'

'To be honest, I kind of feel like I'm sleepwalking into this whole thing.'

'I don't like the sound of that,' said Samia.

'Well, he seems keen and he's basically proposed through

Zayd.' I shut my eyes and tried not to think of my childhood dreams – the ones where the man declares that he can't bear to live without you and sweeps you off your feet to live a dream life happily ever after.

I sighed again and looked at the two of them. 'He says I'm a nice sister. That he thinks I will make a good wife. Yadda yadda yadda...'

Rania wrinkled up her nose. 'Oh, I see...'

'It's that whole 'cookie cutter wife' thing, I suppose,' I continued. 'I tick boxes, as far as he is concerned.'

'So, no talk of uni, then...'

'He didn't give me a chance, to be honest! He's very sure of himself, very confident. And, boy, can he talk!'

'But wait, you mean you haven't even told him that you still want to go to uni? That you want a career?'

I squirmed in my seat. 'He never gave me a chance...' I squeaked. 'Besides, the whole family seems to have taken it for granted that it's going to go ahead.'

Rania frowned at me. 'I want you to stop the pathetic victim act, OK?' she snapped. 'I mean, whose life is this? Yours or theirs? Amirah, if you go into this without being really clear on what you want and who you really are, you will regret it for the rest of your life.' And she took a sip of her juice. 'And I will never forgive you.'

I took a deep breath. 'Look, I've been through a lot in the last few weeks and, just when I thought things were going to finally get easier, they've just become more complicated. Maybe uni isn't for everyone. Maybe it's fate for me to get married now. Yeah, sure, I would love to paint, study, travel and settle down with my soulmate who will totally get me. Of course I want to have a life of fun and adventure and all that stuff we read about. But maybe that just isn't realistic for girls like us.' I shrugged. 'For girls like me, anyway.'

* * *

After talking with the girls I had gone to see Auntie Azra and tell her about my mixed feelings about Hassan's proposal.

'Do you want to marry the brother, Amirah?,' she had asked me. 'There's no shame if you do, I mean, he seems like a very suitable young man. But you have always shared your hopes and dreams with me – and you were planning to try a different university course, weren't you? Is marriage what you want at the moment?

'No, it isn't. But I don't think I can fight anymore. I love to draw. I love art. But things have become uncomfortable at home again...' I bit my lip, careful not to say too much about my mother's marriage situation. 'It's another way out of the house, I guess...'

'A way out?' Then Auntie Azra's face had showed her disapproval. 'Amirah, you're not going to be one of those girls who sees getting married as a way out, are you? Too many young girls in this community are dying to get married to get away from their problems at home, or to get a bit of freedom. But let me tell you something: if you rush into marriage to escape your problems, you may find that they follow you anyway.'

She had come to sit on the floor cushion next to mine and took my hand. 'Get married whole, Amirah, that's what I tell my girls. Don't get married weak and needy, looking to your husband to make your world the one you dream of. What a burden for him! What high expectations. How on earth will he ever be able to fulfil all your needs? He's still learning, himself. And what happens when he fails this huge task you've set him without his knowledge? You become bitter and disappointed. And that's no way to be, trust me.' She caressed my cheek. 'Mashallah, you're a lovely girl, Amirah. You are strong and loving, brave and determined. You have much to offer the world – and your future husband. Don't ever believe that you are anything less than gold. OK?'

And that had been Auntie Azra's take on it.

But once I went home, it was a different story. There, I couldn't help feeling that it would be easier, more sensible, more befitting to settle for what was right in front of me, what was realistic.

Hassan was a good brother, I knew that. And he was nice-looking, considerate. He was educated, solvent, had a plan in life. And, most importantly, he wanted to marry me. How many girls would turn down such a catch? Not many.

I would be crazy to let him go, I knew that.

I knew all that.

And yet, a tiny part of me was holding out, hoping against hope for a better alternative, one that would bring my heart ease.

And make me happy, *deen*-wise and as Amirah.

Bottom line: I wanted it all, *deen* and *dunyah*.

43

Everything seemed to be winding down, now that the summer was fading. Summer school would be over next week and I was glad – I didn't think I could bear to see Zayd, all smiles about his sister getting married – but saying goodbye to Abdullah was going to be hard. We'd grown attached to each other over the past few months.

'Maybe I can help you practise when summer school is over,' Abdullah signed at the end of the day. 'You could come to my house.'

I smiled sadly. 'Don't think so, my friend. You'll be going back to school soon and I'll be going to Mexico to practise all the great sign language you've taught me, mashallah.'

Abdullah frowned. 'You mean I won't see you anymore?'

I bit my lip then tried to smile at him. 'Well, maybe one day we'll meet again. You can come out to Mexico to visit me! Wouldn't that be amazing?'

Abdullah frowned and chewed his bottom lip. 'Is it far, Ali? Can I catch a train there?'

I chuckled and knelt down beside him and opened up Google Earth on my phone to show him where Mexico was on the map. When he saw it and worked out how long it would take to get there, he turned to me, blinking away tears.

'I'll never see you again, Brother Ali,' he signed. '*As-salamu 'alaykum.*' And he turned and ran back inside, leaving me feeling awful.

A couple of nights before, I had finally managed to pluck up enough courage to speak to Dad about what had been on my mind for the past few weeks: my immediate future. I knew now that I really did not want to study Law and that I wanted to take a year out to work in Mexico. Amazingly, after quizzing me for what felt like hours, Dad agreed!

'Son, I sincerely hope that you will not get blown off track when you're on your gap year. You have to keep your eyes on the prize and, while that may not be a Law degree, you will have to get a good degree to be able to compete in the job market. I don't need to tell you how tough it is out there. Law is a sure thing, which is why I was so happy when you chose it. If you lose focus...'

223

'I know, Dad,' I replied, 'But I really feel that this is the right thing for me right now. I definitely intend to go to university, inshallah, but I want to make sure that I know what I'm doing and not just studying for the sake of a piece of paper. That would waste my time and your money. I want a degree that will pave the way for a solid future doing something I'm passionate about... does that sound totally naive and foolish?'

Dad patted me on the back and smiled. 'No, son, you sound just like I did when I was your age.'

'And, now that you've got that new job in Bedord and Jamal is sorted as far as school is concerned, I don't feel that bad about leaving you guys.' Although I was still waiting for confirmation from the deaf school in Mexico regarding my volunteering to work for a year, I was pretty confident that it would come through. 'And it will look great on my CV, too,'

I smiled.

Dad grunted. 'Intentions, Ali. Remember to purify your intentions...'

* * *

But Zayd managed to put an end to my winning streak. He had been distant with me ever since the night he saw me with Amy and I had never had an opportunity to explain myself.

Finally, after days of trying to catch him alone and waiting for him to initiate a conversation, I decided to take matters into my own hands. 'Zayd, bro!' I called out to him while he was on his break at the summer school. He looked around, making sure I was talking to him. Then he looked at me, unsmiling, and said, 'What's up?'

'I need to talk to you, man.'

He raised an eyebrow. 'Really? What about?'

I took a deep breath. 'I want to talk to you about your sister, Amirah.' I forced myself to keep talking even though I could see from the way his nostrils flared that he was getting annoyed with me. 'Look, I know that your friend is interested in Amirah and that's great. But I have been wanting to approach you for a long time about her. I want to have a meeting with her. For marriage.' There, I'd said it. I looked into Zayd's face then, defiant, expecting him to be glaring at me. Instead, I read amusement in his eyes.

I faltered, his expression catching me off guard. 'I... I have reason to believe that she has feelings for me.' I gulped as his face darkened, but I rambled on, 'And I've done my research and want to meet to see if there is any way of taking this forward.'

'Bro,' he said at last, his voice dripping with condescension. 'Don't get me wrong: you're a nice brother. A bit weak, but nice, still. But what on earth do you think you have to say to my sister – *my sister* – about marriage?'

'Like I said,' I said quietly, carefully, marshalling my thoughts, 'I think that she may already have feelings for me. And I want to look into a halal relationship – I'm not interested in doing haram.'

'It's not gonna happen, bro. No way.' His certainty shocked me.

'Why's that, Zayd? Has she said something to you? Has she agreed to marry this Hassan guy?'

'It doesn't matter what she says,' he said, shaking his head. 'I'm her guardian and I have to look out for her best interests. She may have feelings for you until Judgement Day but there is no way I am letting my sister marry some *da'eef*, tattoo-wearing brother who... who... Let's just say that he doesn't always keep the best company, yeah?'

Something inside me flipped. I was seething. 'You are way out of line. How dare you stand there and judge me? I saw you that evening, you know? And I've been waiting for you to come and ask me about it but no, you just went and made assumptions, completely forgetting that you are supposed to assume the best about your brother, not the worst. And the seventy excuses, Zayd, what happened to those? I'll have you know, that girl you saw me talking to knew me before I was practicing and there is absolutely nothing going on between us. And you know what makes it worse? You don't even know me! You haven't even tried to get to know me and you have the nerve to tell me I'm not good enough for your sister?'

'Well, you're not.'

'I think she should be the judge of that, don't you?'

'No, I *don't*. My job is to keep her safe from players like you. My job is to make sure that she marries a pious brother who will do right by her and give her her rights. That's my job and that's what I'm trying to do. So, if you'll excuse me,' he brushed past me, 'break time is over.'

I was shaking by the time I turned around and saw Usamah stop Zayd and pull him aside. What a piece of work: arrogant, judgemental, controlling. He could go jump off a cliff for all I cared.

The worst thing was that I didn't even know who to be angry with: Hassan, for wanting to marry the girl I had been dreaming about, the girl who I was sure was – or had been – thinking of me? Zayd, for shutting me down at every opportunity? Dad, for putting me in this situation in the first place?

And what about Amirah? Wasn't I angry with her as well? I mean, what did she mean by giving me all these subtle hints, these moments of connection, and then going off and marrying some random guy? Did she really have no feelings for me at all?

But, of course, after the anger and jealousy had been sweated out, I would come back down to earth. The cards were stacked against me. I had nothing to offer Amirah: no job, no education, no home, no family support, no plan. Just a lot of unanswered questions.

And I couldn't be angry with her. She had no idea how strong my feelings were for her.

My guess was that, in the big scheme of things, she was better off with that brother Hassan who could actually get his affairs in order and look after her properly.

But that cold, calm realisation didn't stop me from wishing that things were different, that they could be different.

It felt like the end of an era. Sure, I had a year in Mexico to look forward to but, I'd be going alone. It felt like I was settling for second best.

44

I was in the garden, painting with Abdullah, when Zayd told me the news.

My little brother and I were working on a piece together: he was painting one half of the canvas in his neat, methodical way, and I was giving the other half my trademark, Picasso-style treatment.

'*As-salamu 'alaykum*, Ams,' Zayd called me from the patio door.

'Hey, *wa'alaykum as-salam*, Zee!' I called out, full of enthusiasm as I ran up to him. 'Have a look at Abdullah's work. He's got real talent, mashallah, seriously.'

Zayd flashed a small smile at Abdullah then looked back at me. Immediately, a shiver ran through me and the hairs on my arms stood up.

His eyes.

He'd been *crying*.

I reached out to him. 'What is it, Zee?' I asked, although I already knew, really. 'What's happened?'

'Abu Malik already spoke to Hassan,' he said at last.

'And...?'

He looked away and shook his head. 'It's off, Ams. He doesn't want to go ahead with the marriage. I'm sorry, Ams, really, I am.' And then he started crying for real.

I just stood there, numb with shock.

Off? Just like that? There had to be an explanation.

'What exactly did he say, Zayd?'

'Well, I caught up with Hassan after the *salah* and told him that I wanted to give him a bit of background, tell him a bit more about your journey. That's when he told me that he had already spoken to our stepfather and that he had told him some pretty disturbing things. To be honest, I was pretty upset that he didn't get in touch with me straight away to confirm what he had heard...'

My head started to hurt. 'What did you tell him?'

'I told him that you weren't always practising... and that things had been tough for you at home with Mum not well and me away in Saudi...'

'Yes, and..?'

'And that you ran away for a while... He asked me what happened when you went missing. Where you were. Whether you're still...' He looked away and I could see that he was too embarrassed to say it.

'Whether I'm still a virgin?' I said, my voice flat.

Zayd's face was pained and he couldn't look at me.

I looked away then, my face hard. 'And what did you tell him?' My voice was like ice.

Only then did he look at me and the fierce pride that I saw on his face took my breath away. 'I told him that I had never asked you. And that I never would.'

Then it was my turn to start crying.

Zayd, oh, Zayd, who had stood by me through everything, who had never given up on me. How would I ever be able to pay him back?

229

I never would.

I put my arms around him and hugged him hard, for a long time.

Abdullah came up to us, his head on one side. 'Are you sad, Amirah?' he signed, pulling a face.

'No,' I signed back. 'I'm not sad at all, alhamdulillah. Come here, come and join us.'

And he did.

* * *

I had first tasted the Darkness when I was a tortured 15-year-old wannabe Goth girl who was angry with the world.

Zayd and I had always dealt with the ups and downs of Mum's moods and marital issues together, supporting each other, exchanging knowing glances, covering for each other. Then he had had to go and accept that offer to study at a university in Saudi Arabia and leave me to cope with Mum all on my own. That was when things became really hard for me. Of course, I didn't say anything to him – he was so happy, couldn't believe how lucky he was to have been given such an amazing opportunity. But as soon as he got on that plane to Jeddah, all the responsibility of looking after Mum and keeping the family going fell on me.

'How's it going, Amirah?' Zayd's voice was always full of concern, his tired-looking face hazy on Skype. He had started growing his beard and it made him look older, almost like an Arab. I didn't think it was fair to let our lives mess up his studies and make things hard for him. So I would smile and said, 'Alhamdulillah, bro, we're fine. D'you want to speak to

Taymeeyah? She's dying to tell you all about her new teacher...'

And I would get off camera as soon as I could. I didn't want my brother to see my breakouts or the fact that I had lost loads of weight.

Such dark days.

Mum suffered from depression quite a bit. Of course, I didn't know that was what it was at the time. All I knew was that, all of a sudden, she couldn't cope anymore: the kids would get to school late, their uniforms unwashed, no packed lunch, homework book not signed.

And it all fell to me: getting the kids ready for school, sorting them out afterwards with snacks, homework, times tables, preparing dinner, reading to them before bed. That was on top of studying for my GCSEs. I had high hopes, in spite of everything. My school was pretty rubbish but I knew that the only way out of the future I could see stretching ahead of me – Mum's life – was to make sure I didn't mess up my education.

But I tell you, there were mornings when I just wanted to pull my duvet over my head and let them all get on with it, sort themselves out without leaning on me, expecting me to be there all the time. There were other times when I just wanted to run, run far away from it all: the pressure, the relentless nagging about everyone and everything. Because when Mum did emerge from her fog, all she had for me was questions. Questions, questions and more questions:

'Were you at school today, Amirah?'

'Have you prayed, Amirah?'

'Who were those boys I saw you talking to, Amirah?'

'Why is your scarf so small, Amirah?'

'Who are all these boys on your Facebook, Amirah?'

'Where were you all afternoon, Amirah? Why weren't

you answering your phone?'

At first I was good, respectful, patient. I tried to answer Mum's questions truthfully – but that didn't stop the suspicion or the accusations. As the weeks turned into months, I stopped answering her. I just stopped talking. After a while, Mum became used to the silence, to the sullen stares. Then, when she had run out of questions, I would look at her and say, 'Are you done?' She would just wave me away then and go and yell at the kids about the mess they were making.

She didn't know anything about me, not because I didn't tell her but because she never asked. Never asked the right questions. Everything she said was like an accusation, like she already knew that I was up to no good.

And what happens when you suspect someone all the time is this: they start to live up to your expectations. I dyed my hair platinum, then purple. Took off my hijab when I was out. Got a few piercings – nose and ears – and would have pierced my tongue if my brother hadn't told me that it was considered a form of mutilation in Islam and that he would kill me if I tried it.

Of course Mum went crazy every time, shouting, crying, threatening me with all sorts. 'You're behaving just like one of those trashy girls out on the street! D'you want to end up in the Hellfire? Is that it? Don't you want to be Muslim anymore?'

No response, of course.

'You were raised as a Muslim, Amirah!' she would scream at me. Like that made a difference. Because, if you don't embrace it for yourself, it will always just be a set of meaningless rituals, a bunch of restrictions that come between you and what you really want to be doing.

♀ AMIRAH

Sometimes, I wished I could do something really bad, something even worse than what she was accusing me of. What difference would it make? Practically everybody else was. If Mum had bothered to open her eyes, to listen, even to observe her friends' children, she would know what was really going on with kids my age. And she would say 'Alhamdulillah' that her daughter wasn't skipping school, taking boys around the back of the bike shed or sneaking out to do drugs in the park. She would know that I was just trying to figure things out, to find out who I was, where I was going.

In the end, it became too much. I couldn't take the feeling of being trapped anymore. Every day, I couldn't stop thinking about getting away from it all. So, one day, I did. Jumped on a coach to Brighton with a girl who had invited me from school, and didn't look back.

I was out there for a week with her and her friends, tasting the Brighton party lifestyle, with all its ups and downs: throwing myself in at the deep end, just to see whether or not I would drown, whether life away from Islam was really as bad as Mum and everyone else always made out.

At first, it was fun, of course. I felt free, at last. I took off my hijab. I got some more piercings, almost got a tattoo. And partied. Hard.

It was a miracle that I made it through the week relatively unharmed. But the day dawned on the following Sunday morning after I had left London and I knew that I was done. I looked at the bodies that lay at varying angles all over the floor of the flat we were crashing in and felt a shudder of revulsion. We were hungover, dirty and broke and my friend had picked up some dubious guy with dreadlocks and a body odour problem. This wasn't what I wanted. So I plugged my

AMIRAH ♀

phone in to charge and, as soon as it switched back on, I rang Zayd's old mobile number. Somehow, even though he was supposed to be in far off Saudi Arabia, I knew he would answer when I called.

And he did.

Alhamdulillah.

When I came back from Brighton with Zayd, it was the beginning of a new chapter in my life. Everything changed after that. I became a new person.

Most people would think so what, she went on a bender for a week. That doesn't make her a tramp or a criminal. But, I wasn't raised like that. My Mum didn't ever expect me to go against what she taught me as a Muslim. She thought that her *tarbiyah*, her nurturing, would be enough to keep me on the straight and narrow. And, mashallah, for some kids, that is. But for others, like me, the outside forces are too strong. I had my own ideas, my own thoughts and opinions that I needed to sort out. I wasn't prepared to take my Mum's word for life. So I dabbled. Others experiment. They push the boundaries. I'm not defending it or condoning it from an Islamic standpoint: it is what it is. You either deal with it or stick your head in the sand. My Mum, like most parents, unfortunately, find it easier to breathe down there than face reality. As I said before, as a young Muslim, you need to embrace the *deen* for yourself. Brighton was what convinced me that I wanted to come back to my life, my home, to Islam, and I was grateful for that.

Unfortunately, people are nowhere near as forgiving as God is. My name was mud for months after I came back, until we decided to leave the area and find new schools and a new community. Then things had started looking up again.

But now the Darkness was coming again, catching up

234

with me, leaking into my present and my future, poisoning everything.

No wonder Hassan didn't want to have anything to do with me. Why on earth would anyone want me, with all my issues?

AMIRAH ♀

45

I invited Dad and Jamal to the finale of the summer school. Even Umar had agreed to come down for the weekend, now that he knew we were leaving South London for good. My own plans had shifted up a gear: the invitation email from the school for the deaf in Mexico had come through and I had already applied for a Mexican visa. We had planned a football tournament and barbecue for the boys and, best of all, the Deen Riders had agreed to spend some time with them.

'I think it would be fantastic for them to see that you can be Muslim, responsible and hip, all at the same time,' I had said to Yusuf. I just knew that the brothers on their bikes would be a hit with our kids.

'We'll be there, inshallah,' Yusuf had replied, nodding with approval. 'Working with the youth is one of our most important missions.' He looked away briefly then said, 'My sister Yasmin sent some goodies for the kids.' And he handed me one of the now familiar cake boxes.

I felt my face burn. 'Listen, Yusuf,' I stammered. 'I am so sorry for that misunderstanding about your sister. I never meant to...'

Yusuf laughed and scratched his jaw through his beard. 'No hard feelings, bro. It was my fault, really. Just got a bit over excited, y'know.' Then he raised his eyebrow and gave me a sly look. 'But does that mean that you aren't interested in meeting my sister or aren't interested in marriage, full stop?'

I mulled that one over. 'Hmmm, let's just say what I want is out of reach right now.'

It was ironic that Dad had had a change of heart about marriage, now that the girl I wanted was promised to someone else.

We had prayed Fajr together that morning.

Afterwards, I had sat on the worn prayer mat, making *dhikr*. I didn't look to my side, where I was aware that Dad was still sitting, probably making *dhikr*, the *mus'haf* at his side, ready. That was one thing I had always admired about Dad: even though languages didn't come easily to him, he had never given up trying to master Arabic or working on his ability to read the Qur'an. But, even now, he still made mistakes.

237

As I sat there, I heard him start to read from *Surah al-Baqarah*. I listened to his gravelly voice, painstakingly pronouncing the Arabic letters, pausing where he was meant to pause, elongating where he was meant to make the sound long.

When he got to the twelfth *ayah*, he stumbled, as I knew he would. He always had trouble at that bit.

I turned towards him. 'Dad, that bit's like this...' And I recited it correctly, the way Mum had taught me.

He gazed up at me, his eyes filling with tears. 'That's just how your mother used to recite that *ayah*...' And, all of a sudden, I saw the way grief and loneliness had marked my father's face: lines where they hadn't been before, dark circles under his eyes, a dullness to his eyes that I had never seen before. My heart broke for him.

'Dad...'

'Son, come here.' He beckoned, and I moved to sit next to him. He put his hand on my shoulder and took a deep breath. 'Son, I've been thinking about what you said about marriage since the day you mentioned it. I thought about it all night, I couldn't sleep. You may not know this, but your mum and I always discussed family decisions after you boys had gone to bed. Sometimes, we'd stay up all night, thrashing things out. Your mother was so wise – and such a great person to confide in. I miss that...'

'I know, Dad. So do I.'

'You know, she often disagreed with me about your kids, about how we should raise you, particularly as you got older. She thought I was too lax with you, that I didn't lecture you enough.' He chuckled. 'Sometimes I think she wished I was a bit less liberal and a bit more authoritarian. But I told her, that's just not my style. Especially not with you boys. I let her take that role.' Then he sighed and rubbed his eyes. 'But now, here I am, the kind of father I swore I would never be: one who doesn't listen, who pushes his own agenda all the time, who forces his kids to do what he thinks is right, without guidance.' He looked up at me again with those tired, tired eyes. 'Forgive me, son.'

I shook my head. 'There's nothing to forgive, Dad. You did what you thought was right.'

'I know, but that's not the bottom line, is it? I know what your mum would have wanted for you: to spend your life in a purposeful way, doing what brings you fulfilment. To find a nice girl and marry her, if that's what you both wanted. She was already worried about you not finding someone, or falling

238

into *zinah*. I used to laugh and say that if my boys couldn't control themselves, they had no business getting married. But I spoke to Imam Talib last night and asked for his advice, something I really should do more often...'

'What did he say, Dad?'

'He told me to be pleased that you were looking at marriage as a serious option; so many youth are in haram relationships and the thought of marriage doesn't even cross their minds. And he said to take you seriously, to trust you more.'

I had been speechless at his words. What a turnaround. I could hardly believe that this was my father speaking.

'Ali, was there a particular girl you had in mind when you spoke to me?'

I had swallowed hard and shaken my head, 'No, Dad. I think I may have missed the boat on that one.'

239

Yusuf's voice snapped me back to the present. 'Ah, I see. So you'll have to wait a bit longer for your little halal love story, eh? Never mind, Allah is the Best of Planners. If He wills, it will be. You've just got to be patient. You never know, she could be just around the corner.'

And, no sooner had he said that, than I looked up to see Amirah, coming into the car park with her three siblings. I swear, it felt just like the very first time I saw her, at the basketball courts.

The whole world dimmed and dropped out of focus. Sound made no sense.

She was as lovely as ever, even more so, now that I knew that she was truly out of my reach.

And when I saw that she was wearing those red trainers, just like the first time, it was all I could do not to cry out to her, to have her look my way, to smile at me, even if it was for the last time.

She waved goodbye as her little sister and brother ran off to meet their group leaders. They were going to be rehearsing for the parents' show that evening. Abdullah was left standing next to her, clutching a rolled up poster under his arm. She gave him a hug then signed that she had to go and that she would be back later, inshallah.

No.

I wasn't about to let her walk away like that, not without hearing her voice again.

'Amirah!' I didn't care who heard me or who saw me. I rushed over to where she was standing with Abdullah then stopped at a respectful distance.

'*As-salamu 'alaykum*, Amirah,' I said, breathlessly.

'*Wa'alaykum as-salam*, Ali. How are you?'

What was it about her that had changed? I expected her to be a bit formal with me, a bit distant now that she was engaged, but it wasn't that. She seemed... *sad.*

I was caught off balance by it. I no longer knew what I had been planning to say, why I had called out to her. So I knelt down and spoke to Abdullah instead. 'What have you got there, Abdullah?' I signed, smiling at him.

'Something for you,' he grinned, showing the gap between his front teeth. 'Open it.'

I unrolled it carefully, wondering what it could be, wanting to keep unrolling it forever if it would keep her standing there.

Eventually, I held it open in front of me, a piece of artwork unlike any I had ever seen. It was basically a thank you letter from Abdullah, but drawn in sign language symbols. Each set of hands was a word and each word was in a square, drawn or painted in different media: oils, charcoal, pastel, pencil, acrylic.

It was a true work of art, there was no doubt about it.

I glanced up to see Amirah, smiling at last, looking proudly down at Abdullah.

'Did he do this on his own?' I asked her. 'It's amazing.'

She shrugged. 'He's gifted, mashallah,' she said simply. 'But I have been doing my own kind of art therapy with him, helping him communicate better through art.'

'That is so cool,' I said, shaking my head. Then I turned to Abdullah and, for a moment, I felt dangerously close to tears. 'No one has ever given me anything as wonderful as this, bro. Really. *Jazakallah khayran*. I'll treasure this forever.' And I had to blink several times to keep the tears from falling.

Abdullah threw his arms around me and held me tight, sniffing. 'I'm going to miss you, Brother Ali,' he signed, his lips trembling. 'I wish you could stay with us forever.'

'Ah, man, don't do this to me...' I said, rubbing at my eyes.

I heard a sniff and looked up to see that Amirah was crying too. 'He's grown so attached to you, mashallah,' she gulped. 'And he doesn't get close to people easily.' She blew her nose and tried to compose herself. Then she looked me in the eye and said, 'Thank you for taking such good care of him. I didn't know who I was going to be able to trust him with but I knew that, if he was with you, he would be in good hands, mashallah.'

I ducked my head. 'It's nothing. He's like my little brother now, isn't he.'

Amirah smiled through her tears. 'Yeah, I suppose he is.' Then she must have become aware of where we were and the people around us because she started to look at her watch, adjust her bag strap.

'I've got to go,' she said at last.

No, please don't go. Stay here and talk to me. What can I say to you to stop you walking away?

'Hey, I hear congratulations are in order...' I said brightly, trying not to betray any of the emotions I was feeling, or what it cost me to congratulate her on her upcoming wedding.

She looked blank for a second, as if she hadn't caught my meaning. Then she said, 'Oh, you mean Brother Hassan, Zayd's friend?'

I nodded, swallowing the bitterness that was threatening to rise.

She smiled then, a small smile that seemed to contain such sadness that it tore at my heart. As if, if she wasn't careful, she would dissolve into tears, right there. 'No, no congratulations needed. It didn't go through in the end. Let's just say there were some compatibility issues...' And, with a sad little smile, she signed with those tiny hands, 'Now I'm as free as a bird...' before walking away through the crowd.

I stared after her as she walked away, my heart in my mouth, total chaos in my head.

What did she say? Free as a bird? Did that mean...?

Look back, Amirah. Look back at me. Just once. Just so I know.

But she didn't. She just kept right on walking, never once turning her head.

I felt a presence at my side. I glanced round and saw that Usamah was standing next to me. He stood there with me for a few moments, not saying anything.

When at last he spoke, he said, 'You know, bro, if you

don't go after her, you'll regret it for the rest of your life. You know that, right?'

I nodded. 'But Zayd... my plans... how do I know...?'

'Like I said, you'll regret it for the rest of your life.'

And I knew that he was right.

There was only one thing to do. 'Amirah!' I called out to her, waving for her to stop.

She was already by the gate but she heard me and stopped and turned to see me running towards her.

When I reached her, I saw her face was full of questions.

'Amirah,' I said, trying to get my breath back. 'I don't know what happened between you and the brother, Hassan, but I want you to know that I'm not sorry.'

'Pardon?' There was a touch of annoyance in her voice and I had to steady my nerves in order to carry on with my unplanned confession.

243

'I'm not sorry because... I couldn't stand the thought of you marrying him. Because I think you're the most amazing girl I've ever met and I haven't been able to stop thinking about you since that first day...'

'At the basketball courts..?'

'*Yes.*' Relief flooded through me. She remembered. 'You've been on my mind since then. And, at first, I tried to fight it but, as time has gone on, I've come to realise that you are someone special. Too special to pass by. And I know it sounds weird because we've not really spent time together and all that – but there is something about you, Amirah, something that speaks to me on so many levels. And...' Then I faltered. 'I know I'm going out on a limb here but... do you feel... *anything* for me? I mean, so many times, I thought I saw something, a sparkle in your eye, a look, a cheeky grin, that made me think that, yes, you felt something for me, too.'

My heart thrummed while I waited for her answer. But she just looked at me with those troubled eyes and I began to feel a bit desperate. Had I totally misread the whole situation?

'Please, Amirah,' I said at last in a low voice. 'Don't play games with me. I don't have much time – I fly to Mexico in a few days, inshallah. If you'll have me, I'll come and see Zayd tonight and we can take it from there, as fast or as slow as you want.'

She stared at me then. 'If *I'll* have you?' She smiled a tiny smile. 'Why, what did you have in mind, Ali?'

Communication at last!

'I don't want a lot, Amirah. I just want to be with you,' I said with a shrug. 'I want to wake up with you to pray Fajr. I want to learn with you, grow with you, see the world with you. I want you to be the mother of my children. I want us to grow old together, inshallah. That's all.'

'Just to be together for the rest of our lives then, yeah?' She laughed and I swear it felt so good to see that sadness disappear from her eyes.

Yes, I thought, *that's it. I want to make you smile like that every day of your life, for the rest of your life, inshallah.*

She opened her mouth to speak then closed her eyes. After taking a deep breath, she said, 'Ali, I'm going to be totally honest with you. I've been thinking about you since that time at the basketball courts, too. When I imagine my dream guy, he is you, in every way. Everything you are telling me is what I have always hoped someone would tell me, one day. Allah knows, I've prayed for it.'

I grinned. This was it. This was the beginning of the rest of my life, the moment I embarked on the greatest adventure ever, with her at my side. I opened my mouth to tell her that she had made me the happiest brother ever, but before I could form the words, she said, 'But that's all it is, Ali: a dream. And in real life, dreams rarely come true, especially for girls like me. It wouldn't be right for you to come and see Zayd. You think I'm so amazing but, trust me, you don't know me. If you did, you wouldn't be standing here, talking to me.'

I was totally thrown off balance. What was she saying?

'Go, Ali. Go to work in Mexico. I'm sure it will be amazing out there. You've got so much to offer – I saw that with Abdullah – you deserve someone better than me.'

And she turned to go.

'Amirah, no! Wait! What are you talking about? Please, just give me a chance to prove myself to you. Give me a chance... please?' I felt tears sting my eyes. Of all the things I had expected, I hadn't expected this.

245

But she simply smiled that sad, sad smile and said, 'Forget about me, Ali. I'm broken and I have too much baggage...'

'Baggage?' I cried. 'Who doesn't have baggage? I've got more than enough for the two of us. But that's just it: we can heal together. You don't have to do it on your own. Isn't that what Allah says in the Qur'an, that husband and wife should be like garments? And what do garments do? They shield, they protect, they give comfort... I'm not looking for someone perfect – I'm far from that myself. But you're my dream girl, Amirah, and I want you, baggage and all.'

She was in tears by then and, shaking her head, she cried out, 'Forget this dream girl, Ali, because that's all she is: a dream. And everyone has to wake up one day.'

And she turned and ran away, out of the gate, leaving me standing there, my heart in pieces.

46

I was like a dead woman walking: blind, deaf, feeling nothing. I bumped into people on the High Street and simply walked on, numb.

It was all too surreal. Had all that really happened? Had Ali Jordan – Mr Light Eyes himself – really confessed that he was crazy in love with me? That he wanted to *marry* me?

And had I really told him *no*?

Fresh tears sprang to my eyes and I ignored the looks I was getting, walking on and on, towards the end of the High Street.

You've done it again, Amirah, I thought to myself. *You've run away. Rather than face the situation and deal with it, you've run away. When are you going to stop doing this?*

Once again, I relived the conversation with Ali: confusion at first, then the penny dropping, followed by the elated, wildly beating heart, and then the Darkness again, eating away at my confidence, smothering my happiness, making me feel like I didn't deserve any joy, certainly not the joy that Ali was offering. The Darkness told me I was worth nothing, that I was just a dirty little tramp, just like Abu Malik was always saying.

So, he would fly to Mexico; his family would move away,

and everything would go back to normal on Seville Close. Rania and Yasmin would go off to university, Samia would go to Egypt to study Arabic. Zayd would most probably continue with his job and start looking for a wife. The children would soon be back at school.

That left me, treading water, knowing what I wanted but afraid to dream again. Afraid to make a move.

I went to the park. I wanted to lose myself in the calm of the shaded hill under the trees, to feel the Qur'an heavy in my hands and find myself in Allah's words. I wanted to prostrate on the grass at last.

I found a sheltered spot and put my coat down so that I could pray there. With my forehead to the ground, I began to speak, to really speak to Allah, pouring my heart out, asking for His forgiveness, His mercy, His guidance. I spoke to him about Ali, about Mum, about Abu Malik, about my dreams and fears. My tears soaked the coat beneath my face and I could feel myself shuddering as sobs wracked my body.

All the prophets had been tested. The Prophet Muhammad peace be upon him, had been tested. The early Muslims had been tested. So we would be tested, too. That was one thing Mum had always taught me that I knew to be true.

Once I had finished praying, I was able to get my breath back, to calm down. After pouring my heart out like that, I felt cleansed, and a little stronger. All the things I had been through had worn me down, down to my lowest level. Only my faith could pick me up now.

I opened my bag and took out the Qur'an Uncle Faisal had given me when I had finished memorising the thirtieth part of the Qur'an. I'd kept it all these years. My eyes scanned the Arabic script, picking out familiar words, words that I understood, words whose meanings had been explained to me. Then, I saw the lines that soothed my heart: 'Verily, with difficulty, there is ease. Verily, with difficulty, there is ease.'

That was a promise, a promise that things would eventually get better, that every cloud did have a silver lining. That it was worth holding on for another day.

* * *

Mum cooked roast lamb for dinner that night and, although the smell of garlic and rosemary was amazing, I didn't have any appetite. I wanted to retreat to my room, away from the noise for a while.

But I didn't get to. Mum insisted that we all sit down to eat together.

'As a family,' she kept saying.

But sitting across from Abu Malik, watching him eat the food Zayd had paid for, food Mum had cooked, made me feel sick. Mum was trying to get everyone to talk and be sociable, but neither Zayd nor I were much help. For once, I couldn't put on an act to make her think everything was OK.

'You've hardly touched your food, Ams,' she said at one point, looking at me with concern. 'Come on, eat up.'

'Yeah, Amirah,' Abu Malik put in his twopence worth. 'You're too skinny as it is – no man wants a woman who's all skin and bone!' And he slapped my mum on her thigh. She giggled and pushed his hand away.

'Amirah knows I'm only teasing her, don't you, girl.' And he had the nerve to wink at me, right there, in front of my mother, in front of Zayd. I cut my eye at him and looked away, but not before I caught Mum looking at him, a frown on her face.

Then she turned to Zayd. 'What's the latest with Hassan, Zayd? Are we still meeting his family this weekend? You know you have to remind me about these things or I completely forget...'

'Didn't Abu Malik tell you, Mum?' Zayd shot him a cold glance.

'Tell me what?' asked Mum, frowning.

'Well, the brother asked me about Amirah,' he said, digging between his teeth.

'Asked you what exactly?' Zayd's voice was hard.

'What she's like, innit,' was Abu Malik's response. 'So I told him, OK?'

'You had no right to go spreading lies about my sister!'

'Wait, just wait! What did you tell him?' Mum started shrieking. 'Will someone please tell me just what is going on here?'

'Kids,' I said, nodding at them, 'take your plates and go and eat in the kitchen. Quick!'

They all scuttled out, glancing back at us.

'Ams? Zayd? *Tariq*? Can someone please tell me what the hell is going on!'

I looked down. I had been dreading this moment. 'Hassan doesn't want to marry me anymore, Mum,' I said softly, trying to stop the tremble in my voice.

Mum looked at us all, from me to Zayd, to Abu Malik and back to me again, confusion written all over her face. 'What?' Her voice was now a hoarse whisper. 'Why? How?'

Zayd took a deep breath and, looking right at my stepfather, said, 'Well, Abu Malik thought it would be a good idea to tell the brother some wild stories about Amirah's past...'

'Like I said, he asked me what I knew, so I told him,' Abu Malik replied.

'No, don't try and sugar-coat it. You went and told Hassan a whole heap of lies about Amirah's past, stuff you heard about her, things you never even verified. You know what the worst thing is? Amirah and I had already agreed to talk to him about Amirah's teen years and what happened when I was in Saudi, but when I went to speak to him, he'd already been poisoned by your garbage!' Zayd kissed his teeth and pushed his chair back from the table. 'I've lost my appetite. I'm going out.'

Mum was still staring at her husband, her mouth open. I could see her hands starting to tremble. 'Did you tell Brother Hassan lies about Amirah? Did you?' she rasped.

Abu Malik looked over at her and said, in his fake apologetic voice, 'No, babe I wouldn't do that. I love Amirah like my own daughter, you know that... But a man has the right to know who he's marrying. And I thought it would be better coming from family...'

'From *family*?' Mum squinted at Abu Malik and, for the first time, I heard her raise her voice to him. 'How *dare* you? How dare you stick your nose in my daughter's business? What gives you the right, eh? What gives you the right to mess things up for her?'

'I was only doing the right thing! I told Zayd...'

'The right thing? The *right* thing? You wouldn't know the right thing if it slapped you across your face!' She got up violently and her chair toppled backwards. 'It is from a person's *iman* to leave alone that which does not concern him,' she said, emphasising every word by stabbing her finger on the table. 'Sound familiar? Or can you only take the *deen* when you're the one dishing it out?'

Zayd and I looked at each other, unable to believe what we were seeing, what we were hearing. Neither of us had ever heard our mother challenge any of her husbands, certainly not in front of us. This was a different woman in front of us, taking offence on behalf of her daughter, telling her husband where he could stick it.

'*Out*,' she was saying now, her voice low and menacing. 'I want you out of my house.'

'Oh, come on, babe, not all that again! I was only trying to help...'

'*Out*!' Mum shrieked, flipping his plate into the air in front of him. The unfinished lamb and mashed potatoes sailed through the air and landed on his T-shirt and in his lap. Then Mum really lost it and started throwing things at him – cups, spoons, the salad bowl – screaming for him to get out, out, out.

Zayd and I just stared, fascinated, covering our ears when the plates started smashing on the floor.

It sounds mad but, even though Mum was totally losing her mind, I had never had more respect for her than I did in that moment.

As soon as Abu Malik had stumbled out of the door, shouting abuse at Mum, calling her all sorts of names, both Zayd and I jumped up and hugged her hard, holding her trembling body between us.

Mum wiped the sweat from her forehead. 'Good riddance,' she said huskily. 'Alhamdulillah, we're free of him.'

Yes, Mum, that's right, I thought.

***

I wanted to tell her. I wanted to get it off my chest, what I had been holding inside for so many months.

So, I made her a cup of herbal tea and sat her down. And I told her about Abu Malik: the teasing that became more persistent, closer to the red line. The fatherly affection that had become something darker, something that made me feel uncomfortable, that made me want to cover up in front of my own stepfather, to make sure I was never alone in a room with him. And then the time I woke up to find him in my bedroom, right by my bed, claiming to have lost his way in the dark before tip-toeing out.

By that time, Mum was sobbing, clutching my hands, saying sorry over and over again. I didn't say anything but felt a strange kind of peace wash over me: I felt like a huge weight had been lifted off my shoulders. I didn't have to carry my awful secret on my own anymore. Finally, I could start letting go and moving on.

'He'll never set foot in this house again, Amirah,' Mum sniffed. 'I swear.'

'Mum, I didn't tell you to hurt you or to get back at him. I just want you to know who he really is. What he's capable of. And that you need to protect Taymeeyah, too.'

Mum nodded. 'I know that, Amirah. May Allah bless you, girl. I don't know what I would do without you.'

I turned away then, afraid of looking into her face.

Mum spoke again, her voice firmer this time, turning my face towards hers. 'You are beautiful, Ams, and a special young woman. And... I know I haven't told you this but... I'm proud of you. I am. You've come so far, mashallah. I know I used to go on at you and give you a hard time, and I know I haven't always been there for you, but I want you to know that

I am proud of you – in every way. You are so much stronger than me, mashallah, and I know that Allah sent you to me as my ease in this life, as my rock. I pray that He rewards you always for that.'

I was so surprised by her words that tears sprang to my eyes immediately. Her words were like the first drops of rain on my heart, a heart that felt dry and barren. I had sealed it off long ago, when it came to her. And now, here she was, telling me all the words I had been longing to hear for so many years: I'm proud of you. I'm sorry.

She put her hand on my shoulder and I grabbed hold of it and held on, as tight as I could, tears running down my face. And, as I looked at her in the mirror, I saw that she was crying, too.

And I knew then what I had to do.

253

47

My bags were packed. The house was empty. Dad, Jamal and Umar were in the car, waiting for me. Part of me couldn't wait to be on that plane, on my way to a new adventure, part of me wanted to stay here on Seville Close, waiting, waiting to see whether she would come and say goodbye. Whether she would change her mind.

But we were running late. Dad started beeping the horn and Jamal was pulling me by my hand into the car. I looked out of the window, hoping against hope.

But the door remained closed and the curtains shut.

It was time to say goodbye to Seville Close.

I just hoped I would get my heart back one day.

48

'Come on, Rania,' I said, checking my watch for the fiftieth time. 'We're not going to make it if you don't break a few speed limits!'

Rania gave me the side eye. 'Actually, I've already broken more than a few.' She squinted at the speedometer. 'And I will be forwarding the fines to your address, lady.'

'Fine, fine,' I huffed. 'Just step on it!'

In the back seat, Zayd chuckled. 'You two are crazy.'

I turned to face him. 'Zee, you know I owe you big time for this.' And then I turned to Rania. 'And you.'

'Well, Ams, this might just be the craziest thing you've ever done. But inshallah, none of us will live to regret it, eh?'

'Inshallah,' Zayd mumbled. I knew how awkward he probably felt sitting in the back seat of Auntie Azra's car with Rania in the driver's seat, but he was doing a good job of holding it down. He was doing this for me.

***

'Amirah, what you're trying to do is madness,' Zayd had told me. 'Pure madness. And, as your *wali*, I'm responsible for you; I can't allow it. Really, I have to put my foot on the brakes here.'

'Zayd,' I said, my voice as calm as I felt. 'I'm a big girl now. And I think it's time for you to respect my choices, my decisions. I agreed to meet Hassan out of my love and respect for you. I was even prepared to marry him, just to please you, even though I knew we weren't compatible. Now, I need the same love and respect from you.' I felt strong and confident: I had done all my research; I knew all about volunteering and visas and gap years and art therapy courses that could be deferred until the following year.

'I understand that, Ams, but this doesn't make any sense! Where will you live? How will he provide for you? '

'"If a man comes to you with good *deen* and character, marry him". Sound familiar, Zee? And you know the brother. You know what he's worth. Now, I know that you had your heart set on me marrying Hassan or, at least, another brother like him, but, to be honest, that's not what I'm looking for. And I'm not a child anymore, Zayd, I grew up long ago. Maybe this brother can't offer me what others can but the point is this: what he has is what I want.'

'And what would that be, dear sister of mine?' I could tell from his smile that I was winning him over.

I grinned at him. 'Now, if you had asked me that in the first place, instead of making assumptions or trying to force me into a box, none of that stuff with Hassan would have happened.'

Zayd hung his head and I felt a stab of remorse. I didn't blame him for what happened, not really, but I wasn't prepared to allow myself to get guilt-tripped into turning into some kind of cookie cutter clone. 'I want a companion in this life and the next. Someone who gets me. Who is into *me*. Not just the fact that I wear hijab or come from a religious family or will be an obedient wife or just because I love kids. Someone who loves my sense of humour, who appreciates my art, who shares my passions. A true partner who will respect me, honour me and make me feel like a princess, all at the same time.' Zayd rolled his eyes but I just smiled at him. 'Zee, one thing you need to realise is that good Muslim women come in all forms. There isn't one officially sanctioned version. Just look at the Mothers of the Believers: they were all different, with characters and personalities all of their own. The only thing they conformed to was the love of Allah and His Messenger, *sallallahu alayhi wa sallam*, and their commitment to Islam. So why are we made to feel that we need to conform to more than that?'

I could tell from his expression that he was listening, digesting what I was saying.

'Zayd, you know me. Better than anyone else, you know where we've come from and what we've been through. You know that this life we have here isn't for me. I've always wanted something different, something more. Now I've got a chance to live a different life, to be true to myself *and* my Islam, to complete half my *deen* in a way that suits who *I* am. Please don't stand in the way of that.'

He didn't say anything for a long time. Then he nodded, got up and gave me a hug.

And I knew that he was in. Now, he had to start doing his research.

Auntie Azra was in, too. She had had tears in her eyes as she pressed the ticket into my hand.

'My gift to you, Amirah,' she said, her voice hoarse. 'May Allah bless it for you, my dear. Go, fly...' Then she'd turned away, wiping tears from her eyes. Mum had come up and given her a hug.

'These girls, eh?' she joked. 'They'll be the death of us, I tell you.' She had come to terms with what I wanted to do and, now, she was calm. 'What will be, will be, Amirah,' she had sighed. 'Ultimately, Allah is the Best of Planners.'

Soon, the two friends reunited were laughing, their eyes full of tears. We left them at the house, going through Mum's things, getting ready to paint her bedroom walls, drinking tea and laughing about old times. Mum had wanted to come, along with all the kids, but I had put my foot down. This was going to be difficult enough already without the whole family tagging along.

'Make sure you look after her, Zayd!' Mum had called out to us as we bundled ourselves into Auntie Azra's car. 'Love you, baby!'

I'd hardly had time to tie the laces on my red trainers.

* * *

But now time was slipping and the roads were choked with rush hour traffic.

Rania banged on the steering wheel in frustration. 'We'll never make it, Ams!' she cried, with a desperate look.

I chewed on my lip and made the same *du'a* as I had made before leaving the house: *Please, Allah, if it is good for me, decree it and, if it isn't, remove it from me and replace it with better.*

Ever since I had made up my mind to do this, *Salatul-Istikhara* had become my best friend. The prayer with which we seek Allah's help and guidance. Indispensable.

Rania slipped out of the slow lane as the traffic eased. 'Time to burn some rubber,' she muttered, bracing herself behind the steering wheel.

And while we sped along the motorway to Heathrow Airport, seconds turned into minutes and the minutes kept ticking, ticking, slipping away, while I prayed feverishly, my eyes closed.

* * *

When we got to Departures, Rania pulled over, bumping up onto the pavement. 'OK, you guys go, I'll try and find parking.' And she sniffled a little and blew me a kiss. 'Inshallah, it all works out. See you in a minute!' She wiped away a tear, waved, and drove off with a screech of tires.

At that point, I grabbed my backpack from Zayd and began to run towards the terminal building. Zayd kept close behind me.

Were we too late? Would we find him? And what would he say when he saw me? Was this really the craziest thing I had ever done?

I had to fight through a group of Spanish students on a school trip to get in through the automatic doors.

Once in, I scanned the screens, desperation stinging my eyes. It felt like every change of the display took hours and still, I didn't see the destination I was looking for.

'Ams,' Zayd's voice behind me. 'There it is: Mexico City...' His voice trailed off and I struggled to focus, my eyes scanning the list.

Mexico City: Gate Closed.

Gate closed.

We were too late.

I heard myself let out a cry of anguish, 'Oh, Zayd, no! *No!*' The tears came so fast, I couldn't stop them. I gasped at the force of the pain that shot through me.

How could I have been so stupid?

Why did I walk away that first time?

Zayd let me sob into his shoulder, stroking my hijab. 'It's alright, sis,' he was saying. 'There's a reason for everything. You know that...'

I pulled away from him and wiped my nose. 'You don't understand,' I wailed. 'You weren't there. You didn't hear the things he said to me, the way he looked when I told him to forget about me. Now he'll never know how badly I wanted to say yes, how I wanted to be that girl, the girl of his dreams.' My words were lost in sobs. 'Zayd, I swear, I felt like our souls knew each other before, like we understood each other...' I shook my head, thinking of every little thing I knew about him, everything that made me love him: his respect, his kindness, his generosity, his sense of responsibility, and his humility. And that smile, those eyes, the way he moved...

'Oh, Zayd,' I gulped. 'The craziest thing is that I love him. I do. And now he's gone and I'll never be able to tell him...'

Zayd smiled then and said, in a voice full of tenderness, 'Why don't you tell him now, sis?'

And he turned me around and there, standing in front of me, holding his backpack, was Mr Light Eyes himself and, from the smile on his face and the tears in his eyes, it was safe to say that he had pretty much heard everything I'd said.

'*As-salamu 'alaykum*, Amirah,' he signed to me with those perfect fingers. 'Now are you ready to fly with me?'

260

♀ AMIRAH

49

Zayd's text had been cryptic: *On my way to the airport. Don't leave until I get there. Trust me. V. important.*

Had it been anybody else, I would have disregarded it, but this was Zayd. So I waited for him, waited to see what it was that was so important.

I won't bore you with all the details of the tears and laughter, excited calls to family and friends, Islamic marriages in airport lounges in front of surprised onlookers, new tickets, and words of advice given before boarding.

But I will tell you this: I first touched Amirah when we had boarded our flight to Mexico, as man and wife. At last, I was able to kiss her fingertips and stroke the cleft in her chin. At last, I could feel her touch the mole on my left hand and caress my knuckles. At last, we could laugh about our matching trainers.

We had so much to catch up on, so much to share. But there would be time for that later. The next day, and the next day and the day after that.

In fact, we had the rest of our lives, inshallah.

Glossary

A'udhu billahi min ash-Shaytan ir-Rajeem: I seek refuge with
    Allah from Shaytan the accursed

Abaya: Flowing outer garment worn by Muslim women

Adhan: The Muslim call to prayer

Akh/Akhi: Brother/my brother

Akhirah: The Hereafter

Alhamdulillah: All praise is for Allah

Allah: God

Allahumma barik: May Allah bless it

Amu: Uncle

As-salamu 'alaykum/salaam: The Muslim greeting, 'Peace be
    upon you'

Astaghfirullah: I seek Allah's forgiveness

Ayah: Verse from the Qur'an

Barakallahu feek: May Allah bless you

Bismillah: In the name of Allah

Da'eef: Weak (in religion)

Da'wah: Invitation or call to Islam

Deen: Way of life/religion

Du'a: Supplication

Dunyah: This world

Dupatta: Light scarf, often worn with Asian suits

Fajr: The dawn prayer

Fatwa: Religious verdict/ruling

Fitnah: Trial/temptation

Ghayrah: Protectiveness/jealousy

Halal: Permissible in Islam

Haram: Forbidden in Islam

Hijab: Head covering worn by Muslim women

Ikhwan: Brothers

Imam: Mosque leader

Inna lillahi wa inna ilayhi raji'un: To Allah we belong and to Him we shall return

Inshallah: God willing

Jazakallah khayran: May Allah reward you with good

Juz: Part of the Qur'an consisting of a number of verses

Khutbah: Sermon

Kufi: Skull cap worn by Muslim men

La hawla wa la quwwatta illa-billah: There is no power or might except with Allah

Madrasah: Religious class/school

Maghrib: Sunset prayer

Mashallah: Allah has willed it

Miswaks: Tooth cleaning stick

Mu'min: A righteous believer

Mus'haf: Copy of the Qur'an

Niqab: Face veil

Qiblah: The direction Muslims face to pray

Qur'an: The Muslim holy book

Raka'at: A unit of prayer

Salah: A ritual prayer for Muslims. Performed 5 times a day. One of the pillars of Islam

Sallallahu alayhi wa sallam: May the peace and blessings of Allah be upon him, spoken after the Prophet Muhammad is mentioned

Shahadah: Testimony of faith. What someone says to convert to Islam. One of the pillars of Islam

Shaytan: Satan/ the devil

Shisha: Hookah pipe used to smoke flavoured tobacco

Sujud: Prostration in the ritual prayer

Surah: Verse of the Qur'an

Talaq: Divorce

Tarbiyah: Islamic nurturing/upbringing

Thobe: Robe worn by Muslim men

Urdu: Language spoken by Pakistanis and some Indians

Wali: Guardian

Wudu: Ablution, performed before prayer

Zinah: Fornication

Zuhr: Mid-day prayer

Acknowledgements

This story is for Aaminah. She knows why.

A huge thank you to my beta readers from Hayah International Academy in Cairo, who lived and breathed these characters: Laila, Nour, Malak, Nada, Salma, Kenzie and Omar. And to Sarah el Meshad for making it happen.

I am grateful for the support of my family, particularly my husband and my father, my wonderful agent and my demanding new editor!

Last, but not least, jazakallah khayran to all the young people who have let me into their lives in some way or another, and have helped shape the characters and concerns of this narrative. Auntie loves you all.

About the Author

Na'ima B. Robert, who has South African Zulu and Scottish roots, was born in England, grew up in Zimbabwe and converted to Islam in 1998 at the age of 21 after visiting Egypt as a student. She graduated from the University of London and is founder and editor-in-chief of the UK-based Muslim women's magazine, SISTERS. She has published many picture books with Muslim themes and four young adult novels: *From Somalia, With Love*, *Boy vs Girl*, *Black Sheep* and *Far From Home*. She has also published a memoir, *From My Sisters' Lips*, and a series of children's non-fiction books under her family name, Thando McLaren.

Na'ima B. Robert is married with five children and divides her time between London and Egypt.